PRAISE FOR THE WORK OF DONNA BALL

"A must read."

—*Examiner.com*

"A major talent of the genre"

—*Publisher's Weekly*

"Exciting, original and suspense-laden."

—*Midwest Book Review*

A maelstrom of suspense...gripping, intense"

—*Rendezvous*

"[Ball] knows how to keep a story moving"

—*Kirkus Reviews*

ALSO FROM DONNA BALL

The Raine Stockton Dog Mystery Series
Smoky Mountain Tracks
Rapid Fire
Gun Shy
Bone Yard
Silent Night
The Dead Season
High in Trial
Double Dog Dare
Home of the Brave

The Ladybug Farm Series
A Year on Ladybug Farm
At Home on Ladybug Farm
Love Letters from Ladybug Farm
Christmas on Ladybug Farm
Vintage Ladybug Farm
A Wedding on Ladybug Farm

The Hummingbird House

FLASH

Published by Blue Merle Publishing
Drawer H
Mountain City, Georgia 30562
www.bluemerlepublishing.com

ISBN-13: 9780985774899
ISBN-10: 0985774894

First printing May 2015

This is a work of fiction. All places, characters, events and organizations mentioned in this book are either the product of the author's imagination, or used fictitiously.

Cover art by www.bigstock.com

FLASH

A DOGLEG ISLAND MYSTERY
BOOK ONE

Donna Ball

BEACH PATROL

CHAPTER ONE

If the call had come four minutes later, Aggie would have missed it. This close to end of shift, no one would have blamed her had she ignored it and headed on in, and in fact she considered doing just that. She glanced at her dashboard clock: 6:56 a.m. Then she saw the street sign coming up she muttered, "Crap." She punched the radio mike. "Unit four, responding. ETA, thirty seconds."

The radio crackled again. "Hey, Aggie, you still beachside?"

It was Ryan Grady, her morning relief for beach patrol. Relief was of course a relative word; he'd been nothing but a pain in the ass since she'd joined the Murphy County Sheriff's Department eighteen months ago. She worried what it said about her that she was actually starting to get used to him—and worse, even to enjoy his inanities. Secretly, of course.

She switched on her flashers and made the turn onto Harbor Lane. The swirl of color bounced off the early morning fog, painting tree trunks and the tangled jungle of vacant lots in eerie explosions of blue. "Amazing powers of deduction, Sherlock. ETA

1

now twelve seconds." And she wasn't even hurrying. The one thing she loved about Dogleg Island was that there was rarely any need to hurry. Very little was more than ten minutes away in any direction.

Roy Briggs, Grady's partner, took over the radio. "Say, Aggie, why don't you call it a night? We've got this."

"Too late, big guy," she came back. "I'm on the clock. Besides, I'm not going to take a chance on you two klutzes screwing up my last call of the night."

Briggs's tone took on a plaintive note as he returned, "Grady, how come do you suppose we allow a female to speak to us that way? Rack and ruin, that's what this whole damn department has come to since the powers that be decided to allow female personnel on the force."

Aggie suppressed a smile as she pulled into the shell drive of 210 Harbor Lane. Roy tried very hard to be a jerk, but that was only because everyone knew he was nothing but a great big teddy bear. He did all the Officer Friendly programs for the school kids and always smelled like candy. He had given her chocolate-covered cherries for her birthday. She still hadn't figured out how he knew they were her favorite, or that it was her birthday.

Grady came back: "Careful, dude. You're talking about the woman I'm going to marry."

Aggie rolled her eyes.

Three miles away, Ryan Grady made the turn onto Island Road, which, as the name implied, was the main road on the island, a thoroughfare four miles long and two lanes wide. There was no reply from the radio, so he figured Aggie had decided to take the high road, metaphorically speaking. Grinning, he turned off the mike. They had just crossed the causeway, the road was deserted this time of morning, and he leaned on the accelerator.

Briggs said, "You better watch it, my friend. One day that lady's gonna nail your ass."

Grady said, still grinning, "I wish."

Briggs chuckled. "She'll chew you up and spit you out before you even know what's happening." Then, "Hey, watch it!" He scowled as Grady took a sharp turn and his double-grande extra sweet mocha latte from the machine at the Causeway Kangaroo station almost sloshed over its cup and onto his semi-clean uniform pants. Semi-clean because there were already a few blueberry muffin crumbs sprinkled there, which he dabbed up now with his index finger and licked off.

Briggs had been riding a patrol car in Murphy County for almost twenty years, and he had the girth to prove it. He'd blown out his knee five years ago and had to wear special orthotics in his shoes to get through a shift; he wasn't as fast as he used to be and everyone knew if he had to pass the police physical today he wouldn't have a chance. But, next to Sheriff Bishop himself, Roy Briggs was the most knowledgeable and experienced man on the force, and Grady liked riding with him. Briggs was good at the kind of paperwork Grady couldn't stand, he was steady and patient on a stake out, and he wasn't above bending the rules a little when necessary. Over the past couple of years of riding together, they'd developed an easy working relationship.

"Come on, man, she knows I'm just yanking her chain." Grady eased up on the accelerator as they came onto Ocean Avenue, the main shopping district, where it was possible old Mr. Phelps might be opening up his tee shirt shop early, or Lloyd Croombs might be crossing the street against the light, as he often did, with coffee and a bagel from the Pelican Café as he headed toward his bike shop at the corner of Ocean and Pine. "Besides, she loves it." He punched the mike again and said, "Don't you, sweet cheeks?"

She didn't miss a beat. "Go to hell, Grady."

He chuckled. Ryan Grady was a good-looking guy in a careless, beach-bum kind of way, with sun-bleached blond hair that he still wore in a military buzz cut, and toasted chestnut skin that he got from spending every spare minute on the water. He never lacked for girls, and he never kept any of them long. He'd even managed to convince everyone on the force his flirtation with Aggie was just for fun, a way to keep them both entertained on beach patrol. What no one knew—no one except Briggs, that is— was that Grady had been the one who left the birthday card and the box of chocolate-covered cherries on Aggie's desk, and that he had at the last minute lost his nerve and signed Briggs's name instead of his own. He still wasn't sure why he'd done it. He felt sorry for her, he supposed, all alone on her birthday in a new place. And, if he were perfectly honest with himself, there was more than a little regret that, after a year and a half, he was still stuck in the flirting stage with her. One day, he kept telling himself, he was going to man up and ask her out for real, just for the hell of it. Not that anything would ever come of it. A girl like Aggie would always be out of his league. And that was probably why, as the days went by, he found it easier and easier just to maintain the status quo.

Ryan Grady, thirty years old and eight years on the force, had grown up on Dogleg Island, which wasn't a claim many people could make. His ancestors, a bunch of rough fishermen and squint-eyed sailors, had been among the first to settle the island and had held on through storm, war, plague, and natural disaster, even though, at times, there was nobody left but them. His grandfather Cedric operated the island ferry for forty-five years, earning a state Medal of Honor in 1983 during Hurricane Alice for returning against Coast Guard advice for a group of thirteen stranded Girl Scouts who would have otherwise almost surely been lost in the storm surge that subsequently flooded two-thirds of the island. When the toll bridge replaced the ferry in 2003, it was named the Cedric B. Grady Memorial Bridge in his honor. Most people just called it the Causeway now, but there was an official green highway sign on each end of the bridge identifying it by name, and Grady still occasionally took some ribbing about "his" bridge.

5

He'd gotten a football scholarship to Florida State, spent two years on the bench, lost the scholarship, joined the Coast Guard. He'd returned to Murphy County after his hitch because there was no place on earth he'd rather be. He had dinner at his sister's house every Sunday, and most days after shift he stopped by for a drink with his brother Pete, who owned Pete's Place Bar and Grill on Sixth Street. He lived beachside in the rambling cypress cottage his grandfather had built sixty years ago, and he stowed a wet suit and a surfboard in the back of the squad car, just in case. In every way that mattered, he was perfectly content, even though he found himself thinking more and more these days about how big his house was, and how empty, and how good it would be to come home to somebody waiting for him. Someday, of course.

"Look at that," he said, nodding toward a plastic sign flapping in the breeze over an almost-completed new construction across from the bike shop. *Future Home of the Island Bistro*, it read. His tone was contemptuous. "What do we need with a bistro around here? What the hell is a bistro, anyway? Next thing you know there'll be a damn Starbucks on every corner."

Briggs sipped his coffee. "You can't fight progress, Grady. Besides, I think this place could use a Starbucks."

"All those damn fat cats coming in from New York and Atlanta, building their fat-cat beach houses with their asphalt driveways and chlorinated swimming pools and floodlights turning the beach into a damn runway at night, noise pollution, air pollution, drug pollution..."

Briggs sighed. "So it's gonna be one of those days. Not enough I have to check in early and burn rubber across the bridge so you can see your girlfriend—"

"She's not my girlfriend." Grady scowled.

"Now I have to listen to one of your lectures. I'm supposed to be drinking my damn coffee in the break room and listening to last night's reports."

Grady ignored him. "You mark my word, this is just the beginning. Crime is going to go sky high. Traffic will be bumper to bumper. First thing you know they'll be building gambling casinos and whorehouses right on the beach, and it all started—"

"When they built the bridge, yeah, yeah, yeah. You sound like an old woman, Grady. Next right."

Grady gave him a dark look. "I know where I'm going."

But the truth was that the map he held in his head was fifteen years old and his preferred method of dealing with change was to ignore it. If Briggs hadn't prompted him, he probably would have missed the turn.

Agatha Elaine Malone had half a law degree from UGA, fourteen months training at the Illinois Police Academy, two years on the Chicago PD. She never talked about that. Her department ID described her as 5'5, 130 pounds, black hair, hazel eyes, which was more or less accurate. There was a rumor going around the department that she came from the kind of money that donated hospital wings and went to White House dinners, which she suspected had originated with Grady simply because he thought it would annoy her. He would've been surprised to find out how much she secretly enjoyed it. Aggie had been raised by her grandmother in an unpainted house with a dirt yard outside of Macon, Georgia, after her mother overdosed on heroin when she was six. Her grandmother had taught her that a lady could do without a lot of things—money, fine clothes, a husband—but class was not one of them. Aggie thought Gran would've been pleased that she had somehow developed enough class to make her coworkers think she came from money, even if her coworkers were just a bunch of redneck Gulf Coast deputies living in a town that had barely gotten used to cable TV.

When she interviewed for the job, Sheriff Bishop had asked, routinely, why she'd left law school for the police department. She had a pat answer prepared for that, all about how she preferred practice to theory, and how justice began on the streets but ended in the courtroom, and that answer had been good enough to get her the job in Chicago. Instead, she looked into the sheriff's thoughtful dark eyes and told him the truth: her roommate, brutally assaulted after a football game by three of the star players; the prosecutor gently suggesting that she reconsider pressing charges given the difficulty of obtaining a conviction since she had been intoxicated at the time of the incident—he had actually said *incident,* as though it had been nothing more than an inconvenience; the victim, broken and afraid, dropping out of college and leaving town.

"I realized then I was in the wrong field," she said. "I wanted to be one of the good guys."

Bishop nodded. "I guess I already know why you left Chicago, then."

She returned his steady gaze and replied, "Yes sir. It was the weather."

He smiled and nodded and gave her the job, and it was good to know he understood the weather had had nothing to do with it at all.

Aggie Malone was twenty-eight, rock-steady on the job, and generally well liked around the department. She kept to herself and didn't push in where she wasn't welcome, which was a good thing, and she made points with the other guys by volunteering for beach patrol, a dull and isolated duty that, with the exception of Grady, was no one's favorite. As only the second female deputy ever to be hired by the Murphy County Sheriff's Department—the first being a forty-seven-year-old weight-lifting former prison guard named Maureen who could intimidate most of the men into silence with a single heavy-browed glance—she had had a few concerns about how she would fit in amongst all the good ol' boys. In fact, she'd had some concerns about small-town life in general. But, Grady notwithstanding, she'd been surprised how easy it had been to slip into the routine of this slow, hot, lazy place, to let the sun soak up her ambition and the steam wash away her worries. It was exactly what she needed, and she never wanted to leave.

She parked in front of the house, turned on her high beams, and looked around. 210 Harbor Lane was one of the new McMansions that were starting to spring up along the formerly pristine beaches of Dogleg Island, an unincorporated protectorate of Murphy County, Florida. A short curved drive led from the street to the Mediterranean stuccoed façade of a three-story concrete building with curved balconies and ocean frontage. The three-car garage was on the front of the house, doors closed. The power-operated hurricane shutters were rolled up, but the windows were dark. An expensively maintained bougainvillea and two palm trees flanked the entrance, and a thick morning sea mist obscured the remainder of the yard. Aggie could hear the screech of the security alarm through her closed car windows. She opened the mike. "This is Malone, on site. Also, Sheriff, I'd like to file a sexual harassment complaint."

Sheriff Jerome Bishop, a sixty-one-year-old war veteran, was the first black man ever to be elected sheriff in Murphy County, and he'd held that post for twenty-one years. He arrived at his desk at 6:00 a.m. every morning, seven days a week, including Christmas and Easter, with a reheated cruller and a tall paper cup of tar-colored coffee from the IGA grocery on the mainland. He went home to his wife and a hot meal at 6:00 p.m. every evening, and in between he monitored every word that went back and forth between his deputies on the radio, occasionally interjecting a pertinent comment in that deep baritone of his that was somewhere between James Earl Jones and everybody's memory of their scariest high school principal. He rarely gave orders; he didn't have to. His men—and women—knew their jobs and respected him enough to let him do his. He said now, "Sorry, you'll have to take that up with HR."

The Murphy County Sheriff's Department consisted of four shifts of six deputies each, a 911 dispatcher for each shift, two jailers, an administrative assistant, and the sheriff himself. There was no human resources director, no public relations spokesperson, no in-service training specialist, and when they needed help investigating a crime—which was rarely on this Forgotten Coast—they got it from the state police. They had, however, recently received funding for a new microwave and vending machine in the break room.

Bishop went on, "Meantime, we're on public airways, children, so let's try to stay on task, shall we? I've got 210 down to a Walter and Leah Reichart, Reichart Dental Group. Summer people, right?"

"Yes sir. They're in residence now, though. At least they were the last time they accidentally set off the security alarm, which was two days ago. "

The sheriff returned a grunt of acknowledgement, and the microphone picked up a shuffling of papers. "That must be what they called about. I have a message here. You were nice to them, weren't you, Aggie?" It was a joke. If there was one thing anyone could say for sure about Aggie, it was that she was nice.

"Nice as can be," she returned. "I can't vouch for Roy, though. He caught the one after that."

Briggs picked up the mike. "I'm always nice to rich folks, sir."

Bishop chuckled.

Aggie got out of the car, not bothering to muffle the slamming of the door. She rested her hand on her utility belt and looked around, noting the absence of cars—which could well be parked inside the garage—and, more significantly, the absence of movement behind those darkened windows. There were two more houses on the beach side of this newly developed community, both of them empty, and nothing across the street but a tangled hummock of tupelos and loblolly pines. The sky was lightening to a pale gray now, just enough for Aggie to make out shapes and structures, but half an hour ago this short street would have been as dark as the underside of a tomb.

The whooping of the alarm, which was programmed to cease after five minutes, abruptly stopped, leaving her with the susurration of the ocean and the throbbing flight of the unit's blues on the morning fog. She switched to her collar radio. "It's quiet inside. They may have left."

Grady broke in. "Backup's on the way, baby. ETA one minute."

She made a face, just as though there was someone there to see. "Be sure to bring your Batman suit.
This case is clearly beyond the skills of an ordinary
law enforcement officer." She started up the walk.

Grady said, "Forty-five seconds. And say, Aggie,
about that fantasy of yours. You know the one where
I'm…"

"Buried in an ant hill up to your neck?"

Bishop said, "Focus, ladies and gentlemen."

"It's awfully quiet here," Aggie said. "I'm moving
in."

Sheriff Bishop said, "Hold on, Aggie. You're riding alone today. Wait for the boys."

"You did not just say that."

Bishop liked to pair up the deputies on beach
patrol, not because the beat was dangerous or even
particularly challenging, but because it was so damn
boring. This time of year there were barely three
hundred people living on the whole island, and it
hardly seemed worth the assignment of a patrol car,
but all those miles of beach did make a tempting target for drug dealers and sex offenders and Bishop
didn't like to take chances. So he put two men to a
car on beach patrol, figuring that two of them had
a better chance of staying alert, or at least awake,
than one.

Aggie's partner—her second since she'd been
with the department—had left last week for a higher
paying job, which was a fairly regular occurrence in
Murphy County, and Aggie had discovered she liked
taking the duty by herself. She did her rounds every

two hours, chatted on the radio with the night dispatcher, checked security lights and rattled doorknobs on the shops in town. Around midnight she stopped by Pete's Place for a burger and coffee, and on weeknights in the off season when they weren't busy, Pete or his wife Lorraine would pour a cup and sit with her, talking about this or that. Pete Grady was six years older than his brother Ryan and, in Aggie's opinion, a lot more interesting, and she really liked Lorraine. After her dinner break she'd resume her rounds, slow, quiet patrols down sleeping streets, listening to a little Ray Charles, or maybe a James Patterson book on CD. A big night would involve rousting a couple of teenagers from the backseat of a parked car at Beachside Park, or chasing away scavengers from pillaging the dumpsters outside a construction site. The quiet life was what she'd been looking for when she moved here, and the quiet life was what she found.

Bishop said, "Humor an old man. That alarm's been going for five minutes and nobody shut it off. Could be we've got ourselves a real crime here."

"I thought of that one myself, chief. In which case, don't you think we ought to try to stop it? Being the police and all." As she spoke she turned toward the garage and, taking out her MagLite, shone it inside the windows. There was a little red sports car and a blue SUV parked inside. She frowned and looked back toward the house. Still dark. Had the family taken off for an early fishing trip? Did they have more than two cars?

She spoke into the radio. "Sheriff, it looks like the Reicharts might still be in residence. Two vehicles in the garage, no signs of activity in the house. I think I'd better—"

"Check it out," said Bishop tersely.

"Roger that." She placed her hand on the butt of her sidearm and approached the front door just as Grady and Roy pulled into the drive, the flashing lights from their unit mixing with hers to create a dizzying cacophony of color across the lawn. They had, of course, been monitoring the radio communications and wasted no time joining her. One thing about Grady: he might be a cut-up in his down time, but when it came to business, he was the man you wanted by your side.

"I'll go around back," Grady said.

"Damn fool kids," muttered Roy, who was breathing hard and limping a little just from the hurried walk up the driveway. "I'll bet you anything they're trying to carry a 52-inch flat screen down the beach right now. I got it."

He moved around the east side of the house toward the beach while Grady went to the west. Aggie knocked on the front door. "Police!" she called loudly. "Hello!"

There was no response, but in a moment she heard Grady pounding on the glass door that opened onto the wrap-around deck. "Police!"

Aggie knocked again. The sea breeze was damp and salty, parting her dark bangs and creeping down the collar of her uniform shirt. She wished she hadn't left her hat in the car; she could feel her hair going as flat as a skillet even as she stood there. She smoothed it back self-consciously, aware that Grady was just around the corner.

She tried the knob. To her surprise, it opened. She called, "Police! Mr. and Mrs. Reichart, is everything okay?"

Into her radio she said, "Hey, Grady, I'm going in. The front door is open."

"Aggie, hold on. I'm coming around."

She went in.

The house was built in a pretentious style, with a terrazzo-tiled three-story foyer and an oversized wrought iron chandelier hanging midway down. There was a staircase to the right, and a big open kitchen/family room overlooking the Gulf straight ahead. Aggie knew this from the last time she had answered a security alarm and Mrs. Reichart, a petite middle-aged blonde with the kind of perfectly coiffed bob that never frizzed, even in beach weather, had met her at the door with profuse apologies and invited her in. Her teenage son had accidentally set off the alarm while coming in late, and since it was a new system, neither one of them had been able to remember the code in time to shut it off. Her husband was driving in that night from Atlanta and he *did* know the code; nonetheless, he had managed to set off the alarm again when he arrived. In all, Aggie had made three trips to 210 Harbor Lane that week, not counting this one or the one Roy had made. Some police forces had a limit on how many false alarms they would answer before they started charging the homeowner for the call, but Murphy County did not, and Bishop had never pushed for one. The way he figured it, false alarms were a good training exercise for his officers and kept them on their toes. For Aggie, it was good to break up the monotony, and a way to get to know the people on her beat.

The light switch was on the wall to Aggie's right and she flipped it on. The big iron chandelier prismed light across the tiled staircase and yellow stucco walls, catching the brilliant colors of an oversized oil painting of tropical birds in a way that almost brought it to life. Aggie started toward the front of the house, calling again, "Mrs. Reichart, it's Deputy Malone from the sheriff's department!"

She stopped, listening. The sound she heard was unidentifiable, but distinct, like a chain rattling against metal, or a small door being repeatedly slammed. It was probably just a loose shutter or a Venetian blind slapping back and forth against an open window. But she had not survived two years in Chicago by being careless, so she took out her gun, pointed it at the ceiling, and proceeded cautiously toward the front.

The pink sunrise and cerulean water that swept across the bank of windows lining the big room looked like a giant painting, and it was hard not to stop for a moment and stare. The morning glow was just enough for Aggie to make out the white leather sectional that curved around the center of the room, the glass-topped coffee table in the center of a white fuzzy rug, and, against the wall next to the windows, the source of the noise. A small black and white puppy was confined to a wire crate there, tugging on the metal door with the kind of frantic determination that would either destroy the cage or his teeth before he was done.

Aggie relaxed and reholstered her gun, her expression softening as she went over to the crate. "Hey there, little fellow. Are you missing your breakfast? Time for you to go out?" She knelt beside the crate and the puppy sat down and watched her alertly, as though waiting for her to unlock the door. He had a funny lightning-bolt blaze of white in the middle of his otherwise black forehead and the most amazing blue eyes she'd ever seen. Who knew dogs even *had* blue eyes?

Her radio crackled. "Report, Malone." Sheriff Bishop sounded tense.

She pushed the button on her radio. "All quiet," she replied. "No sign of the family. They left their puppy in a cage so they're probably planning to be gone a couple of hours."

"A cage? Who the hell does that?"

"Anybody who doesn't want their five-thousand-dollar carpet peed on or the upholstery on their designer sofa shredded." That was Grady. "Coming around front. Any signs of forced entry? Vandalism?"

"None." She knew he was disappointed to hear it. They all secretly hoped for a little excitement to break the routine. "And the TV is just where they left it so you can tell Roy to stop looking. Looks like they just forgot to lock the front door. The puppy was making an awful lot of noise so that must've set off the alarm."

"Could be," said Bishop. "Have a look around anyway. Don't forget to leave your card."

"Roger," said Aggie, and clicked off the radio.

She started to get up, and the puppy gave a single sharp short bark. It sounded like a command. She turned back to him, smiling a little.

"Where's your mom and dad, hmm? Did they forget about you this morning?" She glanced around, and then hesitated. There was something splattered on the floor a few feet away, like the puddle made by a spilled drink. Part of it had seeped into the corner of the white rug, darkening the fibers. Her brows drew together and she half-turned, starting to stand. That's when she saw a woman's bare foot lying half on and half off the rug, and next to it a man's. And she knew with instinct honed by two years in Chicago that the liquid that glistened on the floor was not a spilled drink.

The puppy wasn't barking because he wanted out of his cage. He hadn't set off the alarm. She understood then, in a moment of startling clarity and surrealistic calm, that she was very likely living out the last few moments of her life.

She thought, *Damn it, damn it, damn it.* Eighteen months and she'd forgotten everything, everything she'd ever known about staying alive, about being a law officer, about what bad people could do. Eighteen months of routine patrol, of sunrise over the ocean, of kids leaving condoms on the beach and thinking that was the thing she was defending against, that was the worst they could do, forgetting what was out there, forgetting who the real bad guys were. *Damn it.* Eighteen months of hearing fireworks, not gunshots; of seeing neighbors, not perps; eighteen months of feeling *safe,* for Christ's sake, wasn't that why she had come here? And in the process she had forgotten how to be a cop.

She was reaching for her gun when she felt the presence in the room, or perhaps she heard the harsh erratic breathing over her shoulder, and when she looked up she knew she'd never get her gun out in time, never even push the button on her radio in time. He was young and skinny-chested and wild-eyed, naked except for a pair of red swim trunks. Long hair was tangled across his face, wet with pinkish sweat, and there were dark smears on his arms and legs and chest. He held a pistol with both hands pointed straight at her. He made crazy gasping wheezing sounds through bared teeth and he was shaking so badly that the gun wavered erratically back and forth in his hands. That was when Aggie realized that his trunks weren't red, after all, but stained with blood.

Behind her the puppy stood up and gave an anxious little whine, its claws clicking on the metal liner of its crate.

Aggie moved her hands slowly to the level of her chest, palms out. "Hey, it's okay," she said. The puppy whined again and pawed at the cage. She had the oddly rational but completely misplaced concern that a stray bullet might accidentally hit the puppy so she started to edge, very carefully, away from the crate. "I'm with the police and I'm here to help." *Grady, Briggs, where are you? For the love of God, where are you?* Heart pounding, world slowing. *Do your job. Do your job.*

"Everything's going to be okay." She got one foot beneath her and eased slowly from her crouch to a standing position. "Don't be afraid. We're going to take care of this. Okay?"

For a moment some of the crazy terror went out of his eyes. The knotted muscles in his skinny shoulders might have relaxed a fraction and the rattling gasps of breath that blew strands of hair away from his face in gusts and starts actually seemed to ease. Cautiously, she lowered one hand and extended it toward him. "Give me the gun," she said, and somehow she even managed a smile. Or part of one. "Let's not have any accidents. I'm here to help. Let's talk. Everything's going to be okay."

Suddenly the puppy barked, and she instinctively swiveled her gaze.

That was when he shot her in the head.

GATHERING STORM

Twenty-two months later

Chapter Two

Jerome Bishop checked his bait, readjusted the weight, and cast his line back into the surf. All the time he noted, out of the corner of his eye, the approach of the jogger and the dog. They were making good time today. It wasn't even seven a.m.

It was April, and early in the season to be fishing barefoot, but Jerome liked the cold sand sinking between his toes, the splash of icy surf when he waded in to retrieve his line. It woke him up first thing in the morning. Made him remember he was still alive. That was harder to do some days than others.

He'd retired from the Murphy County Sheriff's Department the day after his wife Evelyn had been diagnosed with cancer. On that very same day she had exacted a promise from him. "All right, you lazy-ass would-be ex-cop. You want to deprive the fine people of Murphy County of your protection, you go right on ahead, but you promise me one thing. Every morning that I've got left, you're going to take me fishing, just like we planned all these years, and when I'm gone I plan on looking down from heaven and seeing your lazy ass out there in our spot every single morning, casting a line. You got that, you worthless excuse for a man?"

For eight months they had fished together, in between her chemo treatments. Looking back, he sometimes thought those might have been the best eight months of his life. And now he was keeping his promise, although it sometimes seemed he was doing so with only half a heart.

He placed his pole in its PVC pipe holder next to the two others he had set and returned to his canvas beach chair. There was a thermos on top of the cooler beside it, weighting down the morning paper. Bishop poured coffee into two Styrofoam cups and took up the paper. Ignoring the headline, he turned to the sports section. What do you know about that? The Lady Cougars had trounced the Bears again. High school basketball remained, as ever, a mystery.

The sound of heavy panting and pounding footsteps did not even cause him to look up. He lifted one of the coffee cups and held it out. Grady took it, breathing hard. "Morning, Chief."

"Morning, Captain," he replied.

The dog sat and placed a paw on Bishop's knee. For that, Bishop glanced over the rim of his paper. The dog held his position, regarding him with those keen blue eyes in a way that always made Bishop think he was getting ready to strike up a conversation. He reached into the pocket of his tee shirt and produced a dog biscuit, which he flipped into the air. The border collie caught it expertly in mid-flip.

Bishop produced a lopsided grin, which lasted only as long as it took the dog to crunch up the biscuit.

The debate over what to name the orphaned puppy had been the only thing that kept morale together in the department after the shooting. The majority of the votes had gone to Blue, for the blue eyes. Grady had come up with Harry Potter, after the lightning bolt on his forehead. That might've been a little obscure for most of the guys, but in the end it didn't matter. The only vote that counted had also been inspired by the lightning bolt. His name was Flash.

Grady blew on the coffee to cool it while Flash went off to explore the cooler, the poles, and the surrounding turf. "What're you catching?"

"Not a damn thing. You see the paper?"

Grady took a cautious sip of the coffee. His hair was a little less punk now, as befitted his office, and his skin less tanned, thanks to long hours at the office. But his obsessive eight-mile runs every morning had produced a body that could take down a prize fighter. And there was something in his eyes that made Bishop think he was just waiting for his chance. That bothered him, just a little. Not enough to say anything, but just a little.

"The damn Bears couldn't win if the angel Gabriel himself came down to play forward," Grady replied, sipping his coffee. "We need a new coach."

"I hear you." Bishop turned a page, and took up his own cup. "Y'all doing okay?"

"As well as can be expected, with Richardson dogging my ass twenty-four seven." Jeffrey Richardson was the Special Prosecutor appointed to temporary duty in Murphy County. "You'd think I'd never testified in court before."

"You'll do fine." That was in his James Earl Jones voice. Authoritative, soothing, reassuring. But even as he spoke he could feel Grady stiffen.

Grady took another sip of the coffee and put the cup down on the cooler. "Yeah, well," he said, and his voice, like his face, was grim. "None of us would be going through this now if I'd had better aim two years ago." Abruptly, he turned toward the tide, where the border collie was snapping at the waves. "Flash! Let's go!"

Like lightning, the dog was by his side. Grady absently ruffled his damp fur. He glanced at Bishop. "You coming for dinner tonight?"

"It's Wednesday, isn't it?" Bishop turned another page. He added, as he always did, "What're we having?"

Grady answered, as he always did, "Whatever you're catching."

Said Bishop, "Better order pizza then."

Grady laughed and took off running down the beach, the border collie keeping pace at his side. Bishop watched them for a moment, then put the paper down and lifted his cup toward the rising sun in a small salute. He liked to think Evelyn was watching.

He just wasn't so sure she'd like what she saw.

The headline read: **Testimony in Reichart Murder Case Begins Monday.** Aggie, sipping her coffee, leaned on the kitchen counter and read the article. Clearly it didn't offer anything she didn't already know. But she read it anyway.

It was April, her favorite time of year, and sunrise, her favorite time of day. The windows were open in the tiny kitchen, as was the back door that led to the turquoise painted porch with its coral swing and wicker rockers. The air was wet and cool, smelling of salt and coffee and, faintly, of oranges. Outside she heard Mrs. McCracken's screen door slam as she went out to get the morning paper, and down the street Mr. Montague's miniature poodle barked its early morning warning to imaginary intruders. Beyond that, there was nothing but the sigh of the surf.

Paradise.

The newspaper could not resist reiterating the facts of the case one more time. Too late to worry about contaminating the jury pool; the details had been fodder for every news broadcast and print publication in the country for the first two weeks after it happened—until some even more gruesome crime took precedence—and had been dragged up again at least a couple of times a year ever since. Leah Reichart, stabbed sixteen times. Her husband Walter lying beside her in a pool of his own blood, his throat cut. The police officer shot at the scene. Nineteen-year-old Darrell Reichart, wounded as he fled the scene, testing positive for methamphetamines and crack cocaine, charged with two counts of murder and the attempted murder of a police officer, finally getting his day in court. The more times she heard the story, the less real it seemed.

Considering the fact that in mere days she would be giving testimony that would probably send a twenty-one-year old boy to death row, that was not necessarily a good thing.

The team of specialists who had worked on her case included not only a highly qualified neurosurgeon who had not been able to remove the bullet from her brain that should have killed her, but also a neuro-psychiatrist who specialized in Post Traumatic Stress Disorder. The very excellent Dr. Ferguson assured her that a sense of detachment, even ambivalence, toward a life-changing event like hers was not unusual, and she had great confidence that their work together would help her face the emotions that were associated with that night, and eventually to deal with them. So far the good doctor had fallen short of her goal, perhaps because she spent too much time exploring Aggie's feelings about other things, most of which didn't matter. Or trying to help her deal with the maddening and unpredictable panic attacks associated with things like doors, and shadows, and bridges, which mattered very much. Or conducting endless evaluations on the Amazing Woman With the Bullet in Her Brain which were related to nothing useful whatsoever, as far as Aggie could tell.

Her cell phone rang. The caller ID said it was the office. She answered, "Malone."

There had been a few changes in Murphy County in the past two years. Dogleg Island, perhaps due to the publicity surrounding the Reichart case, perhaps due to the growing tax base made possible by the opening of the bridge and the resultant increase in development, had decided to incorporate. Roy Briggs, who'd taken over as sheriff from the retired Jerome Bishop, recommended Aggie for the newly formed position of police chief. To Aggie's surprise, she'd actually gotten the job. For some reason, folks around here thought of her as a hero, although why being stupid enough to get shot in the head made her a hero she had yet to figure out.

"Chief, we've got a call from Bernice Peters out on Egret Road. She said she chased off a prowler early this morning. And her cat's missing."

Aggie frowned. "Her cat?"

"Yes ma'am. I sent Mo out to investigate but thought you might want to stop by since it's on your way in."

Aggie smothered a smile at the thought of Sally Ann "sending" the two-hundred-plus-pound Mo anywhere, and took another sip of her coffee. "It's a little early for a wild cat chase, Sally Ann. But I'll stop by if I get a chance."

Sally Ann Mitchell was nineteen years old and filled with unbounded enthusiasm for her first real job. She was the first one in the office every morning and the last to leave at night. She brought cupcakes decorated like jack-o-lanterns to work for Halloween and Easter Egg cookies for Easter. She couldn't volunteer fast enough to work overtime, run personal errands for the staff, or take on extra duties. That kind of bouncy cocker spaniel energy and eagerness to please could wear thin after a while, but the fact that she was every bit as good at her job as she aspired to be made up for a lot. Most days the office could run perfectly well with no one but Sally Ann in charge, and some days Aggie let it.

She was going on now, "...said to remind you about the Merchant's Association meeting at 10:00 and you've got an appointment with Dr. Ferguson at 2:00."

Aggie tensed a little at that. It was instinctive. Dr. Ferguson's office was on the mainland and so far no one had figured out a way to get to the mainland without crossing the bridge. Sometimes she could handle the bridge; sometimes she couldn't. What kind of day would this one be?

"Also, the Beachside Park Dog Walkers Association wants to have a costume parade and barbecue on the beach Saturday the twenty-first so I put the permit on your desk. Oh, and I forgot to tell you the dry cleaner delivered your blue suit last night. I thought you'd want it for, you know, court."

Aggie deliberately relaxed her shoulders, although another small frown flitted across her brow that she couldn't prevent. The scent of oranges was stronger now, and as far as she knew there were no oranges in the house. "I'll wear my dress uniform to court," she said, "just like I always do." In the past year she'd been to court exactly twice, both on traffic violations.

Aggie could tell by the hesitation that Sally Ann did not approve. "Yes ma'am. But there'll be lots of press there, from Tallahassee and Atlanta and Nashville and maybe even New York. Maybe even cameras. Maybe the *Today* show."

"I'll be sure to shine my shoes. And Sally Ann." She took another sip of her coffee and caught a glimpse through the window of Grady and Flash as they jogged by. Grady saw her standing there and lifted a hand, smiling. She waved back. "No dog parade. The twenty-first is the opening day of the fishing tournament. The beach will be standing room only—literally—in front of Beachside Park."

"Oh." Sally Ann sounded so disappointed in herself for having made the mistake that Aggie felt compelled to console her.

"See if they'd be willing to move the parade to the sea wall. It'll be less crowded there. We can put up signs for those that miss the memo."

She brightened. "On it, Chief. See you in a few."

The screen door creaked and slammed and Flash's claws scrabbled on the bright yellow linoleum as he hurried into the kitchen, head low, busy tail wagging, bright eyes searching. He'd learned to open and close the screen door the day after they'd moved in here, and could even unlatch the hook lock. Aggie had come to understand early in their relationship that there was no confining him. He came and went as he pleased, not that she'd have it any other way.

She knelt and rubbed his forehead with her own. "How's my best guy this morning? How's my favorite fellow in the world?"

The screen door slammed again. "I'm doing great, thanks for asking," Grady called as he came down the hall. "How's my favorite girl?"

Aggie stood and gave him a stern look as he came into the kitchen, leaving a trail of sand behind. "What part of 'don't wear your running shoes in the house' do you not understand?"

"Sorry." He leaned in from a couple of feet away to brush her hair with a kiss, aware of his sweaty tee shirt and her clean uniform. "You need to put up a sign."

After the surgery, Aggie's formerly black hair had grown in stone white. It was one of the most striking things about her, and most people thought she dyed it that way. She had hated it at first and cried every time she looked in the mirror, until Grady figured out what she was crying about and told her to stop being silly, that the white hair was just where the angels had kissed her good-bye when they sent her back to earth. She had been so startled to hear such an absurd sentiment coming from him that she burst into laughter, and she never cried about her hair again. These days she wore it in a pixie cut that gleamed like a platinum helmet in the sunshine, and every time Grady kissed her hair, it made her grin.

She was grinning now even as she tried to sound stern. "If I make a sign I'm going to pin it to your forehead." She took out the broom and dustpan from the tiny closet and handed it to him. "With a real pin."

He made quick work of the sandy footprints and replaced the equipment in the closet. "You know you wouldn't have this problem if—"

"Don't start."

"This going back and forth between houses is kind of rough on my good buddy here."

"He's young. He can deal with it."

"Marry me. Give the little guy the family he's always wanted."

Flash tracked the conversation with alert blue eyes that moved back and forth between the speakers as though he was following a ball at a tennis match. Aggie's lips tightened with repressed amusement. "You realize he understands everything we're saying."

"Which is why he's on my side."

"Let me explain this to you in words you can understand." Aggie stepped forward and placed both hands on his damp, tee-shirt-covered chest, looking earnestly into his eyes. "Not. Going. To. Happen. I love my house. I love my life. Not getting married. Not moving. Period."

Her house, aka The Conch Cottage, was in fact Councilman Pete Grady's rental house, generously donated to the township of Dogleg Island on a five-year lease agreement as part of the housing package incentive offered to the new police chief—and also, Aggie suspected, because his brother had asked him to. It had once been Cedric Grady's garage, and as such was separated from Ryan's house only by a sand drive and a pepper tree hedge, through which Flash had worn a convenient dog-sized tunnel. There was one bathroom, one bedroom, and a living room the size of a paper napkin. The plumbing was from the nineteen fifties and the kitchen was even older, and the bedroom was so small that when Ryan slept over they literally had to crawl over each other to reach the bathroom, which created an entirely new dimension to the concept of intimacy. She kept her clothes in storage totes under the bed. But she loved the funky bright colors and uneven floors. She loved the porch swing and the spice cabinet in the living room with its multicolored drawers that she used to store everything from shoelaces to sewing needles. She liked that Ryan was next door. And she liked it all so much that she was sometimes afraid that if she changed even the smallest thing the entire fragile wonder that was her life would come tumbling down.

"Besides," she added softly, searching his face, willing him to understand, "we're practically living together. I'm not going anywhere. You're not going anywhere. That's enough, right?"

He smiled the kind of smile that told her he did not understand, and didn't want to understand, but loved her enough to pretend. "If you say so."

She gave his chest an affectionate shove and turned away. "Don't you have a meeting this morning?"

"Damn. What time is it?"

She glanced at the pelican clock over his shoulder. "Seven forty. You better hustle."

"Crap. I'm going to run home and get a shower." He opened the refrigerator door and took out a bottle of milk, gulping down a few swallows.

"I hate it when you do that."

"Bishop's coming for dinner." He recapped the bottle and returned it to the refrigerator.

"What're we having?"

"Whatever he catches." He closed the door and added with studied casualness, "I almost forgot. Lorraine said if you're going across the bridge this afternoon to stop by the bar and she'll ride with you. She wants to do some shopping."

Aggie rested a gaze on him that was quiet and solemn. "Don't do that."

"Do what?"

"Pretend. Pretend like everything's okay. Like you didn't ask your sister-in-law to drive me to my appointment because you were afraid I would freak out on the bridge and like she didn't tell you to tell me she wanted to go shopping because she was afraid of the same thing. Don't pretend like I'm normal. Because I'm not normal, Ryan. I'm incredibly, unbelievably, colossally messed up. And besides that, I've got a bullet in my brain. So don't pretend."

He leaned against the refrigerator, his expression easy and pleasant. "Okay."

Her brows drew together uncomfortably. "But if Lorraine wants a ride across the bridge, I'll stop by the bar."

"Okay."

The frown deepened, but only briefly. "And thanks."

He smiled and winked at her gently. "You know I've always got your back, right?"

Aggie swallowed, glanced away, and then managed a smile. "Yeah. I know."

The silence between them might have gone on just a beat too long, but just then Flash, like water flowing uphill, leapt up onto the barstool and sat there with his front paws on the kitchen counter, firmly atop the newspaper that was unfolded to the headline story. He looked for all the world as though he was reading it. Aggie couldn't prevent the bubble of laughter that rose to the surface, as it so often did when Flash was around. It was as though he was on a mission to keep her smiling, even when smiling was the last thing she felt like doing.

Even Grady grinned, but the mirth faded when his gaze traveled to the headline. He glanced at Aggie, and he said quietly, "You okay?"

"Sure. Fine." But her eyes moved as though of their own volition from Flash to the picture of the accused that was pulsing, larger than life, from the newsprint. The defense team—and he could afford the best—had somehow managed to make sure that the only picture of Darrell Allen Reichart that was released was his high school yearbook photo: clean scrubbed, smiling, white shirt and tie. No wonder none of it seemed real to her. She didn't even recognize the photograph of the kid who'd shot her.

Her throat felt tight and her voice was a little husky as she said softly, "I wonder if Flash remembers." She walked over and dropped a hand onto the silky, curly fur of Flash's neck. "I wonder if he recognizes him."

Grady was silent. Still, after all this time, after all they'd been through, he had trouble talking about it.

Aggie said, "Flash, get down."

The border collie made a soft sound of disagreement in the back of his throat, but sprang down to the floor, dragging the front page of the newspaper with him. Grady bent to pick it up.

"Baby, listen, if you need to talk about this," he began, but didn't seem to know where to go from there.

She shook her head. "I'm good. Really. You're going to be late."

He looked at her gravely. "I thought we weren't going to pretend."

She wished for one brief, intense moment that she could tell him the truth: that all she knew how to do was pretend, that she didn't know whether she would ever be able to do anything except pretend. But this wasn't the time or the place and besides, she somehow thought he already knew.

So she just shrugged. "Go to work," she said. "You've got a meeting, and I've got to see a woman about a cat."

He caught her neck with the back of his hand and kissed her again, and relief was mixed with the tenderness in his eyes. "Call me if you need anything. See you tonight."

"Be safe out there, Grady." These days she never let him put on the uniform without saying that.

"You too, sweetie."

This time her smile was a bit more genuine. "Yeah, I'll watch out for those vicious paper cuts."

He grinned and tugged a short lock of her hair before turning to leave.

But as he was almost at the door she called after him, "Say, Ryan, did you slice oranges for breakfast this morning?"

"Breakfast? No time, honey, gotta run!"

Aggie filled Flash's bowl with kibble, and he took a few polite bites, knowing that better fare would come his way as the day progressed. When she or Grady—usually Grady—had time to make breakfast they always made enough for three, but this morning she had been distracted. The frown returned to her brow as she turned, as though drawn by a magnet, back to the newspaper. She smoothed out the creases left by Flash's paws and read the article again, this time more slowly.

Almost two years after the brutal slaying of Leah and Walter Reichart in their Dogleg Island home,

*the double homicide case will be tried in Murphy
County court. Sixteen weeks of jury selection, pretrial
motions, and postponements concluded with the
judge's decision on Wednesday that no video cameras
will be allowed in the courtroom. Opening statements
are scheduled to begin on Monday at the Murphy
County Courthouse under tight security. The jury
will be sequestered for the duration of the trial.*

*Both defense and prosecuting attorneys
declined to speculate on the length of the trial,
although Special Prosecutor Jeffrey Richardson
confirmed that the State of Florida will be seeking
the death penalty.*

*Darrell Allen Reichart, age 21, is accused of
attacking his father Walter with a knife from their
own kitchen, slicing his throat before turning the
weapon on Leah Reichart and stabbing her sixteen
times. Both Leah and Walter Reichart died of their
injuries. Before fleeing the scene, Darrell Reichart
allegedly shot Murphy County Sheriff's Deputy
Agatha Malone, and was himself wounded and
subsequently apprehended by sheriff's deputies
while trying to escape.*

*Walter Reichart had a successful dental prac-
tice in Atlanta, Georgia. His wife Leah was heiress
to the Atkins Paper fortune. Darrell Reichart was
their only child.*

*Reichart has maintained his innocence of all
crimes, claiming that he came in from an evening
swim to find his parents' bodies. He has repeatedly
insisted that an unknown intruder fired the shot*

that wounded Deputy Malone. He awaits trial in the Murphy County Detention Center, and is expected to enter a plea of Not Guilty.

Aggie turned her gaze to the photograph of the fresh-faced teenager that accompanied the article, willing herself to feel some sense of horror, of anger, of repulsion or disgust...of recognition. She swam with sick fear when she faced a blind corner, was paralyzed with dread by the sight of a door she had never opened before, and succumbed to panic attacks that left her unable to cross a bridge, but at the sight of the person who had tried to kill her she felt nothing.

The sea breeze stirred through the screen door, ruffling the pages of the paper and bringing the scent of oranges. She heard Grady's screen door slam and glanced at the pelican clock again. He was definitely going to be late for his meeting with Richardson.

She picked up her empty coffee cup and turned to put it in the sink. Flash suddenly whipped in front of her, sat, and put his paw on her knee. She backed away, brushing sand from her uniform pants. "Hey!" This time Flash put both paws on her knees, pushing hard.

He barked.

Across the hedge, Grady gave a quick *bleep* of the siren and a flash of the dome light as he pulled out of the driveway; his way of saying good-bye. He had driven a squad car home last night, which he was allowed to do now that he was a captain, probably for the sole purpose of breaking speed records on his way to work this morning. Aggie caught the flash of the dome light out of the corner of her eye, started to give a small helpless shake of her head, and suddenly there was a crash. She stared at the shards of china that appeared at her feet but she didn't really see them. What she saw was Ryan's face, ashen, sweating, terrified, and what she heard was his voice shouting over and over again, "Officer down! Officer down!"

His hand, caressing her face, the anguish in his eyes, his voice whispering brokenly, "Hold on, Aggie, it's okay, you're okay, stay with me, baby, just stay with me."

She thought, *Dude, chill.* She tried to say it but all that came out was gurgling sounds. She was choking on her own saliva.

Ryan shouted, "Where's that goddamn ambulance, Bishop? It's Aggie! Damn it…it's Aggie!"

She realized with no small astonishment that the wetness on his face was not sweat but tears. He was crying. *Oh, Grady. Don't cry. It's going to be okay. Really.* She tried to lift her hand to touch his face, to comfort him, but it wouldn't move. Nothing about her would move.

"Six minutes out." Bishop's voice, calm, in control. "Is she breathing?"

"Yes." His words were short choked gasps. "Breathing."

"I'm en route to you. Describe the situation."

"Chief, it's Briggs."

Into her field of vision came Briggs, the big loveable teddy bear, his face glistening with sweat, his bulk heaving with whooshing breaths, breaths she could hear on her radio and in person, a symphonic echo like the roar of the ocean. "Beach patrol requesting backup." *Whoosh.* "Repeat, urgent backup needed. 210 Harbor Lane." *Whoosh.*

"All units responding." James Earl Jones, clear and calm on the radio. "Four minutes out. What is your situation?"

Whoosh. Whoosh. "Two victims deceased, one male, one female." Whoosh, whoosh. "Suspect down from officer gunfire. In custody. One victim..." Whoosh. "Murphy County Deputy Sheriff..." Whoosh, whoosh. "Seriously wounded..." Whoosh. "GSW to head."

In the background there was barking. "Is the puppy okay?" she said, only again it came out as gurgles. Grady swiped a hand across his eyes and left a smear of blood. Panic rose in waves, *whoosh, whoosh,* and she struggled to sit up. She couldn't move. Nothing moved. *Is the puppy—*

"Okay!" she gasped, and staggered backwards, grasping the countertop for support. Back in her own lime and red kitchen with fragments of a broken coffee cup at her feet and Flash barking an unintelligible command in her ear. She stared at him. He stared back. She lifted a shaky hand to her face and felt the damp skin beneath the backs of her fingers.

Flash barked.

She looked at him, and he regarded her with his head tilted, his gaze probing. She bent to pick up the broken pieces of the coffee cup, aware of a bizarre numbness in the tips of her fingers. She breathed out, long and slow, through her mouth, and opened the hand that did not hold any coffee cup fragments, spreading the fingers. Steady now. That was good.

Flash nudged his small, wedge-shaped head between her elbow and her body in a gesture that was both comforting and comical. She rubbed his head with her knuckles, right on the bridge of his nose between his eyes, in the spot that he liked, and then she pushed herself to her feet. "Weird, huh, boy?" she murmured. Then, regarding him thoughtfully, she added, "Let's not mention this to Grady, okay?"

Once again, all Flash could do was bark.

There is a school of thought among dog lovers, especially those partial to the herding breeds, that the domestic dog is in great part responsible for civilization as we know it today. The survival of early man, so goes the theory, depended on his ability to gather and maintain a herd or a flock, which was not only time-consuming but resulted in a greatly nomadic society which had little reason for or interest in building structures, forming social groups, creating art. Once the dog came in and took over the care of the flock, humans were freed to settle down and till the soil, to trade with neighbors, to build cities and sailing ships and invent the Internet and the iPhone and the concept of the late-night talk show. The weight of this responsibility has given the domestic dog a certain dignity, an awareness of his purpose in life, that is most discernible in the eyes of a border collie.

Dogs, like humans, have depended on their ability to adapt in order to survive. But because their short lifespan allows for as many as ten generations of dogs to evolve within a single human's life time, they are able to adapt, change, and pass on their evolved DNA to their offspring much faster than humans. Before 1960, the dog's brain literally could not perceive the projection of light through a cathode ray that resulted in images being displayed on a television screen. Now they not only can see the images but recognize them, and there is an entire television channel devoted to nothing but programming for dogs.

Though the dog's brain is structurally considered that of a simple mammal, recent research with functional MRI equipment has demonstrated that dogs dream much as humans do, and about many of the same things; they experience the emotions of love, anticipation, joy, and anxiety in the same areas of the brain that humans do. And while the frontal lobe of the canine brain, which houses such functions as complex reasoning, the ability to plan and project into the future, and language, has been found to be undeveloped or underdeveloped in most dogs, the border collie is the exception.

No one is quite certain why the border collie brain should have evolved differently than that of other canines, although the fact that until very recently border collies were bred exclusively for performance is as likely an explanation as any. For centuries this working dog's survival depended on his ability to chart the terrain of a ranch or sheep station that might encompass a thousand square miles, to remember and recognize each member of a flock and to immediately make mental adjustments for births, deaths, and confinements; to memorize and differentiate between dozens of commands that might be given in language, in whistle sounds, or in hand signals, and sometimes in a combination of all three. As a consequence, his brain began to change. The area responsible for long-term memory began to grow to accommodate the hundreds of thousands of details for which he was responsible. The neurons associated with sight and sound began to multiply in order to distinguish and characterize the constant bombardment of essential stimuli his senses received. And his language centers, in response to the need to differentiate between and make associations for the hundreds of new and distinct sounds to which he was exposed in the world of humans, started to develop.

Published reports indicate that at least one border collie has demonstrated the ability to recognize over a thousand words, enabling him to carry out complex tasks at about the level of a three-year-old child. Anecdotal evidence from pet owners suggests this is not unusual, and might even be an underestimate. This breed's survival was ensured by his ability to remember, reason, and adapt to the changing demands of his environment. Just because humans have not yet been able to accurately measure his capabilities does not mean those capabilities don't exist.

Flash remembered every detail of that night of blood and thunder. He understood every word—or most of them, anyway—that Ryan and Aggie spoke. And if he had been able to speak the language of humans, he could have told Aggie why she dropped the coffee cup.

Because he smelled oranges too.

CHAPTER THREE

Ocean City, the county seat of Murphy County, lay on the mainland side of the bridge that connected Dogleg Island to the rest of the state. For the islanders, it was Town. It had a nice marina, a Wal-Mart and Home Depot, 12,000 residents, and a mobile DMV. You could get your hair cut, your dog neutered, and your prescription filled all within ten minutes of the bridge. Ocean City was also home of the sheriff's department, the detention center, and the county courthouse, where the biggest trial of the century in Florida was due to take place next week. Ryan Grady wheeled his squad car into the Reserved Parking space at the courthouse two and a half minutes after his meeting was scheduled.

Allen Edwards, the county prosecutor who was assisting on the case, was waiting for him, along with three or four assistants and Richardson himself. Allen turned and offered his hand when Grady came in, but Richardson barely glanced up from the tablet he was working on. Grady said, "Sorry I'm late." And everyone knew he didn't mean it.

"We understand a law officer's schedule," Allen replied pleasantly, and everyone knew he didn't mean it, either.

Richardson did not look so pleasant. "Let's get on with it, shall we? We've got the testimony of three more people to review before noon."

Allen gestured Grady toward a chair in the middle of the room that he guessed was supposed to look like a witness chair, and he took it. "I'm not sure why we're doing this again. It's not like we haven't been over this a half dozen times already."

"That's exactly why we're doing it again," said Richardson. "The defense counts on the passage of time to blur witnesses' memories and cause inconsistencies in their testimonies. We're going to make certain that what you say on the stand is exactly what you said in the signed statement you gave to the police twenty-two months ago. Mr. Edwards will be playing the role of the prosecuting attorney today." He gave a short nod of his head. "Proceed."

Grady resigned himself to another wasted hour of the usual: establishing his credentials, confirming the obvious, setting the stage. Then the same sequence of events they had reviewed over and over again. The security alarm. The response. The radio chatter.

"So your unit was dispatched to 210 Harbor Lane in answer to a call from the security company regarding a triggered alarm?"

"Not exactly. Deputy Malone was closest, and she took the call."

"And when she arrived she called for backup?"

"No. Deputy Malone was working without a part-ner that morning and my partner and I were just coming on duty, so we offered an assist."

"What time did you arrive at 210 Harbor Lane?"

"7:02 a.m." He knew this only because it was part of the police record, and he had memorized it.

"Was Deputy Malone on the scene when you arrived?"

"She was."

"Take us step by step through the next few min-utes, Captain."

"The three of us proceeded to secure the scene. My partner went east toward the beach, I went west to the deck, and Deputy Malone went to the front door." He recited the facts in a flat dry tone, just as he had been trained to do, just as he had done so many times before, just as though every word did not plunge him right back there into the middle of the nightmare. "I heard Deputy Malone call out and identify herself. I went up the steps to the deck and knocked on the sliding glass door on the west side of the house. I also identified myself. There was no response. Deputy Malone then reported over the radio that the front door was open and she was going in."

Richardson, who until this point did not appear to be paying attention, looked up from his tablet. "Open or unlocked?"

Grady hesitated. It had been almost two years.

"It's important, Captain Grady," Richardson said sharply. "Was the door standing open, or was it merely unlocked? Chief Malone's testimony has been that she tried the door and it was unlocked. Yours should be the same."

Grady's jaw tightened briefly. "Right."

"Start again." Richardson turned back to his tablet.

Allen gave Grady a sympathetic look but said, "Captain Grady, describe your actions when you arrived at 210 Harbor Lane."

And so he started again. Allen asked whether he could see inside the house from the glass doors. He explained that the draperies were drawn and that the interior seemed dark. Allen asked how he responded when Aggie said she was going in.

"I told her to wait, that I was coming around to the front."

Richardson did not look up. "Did you tell her to wait for you, or did you say 'hold on'?"

Damn it, Grady thought. *Damn it.*

"Because the transcript of your original statement says—"

"I know what the transcript says," Grady said shortly. "I may have said 'hold on' but what I meant was for her to wait for me."

"Don't volunteer information, Captain. You said, 'Hold on, I'm coming around' and that is what you will testify to. Go on."

Tightly, Grady related the events of the longest sixty seconds of his life. The way he had decided to turn left and check out the rest of the deck instead of going straight down the steps and around to the front. He could have so easily turned the other way and gone down the way he had come up. He would have been at the front door in ten seconds. But Aggie reported all was well, said the house looked empty, started talking about the puppy. So he continued to secure the perimeter. No one could fault him for that. No one.

"You walked completely around the deck, is that right?"

"Yes."

"Did you see anyone on the deck?"

"No."

"Did you see anyone on the beach?"

"No. I didn't have a clear view of the beach in all directions and I knew my partner was already there. I concentrated my attention on securing the deck and immediate perimeter of the house."

"Did you see anything in your examination of the deck to arouse your suspicion? Any signs of a struggle or forced entry?"

"No."

"Did you report that to your fellow officers via radio?"

"No."

"Why not?"

"Because just as I was about to I heard a gunshot from inside the house."

"Where were you when you heard the gunshot, Captain?"

"I was approaching the front door from the east side of the house, where a second set of steps led down to the walkway in front of the house."

"And upon hearing what you took to be a gunshot what did you do?"

Flat, professional. "I reported shots fired into the radio and I drew my weapon. I advanced into the house and encountered the suspect running toward me."

"Could you describe his appearance please?"

"He was wearing swim trunks, no shirt, no shoes. His torso, legs, arms, and face were splattered with a considerable amount of what appeared to be blood. He was agitated, weeping. He held a pistol in his right hand."

Allen nodded. "Where were you at this time?"

"In the foyer, about six feet from the front door."

"Go on."

"I identified myself and told the suspect to drop his weapon. He refused, at the same time turning the gun on me. Again I told him to drop the weapon or I would fire. He continued to advance, his firearm held in a threatening manner. I fired my weapon, wounding the suspect and disabling him. I called in the shooting and went in search of Deputy Malone."

And so Allen made him go there, made him walk the steps again, listen again to the rasping of his own thin, desperate breath, see again the crimson glisten of blood on travertine, the way it pooled, hot and wet, on the stone, quivering and moving and catching the reflected light, seeming to have a life apart from the life it was deserting. A lake of red death, sucking up the light. Sucking up life.

"I found Deputy Malone on the floor of the great room, immobilized by a bullet wound to the head. I called it in. Approximately four feet away, partially concealed by the sofa, were the bodies of a male and a female. Both appeared to be in their night clothes. The woman exhibited multiple wounds to the torso and throat, mostly obscured by blood. The male had a single open wound across the throat."

"Did you approach the victims to examine them, Captain?"

"No." Grady could feel a fine film of sweat on his forehead, gathering at the corners of his mouth.

"Why not?"

Grady returned a long hard look. The weight of his heart was like a stone in his chest, rising up and down only through the force of his breath. "Because, asshole," he said, enunciating his words with deliberate care, "I was too busy trying to keep the brains of my fellow officer from spilling out into my hands."

Jeffrey Richardson glanced up. "You're a witness for the prosecution, Captain. If you're rattled by our questions, the defense will tear you to shreds. Rein it in. I like the part about the brains though," he added, turning back to his work. "Good visual for the jury."

Grady wanted to punch him out. Instead he turned to the prosecutor and said stiffly, "Sorry, Allen. I didn't mean you."

Allen looked uncomfortable. "I know how difficult this must be for you. Let's move on."

And so they moved on. At least Allen moved on. Grady answered his questions, of course, methodically, professionally. But most of him was still back at 210 Harbor Lane, holding Aggie's face in his hands. When he'd stood up, the knees of his trousers were wet with blood, and later—maybe days later, he wasn't sure—the blood had dried and stiffened and made a crinkling sound when he walked. He'd ended up burning the uniform in the grill in his backyard.

An hour and a half passed. Grady felt like he'd spent the time on a boot camp obstacle course. Finally Allen thanked him for his time and promised to keep him updated. Grady started to get up. That was when Richardson put aside his tablet and stood.

"Mr. Grady," he began.

Grady sat back in his chair, watching the other man warily. "Captain," he said. "It's Captain Grady."

Richardson gave a very small nod of approval. He had drilled Grady previously on the importance of asserting the authority and competence of the police at every possible opportunity. "Captain Grady," he resumed, "you've testified that you encountered the suspect in the entry way of the home, and that he seemed agitated. I believe you said he was weeping."

Grady was cautious. This was new. "That's right."

"Would you say he seemed frightened?"

Grady scowled. "No, I wouldn't say that. I'd say he seemed like a crazed strung-out coke-head mass murderer who just shot a law officer. What is this?"

"This," replied Richardson, "is exactly what the defense is going to ask you. Reichart is claiming that he found his parents' slaughtered bodies and that a third party fired the shot that wounded Deputy Malone. He claims he picked up the gun that was lying next to his father's body in self-defense and was fleeing the house when he encountered you. Answer the question."

"That's bullshit! He was fleeing the house because he'd just murdered his parents and shot a deputy!"

"Answer the question," repeated Richardson firmly.

Grady's nostrils flared with an indrawn breath. He released it slowly. "No," he said impatiently, "he didn't seem frightened."

"How do you know that, Captain Grady?" Richardson insisted. "You said he was weeping, agitated, running toward the door. That sounds like the behavior of a frightened boy to me."

"He wasn't frightened," Grady said angrily. "He was...I don't know what the hell he was, but it wasn't frightened."

Jeffrey Richardson wore steel-rimmed glasses, and behind them his steel gray eyes were completely impassive. He said, "You have no way of determining the suspect's state of mind, is that correct, Captain?"

Grady bit down hard on his back teeth again. In a moment he said, "I have no way of determining the suspect's state of mind at that moment. He appeared agitated, and he was weeping. And," he added coldly, "he had a gun."

Richardson nodded approval again. He said, "What did he say to you?"

Grady stared at him. "What?"

"Did the suspect say anything? You've testified he was weeping. Did he say anything?"

Grady swallowed hard, and looked away briefly. Before that morning, he had never fired his weapon outside of training, but the funny thing was that he remembered very little about the moment he pulled the trigger, the way it felt, what he was thinking. What he remembered was the blood that had stiffened on the knees of his trousers.

He returned his gaze to Richardson and he replied, "He said, 'help me.' That's what he said. 'Help me.'"

Richardson said, "A teenage boy, covered in blood, ran to you and pleaded for help. And then what did you do, Captain?"

Grady replied, "I shot him. I told him to lower his weapon, and when he raised it to fire on me, I shot the son of bitch in the gut."

Richardson looked at him for one beat, two. He said, completely without expression, "Darrell Reichart approached you, begged for help. What did you do?"

Grady shifted his gaze to the American flag in the corner of the room. He said nothing. He said nothing. And said nothing. Then, "The suspect approached me with a firearm in hand. I identified myself as an officer of the law and demanded that he drop his weapon. The suspect raised his weapon in a threatening manner toward me. I advised him again to drop his firearm. He did not, but continued to approach. I discharged my weapon, firing a single disabling shot to the suspect's torso."

Richardson gave a very small, approving smile. "Let's move on."

CHAPTER FOUR

According to geologists, Dogleg Island, like most of the other barrier islands that dot the Gulf Coast of Florida, was separated from the mainland by a great prehistoric seismic shift that tilted the ocean like a giant's wading pool and submerged half the continent. It was officially discovered by the French in 1583—French pirates, to be exact, whose success in the Western Caribbean during the sixteenth century accounted for a considerable percentage of the wealth of France, to say nothing of their own. They named the island Petit Fleur after the tiny wildflowers that blanketed the island, and used it as a source of fresh water and wild boar meat for the voyage home. Rumors persisted, of course, that they had also used it to stash treasure, and every few years a new batch of fortune hunters would show up with dig permits in hand, but if so much as a gold doubloon had ever been found, no one was talking about it.

In 1720 a massive hurricane virtually cut the island in half, creating a dangerous reef of broken boulders upon which hundreds of ships had been lost throughout the centuries. Those sunken ships had yielded up genuine bounty over the years, and the waters off the western shore of Dogleg Island remained a popular destination for recreational divers and treasure hunters alike into the modern day. In 1843, the island, which was then being used by the United States Navy as a munitions storage facility, was dealt another devastating blow by Mother Nature. The storm surge from one of the most powerful hurricanes in recorded history virtually submerged over half of the island. When the waters receded, a deep lagoon was all that remained of the main portion of the island, leaving behind the dogleg shape from which it eventually derived its name.

The lagoon was now enjoyed by fishermen, boaters, and kayakers, and provided a home for sea birds and dolphins. The long narrow "leg" of the island was a wildlife sanctuary managed by the State of Florida. The "haunch" of the island, which was connected to the mainland by the Cedric B. Grady Memorial Bridge and surrounded on two sides by the Gulf of Mexico, was a little over three miles wide at its widest point and twelve miles long. This was Aggie's beat. Which meant, of course, that it was Flash's beat too.

Flash had one job: to take care of Aggie. He knew this because Grady told him so, almost every day. *Take care of my girl, big guy,* and *Keep an eye on Aggie, will you, bud?* In fact, the first thing he ever remembered Grady saying to him was, *I'm counting on you, little guy. Take care of Aggie.* He never forgot his instructions, but the fact was that Aggie needed a lot less taking care of than Grady thought she did. In fact, Flash had observed that it seemed to be Aggie's job to take care of everyone else on the island, which meant it was Flash's job as well. So he had expanded his job description, so to speak, to include keeping track of everyone and everything on the island and making sure that he and Aggie were ready to put right anything that might have gone wrong.

He knew, for example, what time the lights were supposed to come on inside each shop on Ocean Avenue, and what time they were supposed to go off. He knew what time the big yellow school bus flashed its lights at the corner of Third and Main and how many children were supposed to come out of it. Sometimes cars got impatient waiting and tried to go around the school bus before the last child had crossed the street, but they didn't try it when Flash was on duty, you could bet on that. He knew the islanders by name, and he knew the tourists by their smell—suntan oil and rubber shoes, mostly, with the occasional hint of new spandex and chlorine swimming pools. All were equally important to him, and he hadn't missed a day of patrol since he and Aggie had moved out of the sad dark place and into the happy little house across the hedge from Grady.

The majority of the full-time residents—now up to 412—lived in concrete block or wooden fishing cottages from the 1940s like Grady's, most of which had been added on to and updated over the years, and all of which were within an easy bicycle ride along hard-packed coquina roads to the beach. Since the toll booth had been taken down on the bridge, seasonal rentals had become a growing industry, but the season didn't really start until June, and most of the colorfully painted, water-view homes on pilings remained empty this time of year. Then there were the beachfront mansions along what was now known as Millionaire's Row, second homes to plastic surgeons and CEOs and bankers from Orlando and Atlanta, Birmingham and Tallahassee. One of those homes, 210 Harbor Lane, had been closed up tight, utilities disconnected, for over a year. Nonetheless, Aggie sometimes drove by as part of her routine patrol, and sometimes, particularly on quiet foggy mornings when no one was around, she would park in front and just sit there in her patrol car, looking at it.

She did not do that today. Today she turned right before she got to the stoplight in town, took the sand-and-shell road past a vacant lot with a faded "For Sale" sign that proclaimed *Ocean View!*, continued past a row of three mailboxes, a bright coral concrete block house with a Seasonal Rental sign in front, an abandoned single-wide all but overgrown with weeds, and pulled into the short crushed-shell drive of 1312 Egret Road.

The house was a gray one-story on pilings with parking underneath, and Bernice Peters's red Cherokee was in its place there. In the other bay, leaning crookedly against a concrete support pillar, was a bicycle with one red fender and one orange one. The landscaping consisted of a few spiky palmettos and some scraggly looking lantana growing wild around the perimeter of the St. Augustine grass that served as a lawn. But her deck was a lush tropical garden of window boxes and potted plants, trailing vines and fragrant blossoms. As Aggie got out of the car, a screen door opened and a woman in a blue velour tracksuit came out onto the deck, arms folded.

Flash hopped out of the car after Aggie and immediately began to explore, head down, tail waving. Aggie called up, "Good morning, Mrs. Peters."

Bernice Peters scowled down at her. "For some folks, it might be."

"I understand you had some excitement this morning."

"A woman my age doesn't need that kind of excitement. Besides, your lackey's already been here, took her report, said she'd do what she could." She sniffed contemptuously. "Like *that*'s supposed to make a taxpayer feel like she's getting her money's worth."

Flash looked for signs of the excitement, but all he found was the usual: the crisscross paths of snakes and lizards and a toad or two, night dew, and the smell of a big fat rat, which was odd because a cat lived here. There were bicycle tracks in the sand drive, and they weren't more than a few hours old. Mrs. Peters's grandson was here, whom Flash remembered from the time when Aggie and Grady had brought a tree into Grady's house and put lights on it, and everyone he met gave him treats; a truly magnificent time that should have lasted longer. But Aggie didn't need him to inform her about the grandson; she had already noticed the tire tracks and the beach bike that was propped up against the pillar. Mrs. Peters did not ride the bicycle, so it was stored in the rafters beneath the deck unless her grandson was here.

"May I come up?" she said to Mrs. Peters.

"Might as well, I reckon. But if that dog of yours gets sand on my porch I'll have his hide."

Flash, who had one foot on the bottom step and another on the second step, backed off and sat down. Aggie smothered a grin and gave him an affectionate tug on the ear as she passed. "Better not risk it, boy, "she murmured. "She might be serious."

Amenably, Flash moved off to sniff around the trash cans. He was curious about that cat.

"Damn right she is," returned Bernice as Aggie came up the stairs. "Not a thing in this world wrong with my hearing." And with a satisfied nod, she spun on her heel and went back into the house, letting the screen door slam behind her.

According to Ryan, Bernice Peters had married a petty officer in the navy, settled on the island when he retired in 1987, and taught eighth grade on the mainland for the next twenty-five years. Two of her most memorable students had been the Grady brothers, which made Aggie a bit more sympathetic toward her perpetual crankiness. Her husband had died in 2003, but Bernice remained a powerful force on the island, heading up committees, lobbying for high-speed Internet and twice-a-week garbage pickup in the summer, and making sure that no crime, from littering to jaywalking, went unreported on Dogleg Island.

Aggie reached the top of the stairs and hesitated, not certain whether Bernice Peters had intended for her to wait there or follow her inside. It was just a screen door, but the brightness of the morning made it impossible for her to see inside, and she could feel that vague tightening in her chest that felt like uncertainty, but if allowed to grow could become something so much more. Abruptly she turned away to look over the deck rail. The Gulf, just visible between the row of houses that lined the street, was sparkling today, and she could see a boy in a wet suit skating across the surf on a red board. She had a pretty good idea who it was.

She turned as the screen door squeaked open and Bernice pushed through, carrying a tray with two mugs of coffee and a plate of cinnamon rolls. The cinnamon rolls, which were still warm from the oven, confirmed her guess about the boy in the surf.

"So Josh's down for spring break?" she said, accepting the cup of coffee from the tray.

"He is." Bernice set the tray on a glass-topped table and plucked a paper napkin from it, which she thrust into Aggie's hand. "Have one of these sweet rolls. No sense letting them get cold waiting for that boy to come in."

Aggie obliged, peeling off a soft warm roll and licking the sticky icing from her fingers. "How long has he been in the water?"

"Since daylight, I reckon. Beats me how these kids do it."

Aggie made an appreciative sound as she bit into the sweet roll. It really was delicious. "How old is he now?"

"Twenty. Prelaw at FSU." Bernice sat in a plastic webbed deck chair and braced her hands on her knees, giving Aggie a stern look. "Now are we going to talk about my cat or what?"

"Let's talk about the prowler first," Aggie suggested, and took another bite of the roll.

A little impatiently, Bernice repeated the report she had already given Mo. Apparently she had awakened at 5:08 that morning—so noted because of the oversized LED numbers on her beside clock—and saw the shadow of a man creeping around outside her bedroom window. She called out a warning—something to the effect that she had a gun and wasn't afraid to use it—but by the time she looked out the window he was gone. Knocked over two of her potted plants in his hurry, broke one of them. That was when she had called the police, for all the good it had done. No, she had not been able to get a description; it was pitch dark that time of day, for heaven's sake. And no, she had not been able to see which direction he had gone.

Aggie said, "And your grandson slept through all this?"

"He's slept through a lot worse, believe me." Her tone was both exasperated and affectionate. "He was up and ready for the water by the time that police-woman of yours got here, though. Something about this being the only time of day the waves are any good."

Aggie nodded. Although you'd generally catch better waves in your bathtub than in most places on the Gulf, the reef that surrounded Dogleg made for some pretty good surfing at high tide, at least accord-ing to Grady. This was one of the better-kept secrets of the Forgotten Coast, although as more and more people wandered in from the over-crowded beaches of central Florida, it clearly would not remain a secret for long.

When Bernice nudged the plate toward her, Aggie helped herself to another cinnamon roll. "These really are delicious. Thank you." She took a bite and added, "Your cat sleeps inside at night, right?"

"Absolutely. I'm not going to have him prowling around after dark killing my songbirds."

"And you last saw him...?"

"Sleeping on my armchair at ten forty-five last night when I turned out the light."

"Was Josh in all night?"

She frowned. "He was. What does that have to do with my cat?"

Aggie said, "Well, if your cat was here when you went to bed and not here when you woke up, some-one had to let him out."

Bernice gave Aggie an impatient look. "You don't have to be the chief of police to figure that out. Obviously the burglar did it, only I scared him away before he had a chance to get in and take anything."

Aggie finished off the sweet roll and got up, wiping her sticky fingers on the napkin. She walked around the deck, noting the sliding glass door, the entry door with its dead bolt and thumb lock, as well as the windows. "I don't see any sign of forced entry," she said as she returned. "Were both doors locked when you got up this morning?"

She frowned a little. "Well, the lock on the slider rusted out a while back," she admitted. "We don't use it much."

"Did you notice anything missing? Maybe something from the deck or yard, or even under the house?"

She replied adamantly, "Just my cat. I don't keep anything under the house except that old bike Josh uses. Everything else is in my storage unit in town. Mostly Christmas decorations and such."

Aggie took a final sip of her coffee and returned the mug to the tray. "Thanks for breakfast, Mrs. Peters."

The other woman gave a small sniff. "I don't know how you keep body and soul together, as skinny as you are. You tell that Ryan Grady to feed you once in a while."

Aggie smiled. "Yes ma'am. I'll keep an eye out for your cat. Meanwhile, I want you to get that lock fixed, okay? And until you do, get Josh to

69

cut off a broomstick to put in the slider track so it won't open from the outside. There are a lot more people on the island these days. You can't be too careful."

Bernice Peters sighed as she stood. "I know you're right, honey. I just hate to see it." She gave Aggie a narrow searching look and added, "I read in the paper about the trial coming up. Guess it'll be a relief to have it over and done with."

Aggie managed to keep her smile. "It will."

"But a pure horror to have it all dragged up again. Seems to me the island hasn't been the same since it happened."

Aggie didn't know what to say to that. She watched Flash investigate the bicycle, then move around the perimeter, his nose to the ground.

"Well," said Bernice with a brisk nod of her head, "you just look the jury straight in the eye and tell them what happened, then let them do their job. Don't lose any sleep over it."

Aggie said, "Thanks, Mrs. Peters. I'll be in touch." Then, "By the way, I noticed one of the screws on your license plate holder was missing. They sell replacements at the hardware store. You want to get that fixed before you lose your plate."

Bernice gave a dismissing wave of her hand. "You just find Oscar and let me worry about my own repairs."

"Oscar?"

"My cat," returned Bernice impatiently. "That's what we've been talking about, isn't it?"

Aggie was at the bottom of the steps when Bernice called after her, "He has a blue collar with a tag on it. A microchip too."

Aggie waved her acknowledgment and called to Flash as she opened the car door.

Flash finished his circuit of the house, having found nothing much of interest except a beer cap and a couple of cigarette butts buried in the sand, which was disappointing. He didn't like mysteries, and he was worried about that cat.

After the shooting, Aggie had returned to duty as a Murphy County Sheriff's Deputy following four months' leave, but it was obvious in a week that it wasn't going to work out. The men and women who had lined up outside her hospital room, holding a grim and determined round-the-clock vigil for the first two weeks she was there, welcomed her back with applause and a balloon bouquet. No doubt they had received Briggs and Grady with the same enthusiasm—although perhaps minus the balloons—when the two men returned to duty after the shooting, but Aggie was special. She was the last of the Heroic Three, their fallen soldier, a symbol of the resilience and determination that epitomized Murphy County's Finest, a source of fierce loyalty and departmental pride.

Before the shooting, she'd earned the respect due someone who did her job and minded her own business; she was a good officer, a nice girl, and that was it. But during her recovery and rehabilitation, everything changed. Her fellow officers took turns taking care of her small rental house, picking up the mail and mowing the lawn and making sure the AC was running to keep the mold down. Their wives brought her cookies and makeup and magazines and other things to lift her spirits. When the insurance was slow to kick in, the guys all pitched in to pay her rent, and never said a word to her about it. Before the shooting, she had a job, but afterwards she had a family. And that was exactly why she could not remain an employee of the Murphy County Sherriff's Department.

She was everybody's little sister, the department mascot, their most prized possession. Her colleagues fussed over her, coddled her, bragged on her, worried about her. What they did *not* do was see her as an equal on the streets, and they never would again.

Department policy dictated that her first month on the job after a work-related incident be spent on desk duty, which was fine with Aggie. She knew she wasn't ready to go back out on patrol and wasn't sure if she ever would be. Six days before she was scheduled to return to the active roster, the newly elected Sheriff Roy Briggs called her into his office and told her about the police chief job.

She was both suspicious and oddly resigned. She knew as well as he did that she couldn't stay here. "Is this just a nice way of getting rid of me?"

He replied, "No. It's what I hope is a smart way of keeping you. At least that's what Bishop thought."

Ah, Bishop. It was starting to make more sense. Something about his wife's illness coming so soon upon the heels of the trauma they all had shared—Briggs, Aggie, Grady, and Bishop—had drawn them together in a way none of them would have predicted before, and no one from the outside could really appreciate. They had each other's backs. Always.

Aggie nodded thoughtfully. "Why not Grady? It's his island. He's got twice the law enforcement years I do."

Briggs just chuckled. "Grady wouldn't last two weeks, even if he was fool enough to take it." He added seriously, "The islanders are a peculiar sort, keep to themselves, don't take to outsiders, you know what I mean. But they like you, Aggie, always have, even before…well, you know." The short pause was awkward. "You always treated them with respect, understanding their ways…it means a lot. They think of you as one of their own. Their hero, in a way."

Wow, she thought, a little awed. *One of their own.*

"It's mostly administrative," he went on. "Parking tickets, traffic control, parade permits, things like that. You've got the qualifications, what with your prelaw background, and as long as you don't piss off the council, it's a lifetime job. The pay is not much more than you're making here, but still…"

But Aggie wasn't really paying much attention after that. What she was thinking instead was, *They think of me as one of their own.*

The orphan girl from Georgia had found a home. Finally.

Still, she sometimes marveled over how easy it all had been, how natural. She couldn't operate a boat, knew nothing about fishing, and could barely swim, but the islanders welcomed her anyway, overlooking her shortcomings around the water with the same deft tact one might pretend not to notice an ugly mole or facial tic. She was part of a community, an essential part, helping to build the small island that once had been united by nothing but geography and lifestyle into a sustainable and cohesive whole. People recognized that, and appreciated it. But not nearly as much as Aggie appreciated them.

After leaving Bernice Peters, she and Flash drove down Ocean Street, then walked across the dunes to the beach. The sand was damp and cold, and she could feel it through the soles of her shoes. She waited for Josh Peters to slide in from the surf, noted the brief flash of panic in his eyes, asked him a few questions. He answered as she expected. Flash noted that he was lying. So did Aggie.

They pulled up beside Joe Kelso's shrimp truck, which was illegally set up on the vacant lot between Ocean and Pine. The fine for a parking violation on Dogleg was up to $25 per day, but they had agreed when Aggie took over as police chief that Joe's fine would be $5.00 a day. It was cheap rent however you looked at it, but Joe pretended to resent the tickets every time Aggie presented him with one. Nonetheless, he dutifully paid them every week, always in cash, and always complaining.

Aggie and Flash got out of the car. "Hey, Joe," she said as she approached.

He was bald and clean shaven, his white tee shirt and pants inevitably bringing to mind Mr. Clean—except that there was nothing particularly clean about his uniform. He scowled at her behind the vendor window, where he was scooping ice around a tub of boiled shrimp. Most of his product was fresh-caught and raw, tails and veins intact, and when he had boiled shrimp it went fast. He said, "There you are again, out and about harassing innocent citizens."

She tore a ticket out of her book and handed it to him. "That's about the size of it. I'll take a pound, boiled."

He snatched the ticket from her, stuffed it in his pocket, and started weighing the shrimp. Flash, having completed his inspection of the lot, returned and sat hopefully beside Aggie. Joe tossed a boiled shrimp through the window and Flash caught it expertly.

"Say, Joe." Aggie squinted a little in the sun, which was now bright enough to bounce off the sand in a single white sheet. "You haven't seen Mrs. Peters's cat, have you?"

He added another handful of shrimp to the scale, tipping just past a pound and a quarter. He always gave her extra. He said it was for the dog. "Big grey striped fellow, bad attitude, hangs out with a yellow tabby named Holler?"

Aggie couldn't tell if he was joking or not, so she said nothing as he tilted the tray of shrimp into a square of white butcher paper.

"Yeah, I seen him. He's a regular around here. Hightails it down the road the minute she opens the door in the morning, near as I can reckon. Sometimes follows that kid around on the bike. Not today, though. I usually've chased him off a couple of times by now." He deftly taped up the paper bundle, dropped it into a plastic bag with a scoop of ice, tied it with a twist and handed it to her.

"Well, let us know if you do, okay?" She took the shrimp and passed him a bill through the window. "Mrs. Peters is pretty worried about him."

He grunted and put the money in his cash box. "She's got more to worry about than that cat, if you ask me."

"Oh yeah?"

He looked at her narrowly. "That cat involved in a crime?"

"I'm not sure. Maybe."

"Well, when you're sure, you let me know. Then maybe we'll talk."

His lips closed tight in that stubborn islander way, and Aggie knew the conversation was over. "Thanks, Joe," she said. "See you tomorrow."

He braced his hands on the window shelf and assured her, "Damn right you will."

She waved over her shoulder to him as she started toward the car. Flash fell into step beside her, giving one last yearning glance over his shoulder, but no more shrimp were forthcoming.

"Hey," Joe called when she was almost to the car. She turned.

"Maybe you ought to ask me about what else I seen."

Aggie turned and walked back to the shrimp truck, her expression neutral, unchanged. Flash walked beside her, his expression hopeful. She said, "I'm asking."

He leaned on his elbows, edging toward the window. "A fellow goes to work at four a.m., sees all kinds of things. Like this dark blue sedan parked right across from your house, fellow inside had some kind of something, could've been a sawed-off shotgun for all I know, aimed right at the old Grady place. Like he was waiting for somebody to come out or something. I figured it had something to do with that trouble you all are in."

It took her a beat to realize that the "trouble" he referred to was the upcoming trial, and the reason it took that long was because her cheeks had gone numb at the thought of someone aiming a shotgun at Grady's house. She said, "I don't suppose you managed to…"

"Don't even know what we pay policemen for anymore," he grumbled, digging out his cell phone. "Seems to me like the citizens do all the work."

He turned the phone to her, with the screen showing a blurry nighttime picture of a car, taken from behind. Grady's dark and empty house was in the background. But, thanks to what was probably the reflection of Joe's headlights on the tag, the license plate number was actually readable. She took out her notebook and copied them down.

Joe returned the phone to his pocket. "So, how about a pass on this parking ticket?"

"No deal. But if you e-mail that picture to my office, I'll probably be too busy to hand out parking tickets the rest of the week." Aggie placed her card on the counter. "And how about another shrimp for my partner?"

Joe thought about it, then nodded and took the card. "Deal."

He tossed Flash a shrimp, which Flash gulped down in a single bite.

Flash was a bit unsettled to hear about a car parked where it didn't belong. This was his beat, after all; how could such a thing have happened? And he was pretty sure Aggie did not allow shotguns on their beat. He was so disturbed by the possibility that something might have slipped past him that he almost missed the shrimp that sailed his way, but he came to his senses just in time. After all, Aggie had gone to some trouble to negotiate the treat for him, and he wanted her to know he appreciated it.

He and Aggie took care of each other that way.

CHAPTER FIVE

The Murphy County Sheriff's Department was structured fairly simply. Every deputy on every shift rotated through narcotics, detective, and public relations specialties in two-year terms. Every deputy on every shift road patrol, worked traffic, did PR in schools and civic organizations when called upon. Promotions were based on merit and seniority when a position became available.

The first time Grady was offered a captain's position, he laughed it off. Too much trouble, he'd said. Too much desk time. Besides, he had better things to do than be on call twenty-four/seven. All that work could start to cut into his beach time. The promotion came up again after the Reichart incident, and that time he'd taken it. He was an older, quieter, more thoughtful Grady then. He could use the money, he said, and besides, there was something to be said for being assigned a permanent day shift. Murphy County wasn't LA, after all, and even full-time captains almost always made it home for dinner.

He was in charge of six patrol officers and four detectives, and technically in charge of all ongoing investigations. But he had learned from the best that when you had good people on your team, the smartest thing you could do was to let them do their jobs, and he had good people. On his roster at the moment was a child molestation case being managed by B shift investigators, a hit and run that had been turned over to the prosecutor, and a half dozen domestic violence cases. There was a liquor store robbery, suspect in custody, and an identity theft ring they had cracked last week and were just winding up the paperwork on.

New on his desk, as he absently flipped through the reports that had landed there overnight, was a high-speed chase after a traffic violation resulting in a non-apprehension between Lawson Street and Ridgeway Drive, which pissed him off. He'd never lost a suspect in a chase in his life. What the hell were those guys doing out there if they weren't even going to try to stop crime? Worse, the license plate traced back to an island address, and that really burned him. Every man in a patrol car knew that the only reason for a citizen to run from a traffic stop was because he was guilty of something worse—probably drugs—and how many times had he lectured his men that the place to stop drugs on the island was on this side of the bridge? That was what they were here for, damn it.

He knew, of course, that what he was really mad about had nothing to do with a lost suspect and a high-speed chase. He was mad at Richardson and himself and at the utter arrogance of that rich-kid

Reichart who thought he could plead not guilty and get away with it. His mood was bad and getting worse, and he was about to yell out the door for a follow-up on the license plate when one of his day officers rapped briefly on the door frame and poked his head inside. "Hey, Cap," he said, and Grady could tell by the spark in his eyes that the next words were about to change his mood—and his day. "We just got a call from the island. You feel like getting wet?"

Aggie stopped by Grady's house to leave the shrimp in the fridge, then by the police station to leave the license plate number with Mo to check out. Maureen Wilson—known to everyone in the office as Mo—was another Murphy County recruit and Aggie's only full-time patrol officer. To say that Mo was a big, beautiful black woman would be to damn her with faint praise—although the beautiful part, most people would admit if forced to do so, was mostly on the inside. At 5'9" and 285 pounds, not many people messed with Mo, and those who did lived to regret it.

The second night she'd worked for Aggie, Pete had called in a drunk and disorderly in the parking lot of the bar; Mo had arrived to find a man beating up on his girlfriend and had clocked him with her baton without so much as a how-you-doin'. Fifteen stitches and a concussion later, the man threatened to sue, and Aggie solved that problem by charging him with battery, assault with a deadly weapon, resisting arrest, threatening a police officer, and, after a little research on the part of the ineffable Sally Ann turned up two years' worth of back child support payments, child abandonment. The only charges that stuck—battery and child abandonment—kept him in county detention for twelve weeks and gave his girlfriend a chance to get away. Between Aggie and Mo, a partnership was born.

Nonetheless, she did not tell Mo why she wanted the license plate tracked down. Mo had a tendency to overreact, and Aggie already had one twenty-four-hour bodyguard in Grady; two, if you counted Flash. She did, however, ask Mo to keep a casual eye out on the movements of Josh Peters, and she gave her a description of the missing cat, courtesy of Joe.

She had time to return some phone calls—ignoring the ones that were from reporters—before the ten a.m. meeting with the Downtown Merchants' Association. Afterwards, she walked across the street to the Bistro, where the owner had asked for extended parking in front of his restaurant for the night of the seventeenth, when he was hosting a wedding reception. Aggie had already been advised about the wedding and the potential traffic issues by the Beach Chapel, who had routinely applied six months ago for a permit to erect a temporary structure and seat a hundred fifty people on the beach. She spent some time discussing parking alternatives with the Bistro owner, whose eyes were practically glittering with dollar signs after a long lean winter, and as she was leaving Mo phoned with a report on the license plate.

"Man's name is Adam Morrisy," she informed her, "and that's a rental car out of Pensacola he's driving. One of them damn fool no-account reporters, or trying to be. They call 'em stringers, or at least that's what Sally Ann says. Day job at an electronics store, which is probably where he got that fancy spy camera and parabolic mike he's got pointed at your house."

Aggie blinked. "What?"

"I blew the picture up on the computer. Clear as day. Parabolic mike mounted right on the dash."

"A *what*?"

"Lord, honey, you have *got* to get HBO. That no-account lowlife is taking pictures and listening to everything you say inside your house." Then, hopefully, "You want me to do a stake out and haul him in?"

"Thanks, Mo, that won't be necessary." She tried not to sigh as she crossed the street and opened the car door for Flash. "I'll take care of it. And by the way, I know what a parabolic mike is, I just didn't expect to find one here." *Pointed at my boyfriend's house*, she added silently to herself, but of course did not say.

"Hot stuff, right?" agreed Mo with enthusiasm. "We hit the big time now!"

"I guess." Aggie tried not to sound as depressed as she felt. "Don't forget to swing by the school bus stop this afternoon. We're getting more tourists every day and all of them act like they never took the part of the driver's test that tells you what to do when the school bus flashes its lights and puts out the stop sign."

"You be careful going across that bridge, you hear?"

Aggie didn't bother asking how Mo knew where she was going. She told her to call the sheriff's department if there was an emergency—Dr. Ferguson did not allow cell phones in her office—and gave a small unhappy shake of her head as she disconnected and got behind the wheel. "This is really starting to get out of hand, Flash," she muttered. "I can't tell you how glad I'll be when it's all over."

Flash had no trouble hearing what Maureen said over the phone, but unfortunately found that much of what she said was lost on him even under the best of circumstances. As much as he hated to admit it, he didn't have a clue what Aggie was talking about.

So far—and with the exception of the shrimp—he was not having a great day.

Aggie swung by the house to change into jeans and a blazer for her appointment and walked into Pete's Place a little after noon. It was the lunch rush, which at this time of the year meant most of the tables were full. By summer, there would be a line out the door. Flash wound his way through the tables to the bar and sprang up onto the first vacant stool he saw, paws on the bar. Pete had taught him that trick when he was barely old enough to see over the brass foot rail.

Pete came up to the bar, towel in hand, and said, "Afternoon, Flash. The usual?"

Flash grinned a reply that he knew Pete understood, and Aggie laid a gentle hand upon the back of Flash's neck. "Cute, Pete. You know this is against health code. My buddy and I will be eating on the patio."

Pete pointed to the sign over the door that said, *Well-behaved dogs welcome; children must be on a leash.* "Besides," he said, "we pride ourselves on serving police officers."

"I appreciate that, but Flash is not an official police dog."

Pete nodded thoughtfully. "We need to get him one of those vests. I'll bring it up before the council."

Aggie grinned. "Well, until you do, we'll be on the patio. How's the grouper?"

"Frozen."

She made a face. "Bring me a tuna salad sandwich then."

He groaned. "You're killing me, babe."

"And the usual for Flash."

"Coming right up."

He started to turn away and Aggie said, "Hey, Pete."

He looked back.

"What do you know about what kids do around here for fun?"

He lifted an eyebrow. "Kids like the twins from hell?"

That was what he and Ryan called their nine-year-old nephews, offspring of their sister Lucy on the mainland. Aggie shook her head. "Kids like twenty-year-old college spring breakers."

He shrugged. "The usual. Drugs, sex, rock 'n'roll. Sometimes they come in here trying to slide by on a fake ID, but I can spot them a mile away, which is I guess why we're not that high on the hit parade for spring breakers. Usually they get their fix across the bridge at Mickey's or Go Nine, a cheesy joint with fake strippers you don't want to know about. Why?"

Aggie lifted an eyebrow. "Fake strippers? Seriously?"

"Baby, there's a whole world of scams out there you haven't begun to crack. And that one's out of your jurisdiction. What's up?"

She said, "Josh Peters."

Pete filled a glass with diet soda and slid it across the bar to her. "Yeah, he's a slippery one all right. I can't make up my mind whether he's a good kid trying to pretend he's bad, or a bad kid trying to pass for good. I'll tell you this, though, his biggest problem is the company he keeps. He came in here the other night with this punk-ass looking little dude, tats up one side and down the other, soul patch and mustache, one of those bite-my-ass swaggers, he might as well've been wearing a sandwich sign that said 'crack cocaine here.' Had to be forty, forty-five. That kid has got only one reason to be hanging out with a loser like that."

Aggie wasn't surprised, but she was sorry to hear it nonetheless. She liked Bernice Peters. "Did they cause any trouble?"

He shook his head. "Ordered a couple of burgers and beers—I only served one beer, of course—then finished up and left."

"When was that?"

He thought about it. "Day before yesterday, I think. Maybe ten o'clock."

"Thanks, Pete. We'll be on the patio. Where's your better half, anyway?"

"Trying on earrings. She said for you not to leave without her."

Aggie gave a small, almost silent chuckle. Like that was going to happen. "Come on, Flash. Let's go."

Pete had just brought out Aggie's tuna sandwich and Flash's hamburger—lightly seared on the outside, cold and juicy on the inside, no bun, no ketchup, one slice of lettuce—when Aggie's phone rang.

"Chief, glad I caught you." Mo's businesslike tone did not quite disguise her excitement. "You're not going to believe this. Some kayaker paddling too close to shore at low tide hit something, about ten feet off the Tarpon Road access."

"Any injuries?"

Flash could tell by the look on Aggie's face that he had better eat fast if he wanted to eat at all, so he did.

"Nah, that's not the point. The point is what they hit. It was a car. In the water. A car."

Aggie put down the triangle of her sandwich, getting to her feet. "Call fire and rescue, I'm on my way." It was procedure, although they both knew that if the car had gone in the water at high tide—which it must have done, or it would have been spotted long before now—there was no one left inside to rescue.

"Already done. I'll meet you there."

Flash gobbled down the last bite of his hamburger and scrambled after Aggie as she jogged down the steps, calling over her shoulder to Pete, "Got a call! Tell Lorraine I'll call her tomorrow!"

She flipped on the siren and slammed the car into gear almost before the door was closed. Flash loved it when she turned on the siren. He loved it almost as much as he loved the sound of gravel spattering against their back tires as they spun out onto the road.

Barely six minutes later, Aggie pulled the car onto the shoulder of Tarpon Road. Maureen's car was there before them and she was standing beside it, feet planted square, her big bosoms straining against the buttons of her uniform shirt as she interviewed the witnesses. She had a notebook in hand, and the kayakers, a man and a woman, gesticulated excitedly to punctuate their story. Flash, too impatient to wait for the door, bounded out the window and began to look for evidence. He could hear sirens in the distance and he wanted to find out what he could before the big trucks got there and made everything smell like diesel fuel.

All of the roads on the lagoon side of the island ended in public lagoon access; that was where part of the island taxes went, although it had been a point of contention on the ballot when the vote for incorporation came up. Some of the roads had houses on them; some did not. Tarpon Road was devoid of houses, but the owners of the four empty lots paid a tax premium for their proximity to lagoon access, just as the council had planned. This meant that, with the exception of a few raccoons, a lot of rats, some snakes and lizards, and one bobcat that Flash definitely intended to investigate later, the only thing to pass this way in the past twelve hours was a single vehicle. And inside that vehicle was one very bad thing.

Aggie came over to him, kneeling beside the line of crushed grass and broken shells that indicated the track of a tire. "Is this it, bud?" She called him that sometimes. "Is this where the car went off the road?"

Her gaze was already following the line of sight toward the flattened undergrowth that only a few hours ago had obscured the lagoon from view. Now the water glinted brightly across the tops of broken reeds and bushes. Aggie's brows drew together worriedly as she stood up again. "He went off the road here," she murmured, "but got back on it in time to drive straight into the lagoon. Probably drunk."

But Flash did not think so. He backtracked onto the sandy road a few yards and Aggie followed. He made sure she saw what he scented.

"Shoe prints," she muttered.

Yes, shoe prints, but not just that. Not just the smell of leather and canvas and carpet fibers and saw dust and wet sand and tobacco and the kind of briny fishy sour-mash odor that clung to the soles of shoes when a human walked through an alley behind a restaurant where the big Dumpsters were. Something beneath all that, the hot-black smell of burning thunder that he smelled sometimes on Grady, and even on Aggie, and when he did it made him nervous, itchy, and uneasy. But on them the smell was different. On them it didn't make him think of blood.

Aggie got up and followed the tracks a few feet. "Shoe prints right beside the tire tracks. Like someone was pushing the car." She frowned again and knelt beside the tracks, careful not to smudge them. "Hey, Flash. Look at this."

He obligingly came to stand beside her, even though he was much better at smelling than looking. She pointed with a twig to the design made by the sole of a shoe in the sand. "B.A.," she murmured, "clear as day." She took out her cell phone and snapped a close-up shot, then called, "Hey, Mo! Get some tape out of the car and secure these tracks."

Maureen lifted a hand in acknowledgement and started toward her patrol car.

Aggie stood up, dusting off her knees. "It's starting to look like this might not be an accident after all." She did not sound happy. But Flash knew there was even worse coming.

When Flash was still new at the world and learning his way around, one of his favorite activities had been chasing the squirrels that used to dash across Aggie's small yard and taunt him with their chittering little voices from the low branches of a palmetto tree. He did not know then that chasing was almost always more fun than catching.

And then came the day when he actually caught a squirrel, and in the same moment without even thinking about it, felt the bones of its little squirrel neck crunch beneath his teeth. The taste of hot iron blood. The great electric surge of life that was, and then was no more. And then a vast, black, unspeakable emptiness. There was life. There was no life. There was only a huge dark terrible nothingness, and it was the kind of nothingness he never, ever wanted to know again.

Because of him.

Flash had buried the limp, foul carcass in the sand of the backyard with the taste of iron still on his tongue, and then he had crawled underneath the narrow dark space of the porch where he intended to stay forever, where the nothingness wouldn't find him. Aggie called him, but he didn't come. He didn't stir when she placed a bowl of boiled chicken and rice—his favorite—at the edge of the porch, nor did he inch forward to lap from the water bowl she left beside it even though his tongue was sandpapered with thirst. He was afraid that if he moved, the nothingness might come for her too.

Because of him.

Daylight faded and shadows grew. Aggie sat on the ground at the edge of the porch and talked to him, but he closed his ears. Nighttime came, and still she sat there, waiting for him. Sometime before dawn she started to cry. He could feel her sorrow, and it was almost as big and as terrifying as the nothingness. He heard her whisper, "Don't do this, Flash. I need you. Please don't do this. You're all I've got. Please don't leave me."

This was before Aggie knew that Grady loved her almost as much as Flash did. It was before they moved into the happy yellow house. It was in the sad, quiet time, when all they had was each other.

He crept forward inch by excruciating inch, until his chin rested on her lap. She wrapped her arms around him and bent her head to his fur, her tears wetting his neck. That was the night he understood that sometimes you have to do the thing you refuse to do, and face the thing you most fear, for the sake of someone you love. Sometimes you have to go into the darkness.

And that was how he knew, now, what he had to do. He followed the trail, knowing what lay at the end of it. He heard Aggie call, "Flash!" But he did not look back. She called again, with a touch of alarm in her voice, "*Flash!*"

He dived into the darkness.

CHAPTER SIX

Grady surfaced, spat out the regulator, and pushed back the visor and hood of his wet suit. He caught Aggie's gaze onshore and shook his head. "Nothing," he called across to her, and also for the benefit of the other officers and EMTs who were waiting there. Everyone looked disappointed. An empty vehicle meant a protracted search, an unsolved mystery, and a possible gruesome surprise outcome. The lagoon was as deep as the ocean in some places, as tangled and untidy as a swamp in others. Once a person went missing there, anything was possible.

Grady added, "We're searching the perimeter. We'll go fifty feet out, then call in the winch to raise the vehicle. No tag," he added, which everyone on shore knew meant that the chances of the vehicle having been involved in a crime were raised considerably.

Grady was one of the five certified divers on call to the county for search and rescue. He and two others had responded to Aggie's call, along with a contingent of sheriff's deputies and two rescue trucks, one county and one local. A heavy-duty tow truck with a winch had arrived only minutes ago, and was standing by while the other two divers continued to search the bottom of the lagoon.

Aggie knelt close to the water, her arm around a wet and shivering Flash. She had dried him off with a towel and tried to warm him with a space blanket she kept in the patrol car, but he was still shivering, and she knew it was not from cold. She looked at him. He was never wrong.

"Grady," she shouted across the water, "pop the trunk."

Even in the bright sunlight that prismed the water, even across the twenty feet or so that separated them, she could see his skepticism. He called back, "Not procedure to do it under water. We can't bring the vehicle up until we've secured the area. It'll take a while."

She threaded her fingers through Flash's coarse, wet fur and insisted tightly, "Flash found something, and he doesn't lie. Pop the trunk!"

Grady hesitated, but not for long. He looked at Flash too. Flash looked back, shivering. Grady turned to one of the deputies standing onshore and called, "Get me a crowbar."

Mo gazed down somberly at the body stretched out on the tarp before them. "Sure is something how you can go all year without a damn thing happening, then all of a sudden it's everything at once, ain't it?"

Aggie blew out a long breath. "Yeah, sure is."

The victim was a male, looking to be well over forty. He wore a faded red tee shirt with a skull and cross bones printed on front, jeans, and running shoes with no socks. He had not been in the water long enough to distort his features, although there were a few bluish red crab bites on his face, and his skin was pale and flabby. Thinning brown hair slicked back from the forehead, ending in an anemic ponytail. A soul patch on the chin. Bad teeth. Tattoos up both arms and on his neck.

His most distinguishing feature was a bullet hole in the middle of his forehead.

Flash came by, giving the tarp a wide berth, on his way to the patrol car. He already knew what lay there, and he didn't want to get too close. Aggie didn't need him for this. He jumped inside the car through the open window and curled up in a patch of sunlight to dry his fur.

Three more units from the sheriff's department had been called in to blockade the entrance to Tarpon Road, which Aggie thought was overkill. The police photographer took pictures. The coroner took measurements.

"Body in a car trunk." Mo gave a disbelieving shake of her head. "Now, that's big city if I ever heard it." She slanted Aggie a suspicious look. "How'd that dog of yours know there was a body down there, anyway?"

Aggie said, "Dogs have a sense of smell that's five hundred times greater than a human's, even under water." When her colleague still looked skeptical, she added, "He's a trained police dog."

This Mo seemed to accept. "Well," she allowed, "at least it's nobody we know."

Maureen lived on the mainland, just across the bridge with her daughter and her three-year-old grandson, but in the two years she'd worked for Aggie she had come to think of the people of Dogleg as her own. Aggie understood what she meant when she said that, and she didn't feel bad for pointing out, "It's still our case, Mo. And I think I might have a lead on the victim, so make sure we get copies of the crime scene photos ASAP."

Maureen's eyes widened as she looked at her boss. "No sh—I mean, yes sir, on it, Chief." She started to turn away then looked back at Aggie. "You don't mind me asking…"

"I'll let you know as soon as I do," Aggie said. "Meanwhile, I need you to go find Josh Peters, Bernice Peters's grandson, and bring him in for questioning."

Mo's eyes grew even bigger. "Holy you-know-what. This *is* the big time." She hesitated. "Um, bring him in where?"

She had a point. The Dogleg Island police station was a three-hundred-square-foot space located in a strip mall between a beauty salon and a bakery with barely enough room for three desks and a file cabinet. Interrogations were not a priority, and therefore not in the building plan. Aggie said, "We make do with what we have, Mo. Bring him down to the station and call me when you're on your way. I'll meet you there."

"You got it." She moved away as briskly as her bulky frame would allow.

"And Mo."

The big woman looked back.

"Be nice about it, okay? No point in scaring the kid to death."

Mo looked mildly insulted. "I'm always nice."

Aggie smiled and lifted an eyebrow, but didn't argue.

Seth Garrison was the county coroner, an earnest, slight young man with thinning hair and black square-framed glasses who had been elected to the position mostly because no one else wanted it. In this part of the country the county coroner did little more than issue death certificates and, by virtue of the family-owned funeral home, prepare bodies for burial; nonetheless, Aggie turned to him when he had finished examining the body.

"Hey Seth," she said. "What can you tell me?"

He had an expression of controlled horror on his face. He didn't see that many murders around here, and the graphic evidence of what one human could do to another was enough to put anyone into a mild state of shock.

He took off his glasses, wiped them nervously, and replied, "Well, um, hard to say at this point, the ME will know more after the autopsy, of course, and with the temperature of the water and all, there's some math to be done…"

"It's okay, Seth," Aggie assured him gently. "Just an opinion will be fine for now."

A look of mild relief crossed his face and his shoulders seemed to relax a fraction. "Well," he said, putting his glasses back on, "cause of death appears to be that wound on the head. I'd say a bullet, but you know we can't say for sure until they open him up and, well, find it. Hard to say for sure with him being in the water and all, but if I had to give an opinion I'd say he was dead before he was put in the trunk." He hesitated. "As for the time of death, from the state of the body I'd say no more than six hours ago. The crab bites indicate the car went in at low tide, which would have been between three and six this morning. Just a loose opinion, of course," he added quickly. "Don't tie me to it or anything. The ME's office will write a report."

She nodded and smiled. "Thanks, Seth."

She walked over to Grady, who was talking to the two divers from Fire and Rescue. They were still in their wet suits, although they had dropped their tanks and unzipped the necks. Grady had used the back of an ambulance to strip out of the hot neoprene and change back into his uniform, which was rumpled and somewhat the worse for wear. The two divers nodded a greeting as she approached, and then one of them told Grady, "I don't see any point in going back down. If there was anything we didn't find, the tide has it now."

Grady nodded agreement. "Yeah. Thanks guys. I don't think there's anything else to find anyway, but you have to cover your bases."

"Right." The diver gave a small shake of his head and glanced around. "Hell of a thing, huh?"

Grady said, "You got that right."

Aggie waited until the two had departed to ask, "Any opinions about the murder weapon?"

"Well, I'm no expert, but I'd guess a nine-millimeter. Neat, precise. The shooter knew what he was doing."

She nodded. "Some of that body art looks like prison tats to me."

"Yeah, me too." Then he grinned at her. "I love sleeping with a woman who knows what prison tats look like."

She added thoughtfully, "I have to do some research, but that shoe print looks familiar. It might be a uniform boot."

"Military?"

"Probably."

"Well, that narrows it down." The sarcasm in his voice was mixed with resignation. With both a naval training station and a Coast Guard station less than fifty miles away, three-quarters of the male population of Murphy County was either retired or active military.

She shrugged. "It's a place to start. And take a photo of the vic over to Pete. See if he recognizes him."

"Pete?" Grady looked surprised. "Something I should know?"

"Just covering my bases."

"Are you officially asking for assistance from the sheriff's department, Chief Malone?"

One of her eyebrows twitched wryly. "I am officially suggesting we make this a joint investigation, Captain Grady."

"In that case, I have some intel to officially share. High-speed chase on the other side of the bridge around one this a.m. My men lost him between Lawson and Ridgeway." His lips tightened briefly in annoyance, and he jerked his head toward the recently recovered vehicle. "The description was a black Dodge Charger, a lot like this one."

"Do you have dash video?"

"I've got something better. A tag number. Turns out it was registered to Ms. Peters, right here on Dogleg."

"Bernice Peters?" Aggie frowned. "She drives a red Cherokee. And it was still in its parking place at eight this morning."

"Things aren't always what they seem, Chief."

Aggie pursed her lips thoughtfully. "Actually," she said, "they usually are." Her phone buzzed in her pocket and she checked the text. It was from Mo, and she was on her way in with Josh Peters. "That was easy," Aggie murmured. On the other hand, most apprehensions were on an island this size.

She glanced at Grady. "You got this?"

"Yes ma'am. What's up?"

"Bernice Peters's grandson is home from college. He might know some things we need to know. I'm on my way to talk to him now—for the second time today."

Grady gave a thoughtful nod of his head. "You're right. Sometimes things are exactly what they seem. Drugs?"

"Probably. Make sure the photographer gets some good shots of the tire tracks and the shoe prints, will you?"

"Yes ma'am."

"See you at home."

"Don't be late for dinner."

She tossed him a wink and a wave over her shoulder as she turned toward the patrol car.

Aggie was two blocks from the office when her cell phone rang. "What the hell?" demanded Lorraine.

Lorraine Grady was the first best friend Aggie had had since high school—or, if she really thought about it, perhaps ever. Like most of the best relationships in Aggie's life, this one hadn't really begun until after the shooting, when they had bonded over wigs, of all things.

"Dead body in the lagoon," Aggie responded. "Looks like a homicide."

There was a beat of silence. "Damn," replied her friend. "I had my eye on a pair of gold espadrilles at Hali Kalani. Sale ends tomorrow."

"Sorry about the shopping trip," Aggie said. "Can we reschedule?"

"Have your people call my people," Lorraine responded. "Love you, sweetie,."

"You too." Aggie disconnected as she made the turn onto Main Street.

She reached her free hand across the seat and brushed Flash's almost-dry fur. "Thanks for your help, Flash," she said quietly. "That must have been awful, going in the water after a dead body. But it would have taken us a lot longer to find it without you."

Flash did not have the human ability to dwell on unpleasant things in the past, and if it had not been for the slight dampness lingering against his skin he might already have forgotten about the awful black nothingness in the water. As it was now, they had more important business at hand, and he couldn't believe Aggie was about to miss it. On the other hand, it was his job to make certain she didn't. He stood abruptly and barked out the window as Joe's shrimp truck came in sight.

"Sorry, dude," Aggie said, "I know you've earned a treat, but no time for shrimp. We're working a case."

Flash barked again, several times, insistently. Aggie glanced at him curiously, and then she got it. "Right," she murmured. "The guy goes to work at four in the morning."

She made the left turn, pulled the car up beside the shrimp truck, and got out. Flash trotted beside her.

Joe was just finishing up with a customer as Aggie and Flash approached, and he met them with hands propped wide apart on the counter, glaring. Aggie got right to the point. "This morning you asked me if Mrs. Peters's cat was involved in a crime," she said. "Well, I think it might have been."

"Thinking ain't the same as knowing," he pointed out stonily, but there was the faintest flicker of interest in his eyes.

She went on, "You also said Mrs. Peters had more to worry about than a missing cat. Would one of those things happen to be her grandson?"

He didn't even blink.

"Because a man was murdered last night," Aggie said, "and his body was dumped in the lagoon. We think it happened between three and four in the morning. There aren't too many people on the streets that time of day, but you're one of them. Did you see anything this morning I need to know about?"

He scowled. "You're the almighty *po*-lice," he returned testily. "Seems to me you ought to know a whole lot more than you do."

Aggie nodded patiently. "We've covered that, Joe. I just hope I don't find out later you've been withholding information that could have been of assistance in a homicide investigation, because we in law enforcement tend to take a very dim view of that kind of thing."

He stared at her in what might have been taken as a belligerent manner. "I didn't see the Peters kid this morning."

Flash put his paws up on the counter and met Joe stare-for-stare. Aggie prompted, "But other mornings?"

"Yeah, maybe I seen him now and then, all hours of the day and night, especially the night, creeping around where he ain't got no business."

"Like where?"

"Here and there. Down by the park. Over by Marine Street. Riding that bicycle of his toward home before sunup with no reflectors on it."

Aggie nodded. Beachside Park was a known make-out spot after it closed—although what the kids did there was generally a bit more intense than making out—and Marine Street was little more than an alley where, unfortunately, any number of illegal activities might take place. "When?"

"Don't know. Don't keep a calendar. Two, three times this week maybe. Not this morning."

Aggie glanced at Flash, who held his position with his paws on the counter. She turned back to Joe, determined not to make the same mistake with him she had made earlier. "So what did you see this morning?"

There might have been just a twitch of a smile at his lips, the smallest token of respect. "Maybe nothing. Maybe a black Dodge Charger with no license plate, cruising down Nautilus with its lights off."

Nautilus was the cross-street to Tarpon. Less than a quarter mile from where the car had been pushed into the lagoon. Aggie felt her chest catch with excitement, which she deliberately subdued. "Time?"

He gave a single lift of his massive shoulders. "3:30, 4:00."

"I need you to be more specific."

He thought about it. "I left for the docks at 3:30 to pick up my catch. Ten minutes to Nautilus."

"So 3:40?"

"More or less."

"Did you see the driver?"

The look he gave her was both patient and derisive. "Guess you've never seen a car with its headlights off at three in the morning on a road with no streetlights."

Aggie placed her hands on the counter, fingers splayed inches from his, and leaned in. "Joe," she said distinctly, "I weigh a hundred ten pounds on a good day and my last martial arts class was twelve years ago, but if you think I can't kick your ass when I want to, just keep on playing this game."

To add emphasis, Flash barked. He was getting impatient too.

This time the twitch of Joe's lips was more like a grin. "He might've been bald," he admitted. "Only got a glimpse of him from behind. Round-shouldered fellow, long-sleeved shirt. All I saw."

The victim had been wearing a tee shirt, and had a long ponytail. And if the driver was not the victim, he was very likely the killer.

Flash put his paws on the ground and Aggie straightened up, smiling. "Thanks, Joe. You've just earned your citizen of the day award."

Joe replied, disgruntled, "I'd rather have free parking."

"Then get a permit," Aggie replied and turned to go.

"Hey."

She turned, and Joe tossed a shrimp toward Flash. He caught it, naturally.

"On the house," Joe said, scowling. "But that's the last one."

Aggie smiled all the way back to the car. So did Flash.

CHAPTER SEVEN

"So," said Aggie, setting a platter of shrimp and cocktail sauce on the patio table five hours later, "just as I suspected, Josh was stealing his grandmother's license plate and 'loaning' it to his good buddy Arthur Lincoln, who just happened to end up shot through the head in the trunk of his own car in the lagoon this morning. Josh was the so-called burglar Bernice Peters almost caught trying to break into her house this morning, only all he was doing was trying to sneak home after a wild night out."

Jerome Bishop looked both surprised and impressed. "So you made an arrest for the murder? The Peters kid?"

Aggie shook her head. "I wish."

Grady added, "Not even close."

They were on the back patio of Grady's house, an hour late for supper, and Grady was just now lighting the charcoal in the grill. By the time he got back to the office, finished his initial report, and had seen the body into the custody of the medical examiner, he'd been the one who was late getting home. Jerome Bishop had arrived at six with a five-pound red grouper he swore had been hanging from his own fishhook that morning, but which they all knew had come straight from the marina fish market. Aggie had made the coleslaw and Bishop was on his second beer before Grady showered and got the fire started. The sun was setting over the lagoon, and the sky was dove grey streaked with pink. Tiki torches flared and danced in the sea breeze, burning citronella-scented fuel to keep the mosquitoes at bay and making the entire deck smell like oranges.

"The ME locked in the time of death between two and three a.m.," Grady said, "which means he was completely alive when my guys let him outrun them at one."

"That must've put the fear of God into him though," Aggie said. "Because he tracked Josh down at a party at the marina half an hour after that and returned the license plate. Two dozen witnesses swear he was alive when he left the party at 1:30 and that Josh was there until four a.m. Not to mention that if Joe's description of the guy who was driving the Charger at 3:40—with what we've got to assume was Lincoln's body in the trunk—was anything close to accurate, there's no way it was a twenty-year-old kid."

"Also," Grady put in, "he wears the wrong size shoe. The prints we found at the site were a ten and a half. He's a nine."

"Which doesn't mean he's not guilty," Aggie said. "Just not of this crime."

Bishop nodded and helped himself to a shrimp. "Oh, he was running drugs all right. Some kids never change."

"I knew the shoes wouldn't match the footprints, or Flash would have picked up on it when we brought Josh in," Aggie said.

Flash, hearing his name, looked up hopefully at the shrimp platter. Nothing was forthcoming however, so he settled back down to wait.

"You were right about the logo, though," Grady said. "Baer uniform shoe. The guy from the company said it looked like their leather duty chukka, and is sending a list of uniform stores they ship to in Florida. The US Navy is not one of their customers, by the way. "

"That's a relief. At least we don't have to interview every sailor on the Gulf Coast. "

"Officers can order their own uniforms," Bishop reminded them. "And anybody can walk into a uniform store and pick something off the shelf."

"True enough," Grady said, "but officers would spend their money on dress shoes, not utility boots. These boots run around a hundred fifty dollars new. So my guess is we're dealing with somebody who values good footwear. A security guard maybe, or night watchman."

"Maybe a reservist," Aggie added, glancing at Grady. "You get your boots from Baer, don't you?"

"Yeah, but if I'm going to spend that much, I get Gor-Tex. The company guy said these were leather.

Nobody wears leather duty boots at the beach unless they have to."

Aggie sat down in one of the cedar Adirondacks across the table from Bishop. "I know the Peters kid is bad news, but I thought he was going to throw up when I showed him the crime scene photos. You can't fake being that scared. And he gave us enough names of Lincoln's associates to keep the sheriff's department busy for a few days. He has no idea how lucky he is not to be spending the night in County right now."

Grady poked at the coals and stepped back as a flame flared up. "Which is where he would be if you'd gotten a search warrant. You know he's got drugs hidden somewhere in that house."

"No probable cause, no search warrant." Aggie frowned a little as she picked up her beer. "Besides, I hate to do that to the grandmother. It's her house you're talking about. "

Grady shook his head in admonishment. "That's the trouble with you, Malone. You're too damn nice."

"Yeah, right." She glanced at Bishop. "What did you mean about some kids never changing?"

"He's been spending the summer here since he was ten, twelve years old," Bishop said, "and I've been keeping my eye on him just about that long. Never pinned anything on him, nothing serious anyway." He looked at Grady. "We interviewed him in the Reichart case, didn't we?"

"Yeah, him and every other kid in the county his age. You know how they all hang out together, the ones that come back every summer. Reichart tried to use him as an alibi, but Josh wouldn't cop to it. Smart kid."

"I remember now," Bishop said. "The kid was smart enough to drop his bad-news bud quicker than we could spell out his name back then. Doesn't look like he learned much about how to pick friends, though."

"They hardly ever do," Aggie agreed. "Maybe I should have charged him this afternoon. Might've scared him straight."

Grady smiled at her ruefully across the patio. "Honey, if seeing his old drug buddy spend over a year in jail waiting trial for slicing up his folks didn't scare him, I think it might be too late."

Aggie winced. "Good point."

Bishop took another shrimp by the tail and dipped it in cocktail sauce. "Lincoln," he said thoughtfully. "Link. Why is that name setting off all my alarm bells?"

"Maybe because he's been dealing drugs on the coast for over ten years," Grady said. He came over to the table and picked up the bottle of beer he had left there. "It would surprise me if his name hadn't come across your desk once or twice."

"I guess." He frowned a little. "Seems like something more, though." He lifted his shoulders in a small shrug, letting it go. "What about the tats? They tell you anything?"

"Nothing gang-related," Grady said, and Aggie added, "At least not active gangs."

"The dude's pretty old," Grady explained. "Did a stint in Reidsville in the nineties for narcotics, and was back in two years later for homicide—shot a homeowner during a B&E. How he got out on that one in ten years I don't know, but he did. Since then he's been brought up a couple of times, but never convicted. Fell off the radar a couple of years back, as near as I can tell."

Bishop lifted his bottle in a small salute to the two of them. "All in all, a good day's police work, I'd say."

Grady sank down into the chair next to Aggie's and took a long drink from the bottle. "Except for the fact that we've got a dead body and no killer in sight."

"Yeah," agreed Aggie, a little glumly. "Except for that."

Grady stretched forward to swirl a shrimp in sauce and popped it into his mouth. He tossed the tail to Flash, who caught it expertly, crunched it up, and licked his lips. Aggie slid him a look of mild reprimand. "He's had enough for one day."

"You'll get him," Bishop assured them with confidence. "A partner he screwed over, a deal gone bad...the culture is pretty tight in these parts and there aren't that many places to hide."

"It's all hands on deck," agreed Grady. He frowned a little at the bottle in his hand. "I just can't help thinking the timing couldn't've been worse, with the trial coming up and all."

Bishop said, "How'd it go with Richardson?"

Grady drank again. "Okay. The usual. He thinks I'm going to blow my testimony. Jeez, since when is telling the truth not good enough? I wish somebody would explain that to me."

"The defense has a case," Bishop said. "You know it, I know it, Richardson knows it. I wouldn't have believed it two years ago, but they by-God do."

"The murder weapon," agreed Grady, frowning. "We never found the knife."

A large chef's knife had been missing from the distinctive chrome and mahogany set in the Reichart's kitchen. The presumption was that was the murder weapon, and that, most likely, it had been disposed of in the ocean.

"The thing that never made sense to me," Bishop admitted, "is if he killed his parents with a knife, why did he pick up a gun when he heard the police?"

"That's just how the defense is planning to confuse the jury," Grady replied, scowling. "What happened was that the kid set off the burglar alarm to lure his parents downstairs. The kid admits his dad kept a gun in a drawer by his bed ever since their house in Atlanta was broken into the summer before."

Bishop's frown deepened, "Yeah, but that wasn't the gun Darrell had on him. Records clearly show that Walter Reichart applied for and received a concealed carry permit for a thirty-eight special, but the gun we found that night was an unregistered nine-millimeter Luger. The thirty-eight never showed up. I never understood what an upstanding citizen like that, a dentist for God's sake, would have been doing with an unregistered gun when he had a perfectly legal one at home."

For a moment Aggie hesitated, frowning, trying to catch a thought that was just teasing the edge of her memory. Something about the gun that didn't seem quite right. Something about Darrell standing there holding the gun...But it was gone.

Aggie shrugged and swirled a shrimp in sauce. "You know how stupid people can be. He forgot his pistol at home, didn't want to go through the process for another state, thought it was easier to just buy it off the street. Or he could've bought it at a flea market, thinking it *was* registered. We'll probably never know."

Grady made a dismissive gesture with his beer bottle. "Just another way to confuse the jury. The storyline is as clear as day. The kid came up from the beach, crazy drugged out, and set off the alarm. He picked up a knife from the kitchen, sand on the floor shows that's the way he came in. Dad gets his gun, goes down to check out the burglar alarm, and the kid comes up behind him and slices his dad's throat, causing him to drop the weapon. When his mother came down and saw her dead husband, she probably started screaming, wasn't such an easy target—"

"Stab wounds on the neck," Bishop pointed out, "multiple defense wounds."

Flash watched Aggie grow smaller and smaller, tight into herself. He moved close to her.

"Right," said Grady, "so he chased her down, stabbed her until she was dead. Probably didn't plan it that way, but what're you going to do?"

Flash pressed his flank against Aggie's knee. She dropped her hand to his neck.

"Then he threw the knife out the door," Grady went on, "twenty feet or so to the ocean at high tide. He didn't expect the police so soon, but when he heard Aggie come in, he picked up the gun his dad had dropped and..."

"The rest is history," agreed Bishop, absently reaching for another shrimp. "The problem is that the kid claims his folks were already dead when he came in. He picked up the gun to defend himself."

"He was smoking crack on the beach. His tox screen was so high they almost couldn't anesthetize him for surgery." Grady gave a snort of derision. "Hell, he claims he didn't even fire the gun."

"Which is BS because there was gunshot residue in the barrel."

"Not to mention Darrell's fingerprints."

"Of course," Bishop pointed out, "if we want a definitive match, we'd have to have the bullet."

Aggie smiled tightly. "Sorry I can't oblige."

"He means that's what the defense is going to argue," Grady said.

"I know what he means. It's a weak argument."

"The problem is," Bishop concluded mildly, "without a witness, there's no way to prove his story is wrong. Just like there's no way to prove our story is right. I'm just saying. He's got a defense."

"His story is bogus," Grady declared firmly, upending the beer. "Any jury in its right mind will see that."

"Still," said Bishop, "it's a defense. And it always bothered me, about the murder weapon."

Grady met his eyes in the filtered twilight. "Yeah," he said. "Me too."

Aggie stood abruptly. "Ryan, for crying out loud, see what you can do about that fire, will you? If I don't take the fish out of that marinade in the next five minutes it's going to turn to mush."

Flash got up and followed Aggie into the kitchen, wondering why no one thought to ask about the cat.

The timer light on the microwave was flashing when Aggie went into the kitchen. She stared at it, for a moment unable to remember what it was or why it should be blinking. Flash barked once, sharply, and then it came to her: the fish. She had set the timer for the marinade on the fish. Flash barked again and she started to turn to him, but instead of Flash she saw the tiny holes of a white acoustical tile ceiling, and Ryan's face swam into view. He was wearing jeans and a tee shirt and carried a backpack casually over his shoulder.

She was in the hospital. She flung out a clumsy hand for her cup, because the medication that dripped into her arm made her mouth too dry to speak, and he held the straw to her lips. She drank, and then she said, ungraciously, "What are you doing here?"

He put the yellow plastic cup back on the Formica table by her bed. The room was filled with cards and flowers and balloons. There were boxes of chocolate-covered cherries on the nightstand, on her swing-arm table, on the window sill, one for every day she'd been here. She had given most of them to the nurses, but they still kept coming.

He said, "Just routine, ma'am. We like to pay a courtesy call to all our officers who've almost been killed in the line of duty. Good PR, you know."

She shifted her eyes away. There was nothing to look at but the half-opened blinds and an air-conditioning unit outside the window. "I don't want any visitors."

"How come?"

"I'm peeing into a bag."

"Yeah, well, I didn't want to bring it up, but now that you mentioned it, we can avoid that awkward moment."

He smiled, and almost coaxed a smile out of her. But instead tears went hot in her eyes. She hated that. The doctor said it was because of the medication, but she cried all the time and she hated it. Angrily, she shifted her gaze away from Grady, but the tears spilled over anyway. "They shaved my head." Her voice broke at the end. She hated that too.

"Don't worry," he assured her. "Nobody can tell underneath that big-ass mummy bandage you're wearing." He tried to make her smile again, and failed.

She turned her face to the window, the tears flowing freely now. "Go away, Grady. Please…just go away."

But he didn't go away. He swung the backpack off his shoulder and said, "I brought you something."

"No more candy. Please."

"It's not candy."

He astonished her by sitting on the corner of her bed, nudging her gently with his hip. "Scooch over."

She brought her gaze back to him, staring, and the tears momentarily forgot to fall. "What…?"

He swung his feet up onto the bed beside her and set the backpack on his knee. She thought she was hallucinating when the backpack seemed to move of its own accord. Then he unzipped it and a small, fuzzy, black and white head poked out.

She caught her breath. "Oh," she whispered. "Oh my goodness."

Grady watched her carefully, intently. The puppy used its little pearly claws to wriggle out of the backpack and clamber across Grady's jeaned leg to Aggie, expertly avoiding the IV tube and monitor wires as he crawled up her chest and licked her on the chin. She smiled, a gesture that had become so foreign to her it almost hurt her face.

"Oh my," she said. And again, "Oh…my."

Grady said, still watching her, "Do you remember him?"

The puppy snuggled against her neck and she raised one clumsy hand to touch him, rubbing his silky fur. "He saved my life," she said softly. "The doctor said if the bullet had—if it had hit me straight on, I'd be dead. But the puppy barked, and I turned my head at the last minute and...well, I didn't die, did I?" She ducked her chin, rubbing her cheek against the small bony head. "He saved my life." She looked up at Grady. "You got him, right?"

For a moment he looked confused. "Who?"

"The guy."

"Reichart? The shooter?"

"The guy the puppy barked at. The one..." But Grady was looking at her oddly and the thought, half-formed as it was, evaporated like mist as the puppy began to lick her chin. She chuckled as the little guy curled up with his head on her shoulder and closed his eyes. "Look at that. He's not in the least bit scared of all this."

"That's because he found where he belongs." Grady smiled at her. "I'll keep him for you until you get out of here. The guys at the department are crazy about him."

That was the first time she actually started thinking that she might get out of there. That she might go home. She stroked the fuzzy coat. "Thanks, Grady. That's nice."

Grady dropped his gaze, the smile fading. "I want to tell you something. All this time, messing around, acting like an idiot...I thought I'd blown my chance, you know? But that's not going to happen again." He looked at her. "So what I wanted to tell you was...thanks for not dying."

She looked at him, puzzled, and then he took her fingers, and wound his own gently through them. "Okay?"

She was going to answer him, she was certain of it, but just then Flash barked, a rapid staccato string of barks, and she was back in Grady's kitchen again with the microwave flashing and intense border collie eyes fixed on her as though she were a lost sheep he was trying to herd back into the flock.

She whispered, "He was wearing boots."

Flash barked again, staring at her, and Grady came through the sliding door. "The coals will be ready in ten minutes," he said. "Do you want me to make the garlic bread?" Then he glanced at Flash, who had ceased barking but was still regarding Aggie intently from his herding dog crouch. "What's up with him?"

For a moment Aggie had difficulty concentrating on what he had said, but then she smiled quickly. "Hungry, I guess," she said, and turned to get the marinating fish from the refrigerator, "like the rest of us."

She picked up the dish but suddenly her wrist went weak and she almost dropped it. Grady stepped in with a quick, "Whoa!" to save the fish and she smiled apologetically.

"Slippery," she said. "Be careful."

She glanced at Flash as Grady took the dish, but Flash seemed to have recovered from whatever it was that had set him off, because he had taken up a polite sitting stance, his gaze fixed hopefully on the fish. She murmured, "That's the second time today he's done that."

"Done what?"

She frowned a little, absently threading her fingers through her hair, seeking the scar, the indentation left by missing pieces of skull, the place where the bullet shattered her life.

Grady looked concerned. "Baby, you okay? Headache?"

She dropped her hand with a quick smile and a shake of her head. Headaches, with a brain injury, were nothing to be taken lightly, and Grady was ever vigilant. "No. I'm great." She turned to open a cabinet. "I'll make the garlic bread. Ready in seven minutes."

But when Grady was gone she closed the cabinet door and let her fingers wander to the scar on her head again. The right side of her head. She distinctly remembered that the puppy had been on her right. When he barked, she had turned her head. Turning her head had saved her life. If she had turned to look at the puppy, the bullet should have entered on the left side of her head. But the scar was on the right.

She had turned the other way. She had turned to look toward whatever the puppy was barking at, and that was when Reichart had shot her. But what had Flash been barking at?

And why had she not remembered that until now?

DONNA BALL

There was a small covered balcony outside Grady's third-floor bedroom, from which he had hung a rope bucket swing big enough for two From this height you could see the ocean to the left and the lagoon to the right and some spectacular sunsets and sunrises. But at ten thirty at night, all you could see was a blue velvet sky and a hundred thousand stars. Flash liked to sleep out here this time of year, before the bugs got too bad, and Aggie had bought him one of those nice waterproof dog beds from the catalogue, which he politely used when she was around. To tell the truth, though, the bare boards of the deck were more comfortable.

Aggie preferred the swing, and she was curled up there now, feet tucked beneath her, still sipping the beer she had nursed all through dinner, gazing at the stars. The door slid open, and Grady came out. "Dishes are done," he said, crawling into the swing beside her. "Scooch over."

Boxes of chocolate-covered cherries piled on her hospital room nightstand and on the swing-arm table. Grady with a backpack swung over one shoulder, sitting down on the bed beside her as though he belonged there and demanding, "Scooch over." She had been crying, but only a moment later she smiled. She almost always smiled when he said that now, but not tonight. She juggled the beer bottle against the bouncing of the swing as he settled beside her and drew her into the circle of his warmth.

"You're a good man, Ryan Grady," she said.

"Yes, I am."

"There'll never be anybody better for me than you."

"Not about to argue with you there."

"I just wanted you to know that."

He rested his chin atop her hair. "Then why won't you come live with me and be my love?"

Now she did smile, sliding an upward glance at him in the darkness. "I can't believe you just said that."

"I worked on it all day," he admitted.

She absently plucked at the label on the beer bottle with her thumbnail. "I don't understand why it's so important to you. Getting married. It wouldn't change anything. I mean, we're good the way we are." And she glanced up at him in quick inquiry. "Aren't we?"

He tightened his arm around her shoulders in a brief embrace. "We are. We're great. We're the best."

"So why?"

He took the beer from her and sipped it, then returned it to her. "I don't know. I like the idea of being married. I think I'd be good at it. I like the thought of filing a joint tax return, of listing dependents on my health insurance, of being a family. I know it doesn't change anything. But it changes the way you think about things. It…I don't know, it kind of puts your life in the big picture, and you always know where you belong. Does that make any sense?"

Aggie said softly, "Yeah." Because that's what had happened when she came here, when she moved into the little house across the hedge and had known it was where she belonged. She felt comfortable in the big picture of her life for the very first time. And she didn't want that to change.

She took a sip from the bottle. "It's not because I'm not crazy about you. Because I am."

"I'm glad."

"It's just...It's too soon. I'm not ready."

"Okay. You'll let me know when you are, right?" He tilted his head toward her inquiringly, and she returned a smile.

"Sure thing."

"Because I love you, baby."

"I love you too, Ryan. I really do."

In a moment he took the beer from her hand, sipped it, and returned it to her. "How'd it feel today, doing real police work again?"

"Not that great, if you want to know the truth. When I took this job I was promised there wouldn't be any dead bodies dumped in the lagoon."

"You should've read the fine print."

Aggie sipped the beer. "It's been a long time since I went to bed with a case unsolved."

"Hey, we've got an ID on the victim. We've got a time line. We've got the bullet. You already eliminated the kid as a suspect, and thanks to whatever you did to persuade him to spill his guts, we've got a whole list of likelies to track down. Plus we know the perp wears military boots, is between 200 and 250 pounds, right handed, possibly bald or balding. Bishop's right, it's just a matter of time."

She smiled a little and saluted him with the beer. "We make a good team."

"You'd better believe it." He took the bottle and sipped it again.

Aggie was quiet for a time, and then she said, as casually as possible, "Do you remember the day you first brought Flash to my hospital room?"

"Sure do." He dropped a kiss on her hair. "That was the day you fell in love with me."

"That was when I fell in love with Flash," she corrected, and Flash slapped his tail against the deck boards.

Aggie smiled at Flash, and then sobered. "I was thinking about that tonight. And it was like...I don't know, it was like I almost remembered something I forgot to tell you that day, but I don't know what it was. It was weird. Do you remember me saying anything about Darrell?"

Grady rubbed her shoulder in an absent, comforting gesture. "You asked if we got him. You asked that almost every time you woke up for the first few days."

She said, "I don't think..." She hesitated, aware of Grady's patient gaze, his reassuring caress. Waiting for her. She gave a small quick shake of her head. "Nothing. It's stupid. It's just that..." Just that she remembered Darrell standing in front of her, she remembered turning her head, and it didn't make sense. "Just that when you and Bishop were talking tonight I started thinking about it, and I could almost remember something, something about the gun, maybe. Something not quite right. I don't know." She sighed and took another sip of the beer. "Then I realized there was a witness. Somebody who knows exactly which story is true." She glanced at Flash. "If only he could tell us."

Flash thumped his tail again, but it was in a desultory manner. He did not like to think about that night, and he didn't like it when Grady and Aggie talked about it, which wasn't very often. He wished they hadn't brought it up tonight. Suddenly he was thinking about the smell of oranges and the sound of thunder. And blood. And the truth was that even if he could have told them what had really happened that night, he wasn't sure he would have. In a dog's world, some things were simple. It was over. It needed to stay over.

Grady's reply was a little harsh. "We already have a witness. A human one. You. You know what really happened. Stop psyching yourself out."

He took the bottle and drank again, and Aggie could feel his muscles tighten just a little. Funny how it seemed harder for him to talk about the shooting than it was for her, but then she had had plenty of practice talking. She worried sometimes about how much Grady kept locked inside.

She said, "I know. It's just...these last couple of days I can't stop thinking about it. Worrying about it. Trying to get all the details straight in my head."

"Doesn't surprise me a bit." He returned the bottle to her. "I haven't been thinking about much else, either."

"Yeah, I guess." She raised the bottle to her lips. "But at least you've done this before. You testified at the hearing. I didn't."

He cupped his hand tenderly around the back of her neck. He said gently, "You worried about seeing Reichart again, honey?"

She was thoughtful for a moment. "Yeah," she admitted. "Maybe. I guess so. I haven't really seen him since…That's probably it."

"Might be something you should bring up with Doc."

"Yeah." She sipped the beer. "I will."

"What happened with your appointment?"

"Sally Ann left a message. She rescheduled for Friday."

"Want me to go with you?"

"You don't have time. You're in charge of a murder investigation."

"Me? I thought you were in charge."

The swing rocked gently, stars ducking in and out of view. "Ryan, doesn't it bother you a little… I mean, doesn't it seem weird that years can go by without an unsolved murder in this county and then all of a sudden the week of the trial—this?"

His fingers caressed her neck absently. "It bothers the hell out of me. But the big bad world has found us out here on the island, sweetie, just like I always knew it would. I'm afraid we're going to be seeing a lot more of this kind of thing."

She frowned in the darkness. "What I mean is…" But then she gave a small shake of her head and lifted the beer again. "Nothing. It's just, you're right. I hate to think I might not be giving this case my full attention because of the trial."

"You're our star witness, babe, the only one the defense can't shake. All you have to do is read the statement you gave us after the shooting into evidence and swear it's accurate, and you're off the stand. Of us all, you're the one Richardson is not worried about."

She shrugged a little. "That's because I've got the sympathy vote."

"You take whatever votes you can get."

The swing rocked them both in its silent, rhythmic embrace for a time, the stars appearing and disappearing overhead in tune to its back and forth motion. The ocean slapped and sighed hypnotically against the shore two blocks away. Then Aggie said, "I almost forgot. There's a reporter with a parabolic mike staking out your house."

"Great," said Grady sleepily into her hair. "Guess that means I get to go beat the crap out of him."

"First chance you get," she suggested. "No hurry. My guess is, he hasn't figured out yet that the living areas are on the back of the house and outside the range of his mike. No telling what kind of video he has though."

He kissed her ear. "I hope it's dirty."

She tilted her face up to him, curling an arm around his neck. "I always wanted to be a star."

He smiled down at her, eyes glinting in the dark. "Baby, you always were."

Flash sighed contentedly on his bed and closed his eyes, secure in the knowledge that all was right in his world.

Except for that damn cat.

Chapter Eight

Aggie was awake before she heard Flash growl. She didn't want to disturb Ryan, and, if she was perfectly honest with herself, she wasn't all that anxious to start a day that promised to hold no more answers than the last one had. So she lay there listening to the tide come in with its whispering roar, and to the soothing counterpoint of Ryan's breathing, and she tried to fall asleep again. That was when she heard Flash growl softly from the balcony.

She opened her eyes and checked the clock. It was a little after 5:00 a.m. The growl came again, and she eased out of the covers, moving silently through the open doors to the balcony. Her eyes had already adjusted to the dark enough to see the shape of the border collie standing at the rail, head bent to peer down. Aggie joined him, sweeping the pale reflection of the sandy street below with her gaze, the shadowed bushes, the hillocks and trees, until she spotted it. "Seriously?" she muttered.

Flash looked up at her and she sighed, glancing over her shoulder at the still-sleeping Grady. "Sometimes the best man for the job is a woman," she said, and dropped a hand to Flash's head. "No offense."

Flash followed her back into the room, looking not in the least offended, as she silently pulled on her jeans and sneakers. She leaned close to Ryan's ear and whispered, "Back in a minute, babe." He muttered something unintelligible and turned over in his sleep. She slipped his windbreaker over her nightshirt, then silently removed his badge and gun from the nightstand and dropped them both in the pocket. She went down the stairs and out into the night with Flash by her side.

She grabbed a flashlight from the kitchen but didn't turn it on until she was almost upon the parked car. The moon was bright and the shadows clung to the edges of her vision; she kept her eyes focused on the bright ribbon of sand. She approached the driver's side window and Flash went through the shadows toward the passenger side. Aggie directed the flashlight beam through the window and held up the badge, but the driver already had his hands up by his shoulders and his eyes squinted shut against the glare. "License and registration, please," she said.

He was a thin man in his mid-thirties with a receding hairline and a scraggly beard. There was a coffee stain on his plaid shirt, and the inside of the car smelled like stale sweat and long nights. He said, "I'm not breaking the law. This is a public thorough-fare. A man's got a right to sit and drink coffee on a public thoroughfare." Nonetheless, he opened the glove box and took out the papers, passing them to her.

Aggie said, "Actually you are breaking the law, Mr...." She glanced at the driver's license just to refresh her memory. "Morrisy. In the first place, this is not a public thoroughfare. It's a private street owned by the Grady family and made available for public use only through their great generosity. So you can very easily be charged with trespassing. Also loitering, voyeurism, and possibly stalking with criminal intent. Oh, and illegal parking. I'll probably think of some more by the time we get to the station and I pull up the booking forms. Meanwhile, there's good news." She passed the papers back to him with a smile. "Your license and registration are up to date."

He glared at her. "You ever hear of freedom of the press? You and your boyfriend are public figures. I've got a right to investigate a story."

Aggie said, "Roll down the passenger window please."

"What for?"

"The gratitude and good will of an officer of the law who really doesn't want to go back to the house for handcuffs."

He hesitated, still watching her suspiciously, then pushed the button that lowered the passenger side window. He said, "I've got a right to make a phone call."

"Call away. Meantime, that's a nice-looking camera you've got there. Mind if I have a look?"

"No way. You don't take one thing from this car without a search warrant."

Aggie said, "Flash."

Flash sailed through the passenger window and took up residence in the seat beside the uncooperative reporter. For good measure, he curled his lip, baring one canine tooth. Morissy shrank back.

Aggie held out her hand. "The camera, please."

He looked uneasily from Flash to her and back to Flash again. His hand closed protectively around the camera on the console. "This is a two-thousand-dollar camera. I paid for it myself."

"I promise to be careful." Impatience crept into Aggie's voice and she snapped her hand.

"Give her the camera, man, before she pulls my gun on you," Grady said from behind her. "And make it snappy, will you? I haven't had my coffee yet and I get real grumpy before coffee."

Aggie cast a dry look over her shoulder at Grady, who was leaning against the car in jeans and bare feet, looking rumpled and sleepy. She turned back to Morisy. "You don't want to mess with him when he's grumpy," she assured him.

Again Morrisy slanted an uneasy glance at Flash. "If that dog bites me, I'm filing assault charges," he warned.

"He's had his shots," Aggie said. "The camera?"

Reluctantly, and with an ever-cautious eye on Flash, he picked up the camera on the console and passed it through the open window. "Be careful. This is a delicate piece of equipment."

"Oh, don't worry," Grady replied, "we're experts." He took the camera from Aggie and turned it on. "Hey, look at that, sweetie, a picture of a little trash-can. What do you suppose that does?"

"Hey!" objected Morissy, stretching his hand out through the window. Flash growled and he sank back again, resigned. "What the hell," he muttered. "There's nothing there anyhow. You people need to get a damn life."

Aggie compressed a smile and glanced at Grady. The quirk of his return smile was illuminated by the glow of the camera's view screen as he scrolled through a series of very unremarkable photographs: Aggie getting out of her car, Grady getting into his car; Grady running on the beach, Aggie entering the police station. Aggie and Grady walking on the beach with Flash between them. "That one's not bad," Grady said, showing it to her. "Maybe we'll keep it."

"It's the only one in daylight," Aggie noticed, and glanced at the reporter. "What are you, a vampire?"

He scowled. "I've got a day job."

"Oh, right. The electronics store over in Haysville, three days a week. I forgot. That picture was taken last Sunday, wasn't it?"

He didn't answer, but Grady agreed, "Yeah, I think you're right. You're wearing that sundress I like." He glanced at her. "You ought to wear dresses more often. You look hot."

She turned the flashlight beam toward the floor-boards and the backseat of the car. "Where's that fancy microphone of yours? What did you need it for, anyway?"

He shrugged, scowling. "Sometimes websites pay for audio. Didn't get any though. What're those walls lined with, anyway? Lead?"

Aggie switched off the flashlight. "Sorry. Guess we should've been more considerate to eavesdroppers. Also against the law, by the way."

He was undeterred. "So, how about a quote? My boss says Reichart's as good as a free man. Any response?"

"Yeah," replied Grady without looking up from the camera. "Your boss is an idiot." He showed another picture to Aggie before deleting it.

"You got a real reporting job?" Aggie lifted an eyebrow. "Congratulations. Last we heard you were freelance. Who with?"

"*Up to the Minute News*," he replied smugly. "Everything you need to know when you need to know it. That's our slogan."

Grady said, still scrolling through photos, "Never heard of it."

"It's online."

"It's a blog," Aggie said. "These guys just upload crappy photos and half-ass video and hope some tabloid will be desperate enough to fill their space that they'll pay a few bucks for them."

Morissy ignored her. "I mean, you got no material evidence, your only eyewitness is, well, brain damaged, and let's face it, public opinion is not exactly on the side of cops who shoot first and ask questions later these days. Talk on the streets is this is going to be just another O.J."

Grady glanced at Aggie. His tone was mild but there was a glitter in his eyes. "What do you say, baby? Should I break this camera on his face or ram it down his throat?"

"No, don't hurt the camera," she objected. "I want that picture of Flash." She added, "But you can do whatever you want to with his face."

"I'm recording every word you say." Morissy sounded a little agitated and Flash gave another warning growl, just to remind him of who was in charge.

"Good." Aggie rested her forearm on the windowsill and leaned in close, speaking quietly and distinctly. "Record this. The privacy laws in Florida are very clear, and there is nothing to stop a property owner from shooting a trespasser on site. And if I catch you within a telescopic lens' range of this house again, you're going to wish some property owner had taken advantage of that law. Do you understand?"

He tried to look smug, but the effort was somewhat mitigated by the way he kept glancing at Flash. "Is that a threat, officer?"

Aggie straightened up and drew a breath for a no-nonsense reply but Grady interrupted mildly, "It sounded more to me like a well-intentioned officer giving a citizen some friendly advice. Isn't that right, Chief Malone?"

Aggie tried not to make a face. Nothing good could come from a day that started with Grady trying to keep her from losing her temper. Usually it was the other way around. She pulled her expression into a stiff smile and replied, "Right. It's all part of our public relations campaign. We don't want ignorance of the law to be an excuse."

Grady grinned and nudged her, holding up the camera. The photo was a very unflattering shot of her crossing between Marine Street and Evergreen while biting into a chili dog. There was chili on her chin and on the front of her uniform shirt; Flash trotted along beside her with his head upturned hopefully. She'd had to change the shirt before she went back to the office, she remembered.

Grady said, "Little trash can?"

She grimaced and rolled her eyes, but just as he started to push the button, she said, "Wait."

She looked more closely at the photo.

Marine Street was little more than an alleyway that ran between the shops of Main Street and the public parking lot at the corner of Evergreen. There had been a couple of reports of packages being stolen out of cars already this season, so Aggie tried to make sure a uniform walked through the public parking lot once or twice a day just to make their presence known. Apparently, on this day, Aggie had decided to take care of the chore on her lunch hour.

The Hot Dog Emporium was at the north corner of Marine and Main, and Katie's Closet, a consignment shop, was at the south. The remainder of Marine Street was occupied by Howard's Rental and Storage. The rental part did most of its business with tools and outdoor party equipment; the remainder of the long warehouse was divided into separate storage units with private outside access for people who wanted to store things like kayaks, scuba equipment, garden supplies, or just things they no longer used but couldn't quite bear to give up. The older houses along the beach were not built with storage in mind, so almost everyone on the island had one of these units.

Midway down there was a bicycle parked in front of one of the units. A bicycle with an orange front fender and a red back one. Aggie pressed the zoom button and saw the door to the unit was partially opened. She pushed the button that moved to the next photo but it was just another ugly picture of her eating a hot dog, in the parking lot now, and the storage unit was out of view. She checked the time stamp. Tuesday afternoon. Day before yesterday.

She took the camera from Grady, pushed the "delete all" button, and returned the camera to the reporter. "Another piece of friendly advice," she said. "Always back up to the cloud."

He looked at her, then at the camera, tried to bring up his photos, and looked at her again. "Hey! You can't do that!"

Aggie said pleasantly, "Kindly leave the property. This is your only warning."

"It's destruction of private property! It's restraint of trade!"

Aggie said, "Flash."

Flash curled his lip and Morissy tossed the camera aside, quickly turning the key in the ignition.

Flash sailed through the window and sat by Aggie's side as the car roared away, screeching and sliding a little in the sand.

Grady turned to her and held out his hand, his expression dry. After a moment Aggie reached into her pocket and dropped his badge into his open palm. "Mine was at my house," she explained with a shrug. "He didn't know the difference."

Grady tucked the badge into his jeans pocket and held out his hand again. Aggie rolled her eyes, dug into her pocket again, and returned his gun. He instinctively checked the safety and said, "You know you wouldn't have this problem if—"

"Don't start."

"Right." Grady tucked the gun into the back of his jeans and draped his arm over her shoulders as they started back toward the house. "Eggs and grits for breakfast?"

"Sounds great."

Flash trotted happily beside them. The day was already off to a great start, and grits were one of his favorites.

After his wife died, Bishop's son and daughter-in-law in Kansas City had tried to talk him into moving in with them. He never gave it a moment's thought. His neighbors all thought he'd sell the house, move closer to the city, get a little apartment somewhere. Even Aggie and Grady had tried to talk him into moving out to the beach. He'd never understood any of it. It was as though they all assumed that with Evelyn gone he'd want to get rid of everything they'd built together, including the memories. It was crazy. The best part of his life was what they had built together.

The house on 44th Street was in a neighborhood of old Florida houses, built in 1956 and remodeled in 1992, when Jerome and Evelyn Bishop had moved in. It had a wraparound porch with columns on each corner, and a peaked green aluminum roof that had been installed in 2005. There was a huge live oak in the front yard that shaded the whole west side of the property, and nicely landscaped gardens with bougainvillea, saw palmetto, and cedar paths. Evelyn had loved to watch the birds, so every morning Jerome still checked the feeders that were hung from the eaves of the porch. He'd have his coffee sitting at the bright little breakfast table overlooking the backyard where they'd always started their days, then he'd pack up his gear and go across the bridge to fish. Today was different though.

He couldn't get that case on the island out of his mind. Link. Lincoln. Drug dealer, okay, but it was more than that. You didn't get to be a cop for thirty years without developing a few instincts, and there was something about that name, about that case, that was raising every graying hair on his head.

He was on the beach by six thirty, as usual, watching the sunrise turn the lavender sea to turquoise, as usual. He cast his lines as usual, settled back to drink his coffee, and thought about it. Half of police work, he used to tell his men, was thinking. Figuring things out.

By nine o'clock he had decided two things: nothing was biting, and there was no such thing as coincidence in life. He packed up, drove back home, and started digging through the cardboard boxes where he kept his papers from his days with the department. He was always one for writing things down, and Evelyn used to tease him that he had a notebook for every day of the year. When it came to the office, that wasn't far from the truth. He believed in being meticulous, and the notebooks from his last two years in office took up one and a half of the big file boxes.

He didn't have to go through all of them, though. Within the hour he had located the notebook he wanted, and not long after that the pieces of the puzzle began to make sense for him.

Josh Peters.

Darrell Reichart.

Lincoln.

No such thing as coincidence.

"So Flash," Aggie said, "this is what I'm thinking."

Flash, sitting in the passenger seat of the patrol car as they took their usual slow circuit around town on the way to the station, listened alertly. Aggie liked to cruise the streets when the shops were just opening, waving to the store owners and sometimes stopping to chat, just to make sure there were no problems. She told Flash it was because people liked to see where their tax dollars went, but it was also because she didn't like being stuck behind a desk all day any more than he did.

"Bernice Peters said she had a storage unit," Aggie went on, "so I'm guessing it was her unit Josh's bike was parked in front of Tuesday. But she told me all she kept in there was Christmas decorations. So what would Josh be looking for in there in April? On the other hand, maybe he wasn't taking something out. Maybe he was putting something in. But it had to be something small enough to carry on a bicycle." She lifted her hand in greeting to Ken Lindley, who was setting up a display of tee shirts outside the Beach Shack, and he waved back. "The night before he was at Pete's Place with Lincoln. Making plans? Making a deal? Collecting payment?" She glanced at Flash. "All of the above?"

Flash tilted his head toward hers with interest. There was only one way to find out.

"Yeah," she murmured. "I think so too."

She made a right turn and then another right onto Marine, parking the car at an angle in front of the office of Howard's Rental and Storage. At this point, her plan was just to ask a few questions, maybe have a look around, but Flash had another idea. As soon as she parked the car, he heard the sound, and it all started to make sense. He scrambled out of the open window and raced down the alleyway, coming to a stop in front of one of the padlocked doors.

"Hey," Aggie called after him. "What's up?"

He barked at the door and she hurried down the alley to join him. As soon as she reached Flash, Aggie heard the plaintive cries from behind the door, and she gave a small relieved smile and a shake of her head. She took out her phone and scrolled down until she found the number, then dialed. It was answered on the third ring.

"Mrs. Peters," she said. "Aggie Malone, Island Police. I think we've found your cat."

Bernice Peters was there with the key to the unit ten minutes later. "I just don't see how he could have gotten in here," she declared, fumbling with the lock. "This door hasn't been opened since I put the last of the Christmas boxes in here in January." But even she could hear the indignant meowing from inside that proved someone had, indeed, opened the door quite recently.

"Does anyone else have a key?" Aggie asked. "What about Mr. Howard?"

"Well, I suppose, but I can't imagine why he would…" But just then she got the lock out of its hasp and pushed open the door. A startled-looking grey and white tabby cat stood blinking in the square of light. "Oscar!" she exclaimed. "You naughty kitty! How did you get here? You had me worried half to death!"

The cat started to bolt forward, but saw Flash and hesitated just long enough for Bernice Peters to scoop him up. "You poor baby," she said, "you must be starved. Well, it serves you right. Running away from home like that, shame on you."

Flash, pleased with a job well done, moved inside the storage unit, nosing around. He hadn't gone very far before he found something disturbing.

The unit had a concrete floor and metal sides with a high shelf running around three sides, close to the ceiling. The shelf appeared to be empty, but the area between the floor and shelf was stacked with cardboard boxes, leaving only a narrow path to the door. "Wow," Aggie said, glancing around. "That's a lot of Christmas decorations."

"Oh," replied the other woman, glancing around as though noticing for the first time. "Who knows what's in those boxes at the back? Some of the kids' stuff I cleaned out from the garage, I suppose. The only thing I ever bother with are the Christmas boxes. I should get it cleaned out one of these days."

Flash sniffed around the perimeter, then returned to the back stack of boxes. He pawed at the bottom one. Aggie took a small step sideways to obscure him from view, buying time. She said, "Maybe Josh could do it for you while he's here."

She said, "Maybe." Then she smiled, cradling the cat close to her chest. "Thank you for calling me, Chief. You know, I've been pretty upset about the way you treated my grandson yesterday, hauling him in off the street like a common criminal, but I guess you were only trying to do your job. The truth is I never would've thought to look here, and who knows what might have happened if—Good heavens! What is that dog doing?"

Aggie turned. Flash, digging in his back claws, had levered himself up one stack of boxes, and now pulled himself up the rest of the way, springing onto the shelf. Crouching so as not to hit his head, he sniffed and pawed at the corner.

Aggie looked back at Mrs. Peters. "I don't know," she said. "Do you mind if I go in and check it out?"

"Of course, go right ahead. But be careful. How is he going to get down from there?"

Aggie figured that was enough of a permission to search to satisfy any judge, so she went inside. She was pretty sure what she was going to find, and she hated to do it in front of the grandmother. On the other hand, the woman had a right to know what her grandson was doing behind her back, and this time Aggie was going to put the fear of God into the little smartass.

Aggie stretched up until she could tilt the top box enough to get it down. Fortunately, it was light enough for her to lift, and she set it on the ground, using it as a step stool to climb up on the remaining stack of boxes. Mrs. Peters called again, "Be careful!"

Aggie was even with Flash now, who was lying down on the shelf, scratching at the corner of the wall. She took out her flashlight and shone it in the corner, where there was a chunk of concrete about the size of a man's fist loosely shoved into an opening there. "Really?" she muttered to Flash. "All these boxes and he has to punch a hole in the wall to hide his stash?"

Mrs. Peters called, "What?"

Brushing a hand over her hair to clear away a spider web, Aggie turned back to her. "I think there's something behind the wall. Is it okay if I look?"

"Gracious, it's not a rat, is it?"

"I don't think so. Do you want me to find out? "

"Well, okay, but be careful. Don't get bitten."

"Yes ma'am. I won't."

Flash crawled backwards out of her way as Aggie pried the loose chunk of concrete out and shined the flashlight inside the narrow hollow in the concrete block. She had been right; there was a rolled up plastic bag stuffed inside. Aggie reached into her pocket for a tissue, and used that to grasp the edges of the bag and pull it out. The plastic bag she pulled out contained a dozen or so pills and two small baggies of what she was pretty sure was crack cocaine. "Crap," she whispered. She had really been hoping it was only grass.

She glanced over her shoulder to Mrs. Peters, who was cuddling her cat and murmuring something about din-din. Aggie turned the flashlight beam back into the hole. There was something else inside, farther back. She stifled a groan. It looked like another plastic bag. It was heavier than she had expected, and larger. In fact, it was not what she had expected at all.

Flash made a low unhappy sound in his throat and edged forward to look at the dusty plastic bag she had laid on the shelf. Inside was a knife with a mahogany and chrome handle. Its blade was rusty with what could only be blood.

It was not widely known around the department, but the current sheriff and the former one were not as friendly as they once had been. It was nothing overt; they still chatted about sports when they met each other at Rotary meetings, and they'd drink a beer together if they both happened to find themselves at the Shipshead bar at the same time. Briggs had, of course, attended Evelyn's funeral, along with most of the rest of the department, and had said all the right things afterward. Still, there was a coolness there now, a certain reserve between them that shouldn't have been there. Bishop regretted it, but he didn't know how to fix it.

The tension had started right after the shooting. Roy and Grady had been the only operative officers on the scene; Grady had taken down the suspect, but the murder weapon was still missing. Roy had been responsible for securing the beach. In the stress of those following days, while Aggie hovered between life and death and with the eyes of the nation watching the hottest investigation to hit the Florida coast in decades, Bishop might have implied that the knife would have been found that night had Roy actually searched the beach instead of just walking around it.

There was a part of him that still thought so, but it hadn't been right to say it.

When he retired, it was pretty much a given that whoever he recommended as his successor would win the election. He had made the mistake of approaching Grady first, and it got out. Roy took that as another indictment of his competency, since he was not only the senior man on the force but was far more suited to the political and administrative nature of the job than Grady would ever be. When Bishop announced his retirement, everyone expected Roy Briggs to run, and he had already started making plans to do so. It was a blow to his pride not to be the sheriff's first choice, and even though Bishop had enthusiastically endorsed the Briggs campaign when Grady showed no interest whatsoever in the job, the damage was done.

For that reason and others, Bishop didn't often stop by the office, the way he might have done under other circumstances, just to shoot the breeze or keep up with his former officers. He, like everyone else involved, had spent a good deal of time at the prosecutor's office these past months, preparing for the trial, but he did not customarily walk the five hundred steps next door to his old office. So when he appeared there today his progress was measurably impeded by glad-handers and good-to-see-yous, updates on families and promises to get together soon. Roy smiled pleasantly when Bishop came into his office, and Madeleine, the day clerk, brought coffee. He deliberately left the door open as he gestured Bishop to a chair, indicating that he did not expect the meeting to last long enough, or be important enough, to require privacy.

Roy Briggs took his seat behind the desk. "I was surprised to get your call," he said.

All business. That was probably best. Bishop said, "Thanks for taking time to see me. I probably could've handled it over the phone but thought it would be better to stop by. It's good to see you, Roy."

Proving he was, in fact, a good politician, Roy Briggs took the cue. "You're looking good. Lost some weight, haven't you?"

"Can't stand my own cooking."

Roy smiled benignly, pleasantries over. "What can I help you with?"

"Actually, I'm hoping I might be able to help you. It's about the Lincoln case."

"Yeah, hell of a thing." He gave a small shake of his head. "I pulled his jacket. Seems like he dates back to your time."

There perhaps was just the slightest nuance there, the hint of an accusation. Bishop just smiled. "Well, we can't get 'em all, can we?" And without waiting for a reply, he added, "Any idea what he's been up to lately?"

"Number one priority," Briggs assured him.

"Because from what I can tell, he more or less disappeared a couple of years ago. I did an inmate search and didn't find him anywhere in the system, so I'm guessing he moved his operation out of the area."

"Wouldn't surprise me."

"So I started wondering what would bring him back here," Bishop went on, "and what he could've done to get himself killed after managing to stay alive and out of jail for over ten years here on the coast. And more importantly, what it was about that name that kept nagging at me. So I started going through my old notes and found where we had tried to question him in the Reichart case."

Briggs lifted his eyebrows. "Is that right? I don't remember that."

"That's because the interview never made it past my wish list. He was gone by then, and to tell the truth he was pretty far down in the hierarchy so we didn't spend a lot of energy trying to find him. We had a lead that he was Reichart's dealer, and figured it couldn't hurt to interview him, but it wasn't top priority, if you know what I mean." He hesitated, weighing the import of his words before going on. "I should've pursued it, but I didn't. Things seemed pretty much tied up back then. But now, with him turning up murdered like that, I made a few phone calls I probably should have made two years ago."

He looked at Bishop. "Seems that Lincoln didn't just disappear. He's been living it up in Mexico all this time, throwing American dollars around like they were monopoly money. Maybe he saved it up, but he never struck me as the thrifty type. Maybe he made one last big score before he left."

"We would have heard about that," Briggs murmured, his brows drawing together.

"Or," suggested Bishop, "maybe he was paid to leave. And maybe he came back when the money was gone, threatening to tell whatever it was he was paid off not to tell. And he got himself killed."

"That's a lot of maybes," said the sheriff.

"I couldn't agree more. But the interesting part is who gave us the lead in the first place back then. It was Josh Peters."

Now Briggs looked interested, leaning forward in his chair. "That kid Aggie arrested?"

"I don't know why it took me so long to put it together," Bishop admitted with an uncomfortable frown. "Getting old, I guess. It seems I'd brought the Peters kid in a couple of weeks earlier for misdemeanor possession, and I found out he and Reichart used to hang together. A little pressure, and he gave up Lincoln as their dealer." He waited for Briggs to make the connection, but got no reaction, so he added, "It just seemed a little too much of a coincidence that Lincoln should be killed less than a week before the trial, and the Peters kid one of the last people to see him alive. I thought it might help to know the history."

Briggs looked at him intently, and for a long moment. Then he said, "Wait a minute. You don't know, do you? I thought that was why you called."

Now it was Bishop's turn to stare blankly, and feel stupid.

Briggs sat back, and if he was trying not to look superior, he didn't do a very good job of it. "We had a call from the island an hour ago. Aggie found what looks like is going to turn out to be the murder weapon in the Reichart case. And she's taking Josh Peters into custody."

CHAPTER NINE

Aggie stepped outside as Grady's cruiser pulled up, followed closely by four more just like it. Typically male, they carelessly blocked not only her door but the entrance to the beauty salon and the bakery as well. And of course they had their flasher bars going like they were leading a parade. Already doors were opening and curious shoppers were wandering over from shops and cafes up and down the street.

Grady slammed the door of his car, looking annoyed as he approached. "Thanks for the heads-up," he said, a little sourly.

"Hey, he's my collar. You're just the taxi service."

"And this is my case." He pulled a paper out of pocket and handed it to her. "Here's your warrant. I've got two boys ready to start tearing apart that storage shed. Please tell me you had permission to search before you bagged the evidence."

She gave him a look that let him know precisely how ridiculous that question was, then opened the warrant and glanced at it. The door to the beauty parlor opened and the stylist came out, a comb in her hand. Aggie could see a woman with foil squares wrapped around spikes of her hair peering through the window. She offered the warrant to Grady and said, "Do you want to hold on to this or shall I?"

"You might as well," he replied, still disgruntled. "It was your collar."

"Oh, get over yourself." She thrust the warrant back to Grady, and while he turned to dispatch his team to the storage unit, she raised her hand to her neighbor. "Out of your way in a minute, Alice," she called.

To Grady, she said, "Move some of these cars out of here before people start to think you're here to arrest me. Seriously, talk about an excessive show of force."

He scowled at her. "You're in no position to be asking favors. You should have called me before you made the arrest, not after. I guess he's already lawyered up?"

Her smile was a little smug. "Then you guess wrong. His grandmother is still trying to reach his parents. I told her to have the lawyer meet him at lock-up, on your side of the bridge." The smile faded. "I hated to do that. She's a nice woman, and a good neighbor."

Grady winced. "Better you than me, babe. I still have nightmares about the eighth grade."

Aggie said, "Actually, I saved a little something for you. Maybe the best part. But now I'm not so sure I want to share."

Grady bent a humorless look on her. "The prosecutor is expecting us in half an hour. Don't mess with me."

She shifted her gaze to the door. "Come on inside then. But don't get in the way."

Aggie had left Mo guarding the prisoner, and she took her job seriously, thumbs in her gun belt, a scowl on her face fierce enough to freeze water. Flash had taken his position in Aggie's chair across the desk from Josh Peters, his stare unblinking. When Aggie and Grady came in, he jumped lightly down and took up a position perpendicular to the suspect, keeping him in easy sight. Mo removed her death glare from the prisoner and muttered, "We've *really* got to get a bigger office." Then, nodding to Grady, she took a step back to accommodate him. Sally Ann, having abandoned all pretense of attending to her own job, stared unabashedly, drinking it all in.

Aggie said, "Josh, this is Captain Grady of the Murphy County Sheriff's Department. He's going to give you a ride across the bridge to booking. Your lawyer will meet you there."

Josh scowled fiercely. They had pulled him out of bed—no waves today—and he looked more hungover and inconvenienced than worried in his board shorts, beer logo tee shirt, and flip-flops. He was also sporting a pair of handcuffs, mostly because Mo liked to cuff people and, since joining the island police, didn't get to do so nearly as often as she wished.

"This is bogus," he said, barely glancing at Grady. "You've called me in here twice in twenty-four hours and you've got nothing. Nothing. We call that harassment where I come from, and when my lawyer gets through with you you'll be lucky to get a job as dogcatcher."

Aggie stepped behind her desk and sat down. "We've been through this, Josh," she said patiently. "You have an unauthorized copy of the key to your grandmother's storage unit on your key ring. We have a picture of you actually entering the storage unit within the last week. Given your self-confessed association with a known drug dealer, and the fact that your grandmother's age and lack of agility makes her an unlikely suspect for having hidden the drugs, it's probable you will be doing time for felony possession."

He replied, "That's circumstantial. What about that guy, that Howard guy, who owns the place? He's got a key to every unit."

"That's true," replied Aggie pleasantly. "Of course, seeing that he's been in a wheelchair for twenty years, it's pretty hard to figure out how he managed to dig a hole in the wall nine feet above the ground, but we'll certainly question him about it. On the other hand, he was really nice about turning over the security tape from the past two weeks. We'll be looking at it very carefully, but I doubt it will tell us anything we don't already know."

He gave a short shake of his head, along with a muffled sound that was supposed to be a laugh, but was a little too cocky to be believed. "Seriously, you small-town hick cops, don't you have anything better to do? Your whole case is going to be thrown out by the first judge with a grade school education that looks at it, and my lawyer is going to have you for breakfast. I'll never spend a night in jail, I can promise you that. The smartest thing for you to do would be to take these cuffs off me and apologize and I might—*might*, mind you—try to forget this ever happened."

Aggie regarded him for a moment thoughtfully. "Well, Josh," she admitted, "you might be right. Maybe our case is a little weak. Circumstantial, as you say. But Captain Grady here is a really busy man and..." She glanced over her shoulder to Sally Ann. "Sally Ann, honey, it's awfully dark in here. Do you mind opening those blinds?"

Sally Ann almost tripped over her feet in her haste to get to the window and pull the blinds up. As Aggie had expected, three of the sheriff's department cruisers were still there, flasher bars going. She watched Josh's expression change as he noticed, and she finished lowly, "Do you really think we went to all this trouble for a petty possession charge?"

She took out her key ring and unlocked the drawer of her desk. She took out the knife, now secured in its own evidence bag, and laid it on the desk squarely in front of him. Her expression was somber, her tone deadly quiet. "Your name has come up in two separate murder investigations in the last twenty-four hours," she said. "This is bad, Josh. Really bad."

She could almost feel the air go out of his lungs as he lowered his gaze to the object on the desk, and it gave her a sense of satisfaction she probably should have been ashamed of. But she wasn't.

She said, "I'm guessing you thought we were too stupid to find this. But one of the first things they teach us in small-town hick cop school is how to conduct a search. Too bad for you."

He said hoarsely, without looking up, "What is this? Is this supposed to have something to do with me?"

Aggie said, "Did I forget to mention that Captain Grady is also the lead detective in the Reichart murder case?"

Grady said, "Pleased to meet you, Josh."

Aggie went on, "Horrible thing, you might have heard about it. Two people brutally knifed to death. The woman was stabbed sixteen times. Sixteen times, can you just imagine, Josh? The man had his throat cut from behind. We think whoever did it used a butcher knife from the victims' own kitchen. It was part of a set, a pricey chrome-and-mahogany thing that went missing that night and was never found. Until now." She picked up a pen and used the tip of it to nudge the plastic-enclosed package closer to Josh. "See that stain on the blade, Josh? Looks like rust, but it isn't. It's blood. And I'm pretty sure—no, more than pretty sure—that the blood will match one or more of the murder victims. So why don't you tell me what that knife was doing in your grand-mother's storage shed, hidden in the same cubby-hole you used to hide your drug stash."

He didn't look up. In the light that now flooded the room through the open blinds, his face had taken on a sickly yellow shade.

Aggie said, "Bet that felony possession charge is looking pretty good to you about now, isn't it, Josh?"

Josh said, still without looking at her, "I want my lawyer. I'm not saying another word without my lawyer."

"Sure thing." Aggie said over her shoulder, "Sally Ann, try to find Mrs. Peters and tell her Josh has changed his mind about his lawyer. He wants him to come to the island. And then get the prosecutor's office on the line. Tell them it looks like we've got the wrong boy behind bars."

The flash of terror in Josh's eyes gave her another, probably unworthy, stab of satisfaction. She took the evidence bag and locked it back in her drawer as Sally Ann, big-eyed, picked up the telephone. "It'll probably take another hour or so for your lawyer to get here," she told Josh. "Meantime, make yourself comfortable. You need anything? Water? Coffee? If you need to use the restroom, Maureen will take you." Mo took a step closer, glaring, hands on her belt. Aggie just smiled. "Of course, it's a little girly in there. We don't get many male visitors."

She heard Sally Ann say, "This message is for Bernice Peters. This is Sally Ann Mitchell at the police chief's office…"

"Oh dear," Aggie said. "I guess your grand-mother must still be at the storage facility, waiting for the search warrant. It might take a while to reach her." Aggie stood. "Well, just let somebody know if you need to go to the bathroom."

She walked across the room and Flash imme-diately took her place in the desk chair, watching Josh with his fixed border collie stare. Grady fol-lowed her. "Baby, you are good," he murmured.

"You're damn right." She took out her phone and texted Sally Ann to postpone calling the pros-ecutor's office.

"Just the thought of having to pee with Mo watching would wring a confession out of me."

Aggie heard Sally Ann's phone ping and saw her glance at the message. "Yeah, well, you always were a wuss."

He glanced over at Josh. "Do you think we'll find anything else in the storage unit?"

"Nah. Flash would've already found it."

"Yeah, that's what I thought."

Aggie stood with her back to the desk, pretend-ing to check her messages. "How's he doing?"

"Starting to break a sweat."

"I'd really like to wind this up on this side of the bridge."

He lifted an eyebrow. "You think you can?"

"Maybe with a little help from the sheriff's department. I don't think the kid is nearly as ready to gamble his future as he pretends."

He said, "Okay, I'm in." As she started to turn, he added, "Wait. Which am I, the good cop or the bad cop? I always forget."

She smiled and patted his arm. "Just be yourself. You'll do fine."

They returned to Josh.

Aggie sat on one corner of the desk, and Grady leaned his hip against the other. Flash maintained his position in the desk chair and Maureen kept hers two feet to the right of where Josh sat in the visitor's chair. If their intention was to surround and intimidate—which it was—they could not have done a better job.

Grady gave a little nod of his head toward the direction from which he and Aggie had come. "So we were talking," he said, "and this is how I put it together. Tell me if I'm close. You and Darrell, you were big buds back in the day. Smoking pot, drinking, catching the waves and talking trash all summer long. I mean, you had it good—no folks to beat you down, just an old granny who didn't have a clue what her precious boy was really up to, right? Darrell, he didn't have it so good with his folks, except for one thing: they were rich, and he was the only heir. And here you are, just a working-class kid on his way to a state college, you wouldn't mind having a little of what Darrell had, either. So between the two of you, you came up with a plan to off Darrell's parents and make it look like a break-in, and live high on the inheritance. After all, an isolated beach house, two cops on duty for the whole island..." He shrugged.

"People have had worse plans and pulled them off, I guess. But of course, something went wrong. Darrell got himself shot *and* arrested and you must've been sweating bullets all this time, wondering if he was going to give you up. And I'll tell you something— I think he would have, too, if he could've done it without incriminating himself. Because he knew you had the murder weapon safely stashed away all this time. Just in case."

Josh stared at him, jaw tight, nostrils flared. "You're living in fantasy land, man."

"Is that right? Whose fingerprints are we going to find on that knife, Josh?"

Josh looked away; he said nothing.

"Or maybe not even the knife. Maybe just the plastic bag it was wrapped in. Maybe somebody wiped the knife handle down, but it's a little harder to get fingerprints off plastic. So I hope you're really sure you never touched that bag, not even by accident. All we need is a partial."

Josh said, "I told you, I never saw it before. I'm not saying anything else."

Aggie said, "He's right, Grady. Josh has asked for a lawyer. It's a violation of his rights to continue questioning him."

Grady said, "I'm not questioning. I'm giving him an opportunity to volunteer information. I'm trying to help the kid out."

"I don't think he sees it that way." Aggie smiled apologetically at Josh. "If it helps, Josh, I think Captain Grady's theory is pretty far-fetched, myself.

This was clearly a crime of passion. I mean, how do you even premeditate something like that? No way you were in on the planning, if there was even a plan. But you were with Darrell that night, weren't you? Maybe you even saw what happened. Maybe it scared you so bad you've been afraid to talk about it until now. But you've got to start somewhere."

"If you ask me," Grady said, "the kid was better off with my theory. At least then he had something to bargain."

Aggie shrugged. "Can't be helped. He can't tell what he doesn't know."

She looked back at Josh. "So here's the thing, Josh. We know you hid the knife there. You're the only one who had access. That makes you, at the very least, an accessory after the fact, and that makes you subject to second-degree murder charges. Two counts. But what am I telling you for? You're prelaw, right?"

Josh swallowed hard, but said nothing.

Aggie went on thoughtfully, "Of course, if I know the prosecutor, and I do, he's going to go all the way on this one. We're talking Murder One. Life in prison, minimum. If I were you, I'd be begging him to believe all you did was conceal evidence." She shrugged. "That's not so bad, all things considered. Maybe you thought you were helping your friend out. Maybe Darrell has something on you, and that's why you've been hiding the knife for him all this time. But let me tell you that nothing he can do to you from inside prison or out is as bad as what's going to happen if you go on trial as a codefendant in a capital case."

His face was oily with sweat, the scruff of his peach-fuzz beard starting to glisten with it. He tightened his lips briefly as though trying to hold back the words, then he burst out hoarsely, "I wasn't there, I told you! I was at home asleep! My grandmother will vouch for that!"

"Just like she vouched for the fact that you were asleep in your bed all Tuesday night?" Aggie reminded him gently. "I have no doubt that's what your grandmother believes, but the prosecutor will tear her testimony apart in two minutes if it comes to that. Do you really want it to come to that?"

Grady interrupted, "Speaking of the prosecutor, I've got nine messages from him on my phone already. It looks like he's pretty anxious to start building his case, so could we move this along? I need to get the evidence across the bridge."

Aggie looked at Josh helplessly. "There's not much I can do for you if you don't tell the truth, Josh. But if you do tell the truth…if you really are an eyewitness to a double homicide, and if you're willing to go on the stand and swear to what you know… well, that could be huge. I couldn't even begin to guess how grateful we all might be."

He looked at her, lips compressed into a thin white line. A bead of sweat formed on the tip of his nose.

Grady stood up. "Come on, kid, we've got to get going."

Aggie gave him one last sympathetic look and stood as well.

"Wait," Josh said abruptly.

Aggie looked back, nothing but the mildest interest in her eyes.

Josh said, "Okay, I have something to say. Something you want to hear."

Aggie just smiled. "Fine. Captain Grady will be glad to take your statement when you get across the bridge."

"It'll be a few hours," Grady pointed out to her, straight faced. "Maybe not until tonight. Wait, I can't do it tonight, we've got dinner plans. I'll get to it first thing in the morning." He glanced at Josh. "Don't worry, though, our cells are real comfortable, and by morning your lawyer will be there for sure."

Aggie gave him a small shrug and started to turn away again.

"Wait," he said angrily, or perhaps it was simply panic in his voice. "Now. Here. I'll talk to you now."

Aggie raised an eyebrow. "Without a lawyer?"

He frowned, looking uncertain and confused. "Yeah. Okay."

She felt a little bad about that. But it didn't stop her from resuming her seat, taking out her cell phone, and activating the video function. She gave the date and time and added, "This is the statement of Josh Peters, witnessed by Agatha Malone and Maureen Wilson of the Dogleg Island Police Department, and Captain Ryan Grady of the Murphy County Sheriff's Department. Josh, do you waive your right to have an attorney present at these proceedings?"

He stared at her. "A cell phone? You're taking my statement on a cell phone?"

"It's perfectly legal," she assured him. "We'll have it all transcribed for you to sign. Do you waive your right to an attorney?"

"Yeah," he muttered. Then more strongly, "Yes, I do. But I want a deal. You said I could have a deal."

"I have absolutely no authority to offer you a deal on behalf of the prosecuting attorney," Aggie said, very clearly. She could see Grady grinding his teeth and she knew if he had been close enough he would have poked her in the ribs. "On the other hand, the justice system is fair, and if you have information that can lead us to a successful resolution of a major crime, I'm sure that will be taken into consideration when it comes time to evaluate your own charges."

He looked confused for a moment, then said, "Yeah, okay. Whatever." He ducked his head to wipe the sweat off his nose with his shoulder. "Look, here's the truth, okay? That night—the night it happened, the night Darrell's folks were killed—Darrell and I were hanging out on the beach, two, maybe three hundred yards from his place. There's this place where the dunes get kind of high and nobody can see and…" He darted a quick glance from Aggie to Grady and back again. "We were smoking crack, okay? Darrell had some primo stuff and he wanted me to try it, so I did. He was pretty messed up already, I mean before I even got there, and the pipe just sent him over the edge, you know what I mean? So when we heard the alarm going off at his house—"

Aggie said, "You heard the alarm?"

Grady added sharply, "What time was this?"

Annoyance flickered across the desperation in Josh's eyes. "Hell, man, I don't know. I wasn't wearing a watch. It was almost light, but foggy, you know. We had this idea about seeing the sun come up over the ocean, but it was too foggy so we started walking back to the beach house, Darrell's place. We were going to get some beers, you know, only I didn't have any money and Darrell didn't even have his pants. What I mean is, he'd been surfing all day and getting high all night and all he was wearing was his trunks, so he was going to stop by his house and get some cash and then we were going to go hit the all-night mart on the other side of the bridge. We were almost at the house when the alarm started going off and he got all freaky stupid like the cops were after him or something, but I said, 'Dude, it's just a car alarm.' That's what I thought. It sounded different on the beach, and I guess I was pretty strung out, too." He was thoughtful for a moment. "I guess if I hadn't said that, he probably wouldn't have gone to the house. But he did. He said something about turning it off before it woke his folks and started running up toward the house. I didn't feel like running so I just kind of kept on strolling, you know, and after a while the alarm stopped."

"How long a while?" Aggie asked.

He shrugged. "A while."

"Did you see anybody else on the beach? Or maybe on the street above?"

"No, like I told you, it was foggy. It wasn't until I got almost to the house that the sun started coming up. That's how I saw the knife. I mean, I saw it come flying out the window. Not the window, the door. The sliding door on the deck at the top of the stairs. So I went to see what it was, and there was this knife lying there in the sand. I picked it up. I was going to go up the steps, but just then I heard a gunshot. Then there was a lot of yelling and stuff so I just took off. "

Grady interrupted, "You said you heard a gunshot. Just one?"

He frowned. "No. There was another one, I thought I said that, right before I saw the knife."

"Before, or after?" Aggie prompted.

The frowned deepened. "I don't know. Before. I'm pretty sure it was before. I heard something, I looked up, and that's when I saw the knife coming out the door."

"Was the alarm still going off?"

"No. It had stopped. I'm pretty sure it had stopped."

Grady said sternly, "We need more than pretty sure, Josh."

"Look, I'm doing the best I can, okay? It was almost two years ago." Josh ducked his head again to wipe his damp face with his shoulder. "I'm telling you the truth!"

Aggie said gently, "It's okay. Go on."

He took a breath. "So I took off and before long I could hear sirens and it looked like every cop in the state was closing in so I knew something major had happened. It wasn't until I got home that I saw..." He swallowed hard. "That I realized there was blood mixed with the sand on the knife blade. I didn't know what to do. I was going to throw it out, but I didn't want the cops to find it in my grandma's trash. I thought about taking it back to where I'd found it but was too afraid. So I put it in one of those plastic storage bags from the kitchen and I hid it. Later, after I found out about Darrell and what had really happened, I knew I should get rid of it. I knew it was probably evidence. But I figured so far so good, you know, better to just leave it where it was, so I never went back. Not even to wipe my prints off the knife, or the plastic bag." He looked at Grady defiantly. "So that's what you're going to find on the knife handle. My fingerprints, and whoever killed Darrell's folks."

Grady and Aggie exchanged a look. Grady said, "So you lied when the police asked you if you were with Darrell that morning?"

He said uncomfortably, "Not entirely. I said we hung out earlier, and we did, and then I went home, and I did. Maybe I lied about hooking up later. What was I supposed to say? By then I knew what he had done and no way was I going to let anybody place me at the scene of the crime. Besides..."

"You had the murder weapon."

He nodded, once, staring at nothing but the table in front of him.

Aggie said, "Do you have anything else to say?"

He shook his head. "No. That's it. That's the truth. I didn't have anything to do with what happened in that house. I picked up the knife, that's all."

Aggie turned off the recorder on her phone and stood up. Mo muttered, "Taking a witness statement on a cell phone. It's disgraceful." She glared at Grady. "How about telling that councilman brother of yours we need some real police equipment around this place?"

"It's fine, Mo," Aggie replied absently. "Get Josh a cup of water, will you?" She and Grady walked a few steps away.

"What do you think?" Grady asked, his voice low.

"I think he's telling the truth," Aggie replied. "As much of it as he can, anyway."

"Not a very credible witness," Grady agreed. "He can't even remember whether he heard the gunshot before or after he found the knife."

"Doesn't matter. All that matters is that he was telling the truth about not wiping down the knife." She looked at him, cautiously triumphant. "Because if we've got fingerprints, we just won our case."

He returned a grim smile of satisfaction. "You betcha, sweetheart." Then he gave a small jerk of his head toward Josh. "What do you want to do with him?"

It'll be waiting by the time you get across the bridge. I don't guess we really have dinner plans, do we?"

He shook his head ruefully. "Honey, I'll be lucky to get a sandwich out of the vending machine tonight."

"At least you have a vending machine," she pointed out.

"Take it up with the council."

Grady walked over to Josh and pulled him to his feet. "Josh Peters, you are under arrest for possession of Class 1 narcotics and concealing evidence in a major crime."

"Hey!" Josh cried. "That's not our deal!"

"You have the right to remain silent. Anything you say can and will be used against you in a court of law."

"You promised!"

"You have the right to an attorney. If you cannot afford an attorney—"

"This is bogus! You told me—"

Aggie really couldn't listen any more. She signaled to Flash and the two of them went outside to call Bernice Peters.

CHAPTER TEN

Bishop had made up his mind when he retired that he was not going to be one of those old cops who couldn't let go of his beat, the one nobody knew what to do with and everyone felt sorry for. Evelyn had laughed at the resolution and made jokes about firehouse horses who couldn't stop answering the bell, but while she was alive it was easy to put his sheriffing days behind him, almost to forget them. Once she was gone, though, and once the shock and the grief started to wear off, he found his mind wandering back over old cases, he found himself more interested in what Aggie and Grady did with their days than what he did with his, and when he met his friends for a beer—all cops or ex-cops—the conversation would inevitably turn to whatever they were working on. Firehouse horses.

But the one thing he did still know was how to get out of the way when real police work was going on, and he had no intention of being in the building when Grady brought the Peters kid in. But one thing led to another, with people stopping him and wanting to bring him up to date on the case, and even a couple of people from the prosecutor's office pausing to think out loud and get his input on what this might mean for their side. It was only natural, he supposed. He had been in charge during the thick of it, his people had been the primary players, and even though there had been a change of command, in a situation like this time had a tendency to stand still. For all intents and purposes, this was still his case.

So when Grady came in, Bishop was on his way out. He paused for no more than a grin and a "Give the little lady my congratulations."

To which Grady grinned back and replied, "If I tell her you called her a little lady you can kiss your Wednesday night suppers good-bye."

The inner office was a little more crowded than usual, as all the officers even remotely associated with the case wanted to catch up on the latest developments, and justifiably so. There were a handful of people waiting in metal chairs to be booked or interviewed: a couple of complainants in a domestic violence case, a downtrodden-looking deadbeat dad, a woman on a cell phone whose purpose wasn't entirely clear. A man who claimed to be Josh Peters's lawyer immediately surged forward when his client came in, cuffed and escorted by two deputies, and as Grady turned to deal with him, Bishop made his way to the door.

He wasn't quite there when Briggs came out of his office, noticed him, and called, "Hey, Bishop, hold up a minute."

Briggs dispatched the lawyer, the two deputies, and Peters, then turned to Grady. Bishop had to admire the efficiency with which he handled that.

"I've been fielding a call a minute about that knife," Briggs told Grady. "We've got a fingerprint tech standing by downstairs. It was all I could do to keep Richardson from sending him across the bridge. They're not taking any chances on messing this one up. By the way, the prosecutor's office is filing for a postponement due to new evidence, so you might better give them a call—after you talk to Josh Peters's parents, who are on their way down from Knoxville. I'll run the knife down, then I need to see you in my office to go over the statement."

Grady signed the transfer of custody form and turned over the knife, and that was when Briggs came over to Bishop, frowning slightly. "Listen," he said, "it's a little crazy around here right now..." He made a small gesture to indicate the evidence bag. "But if you've got some time later on, I'd like to run something by you. Something you said about Lincoln got me to thinking. Do you want to have a beer at the Shipshead later? I think I can be out of here by nine, nine thirty at the latest."

Bishop tried not to let his puzzlement, or his curiosity, show. "Sure," he said. "If you think I can help."

"Great." He was distracted by a deputy who stopped by to murmur something in his ear that Bishop couldn't hear. His quick scowl was annoyed. "Damn," he said, "looks like I have to make a run across the bridge before I go home tonight. I don't suppose you'd want to make it Pete's Place instead. Say around ten?"

Bishop remembered when he was the one in whose ear secrets were murmured, and he gave a negligent shrug. "Suits me either way. I don't suppose you could give me a hint what this is about."

Someone called to him from across the room, and Briggs looked rushed. "Look, I can't get into it here. It's probably nothing. I shouldn't even get you involved."

"It's okay," said Bishop quickly, probably too quickly. "You take care of business here. I'll see you at Pete's."

Briggs clapped him briefly on the shoulder before he moved off. "Thanks, Chief."

The old familiar appellation made Bishop smile, just a little, and he left the building feeling like himself, like the man he used to be, for the first time in a long time. He spent the rest of the day going through old case files, wondering what it was that Briggs had seen that he had not.

But he never found out.

Flash was curled up beside Aggie on the comforter of her fluffy bed in the tiny room where they sometimes slept. The comforter was printed all over in rosebuds and the pillows had lace around the edges, which sometimes caused Grady to wrinkle his nose when he saw them. Flash wasn't sure why. The pillows, like the rest of the bed, smelled pleasantly of Aggie and Grady and the sweet-tart soap she used—and, of course, of Flash. Aggie sat crossed-legged beside him in her cotton night shirt, smelling of that nice soap, her laptop computer propped up on a pillow between her knees. She said, "This is what bothers me, Flash."

He raised his head to look at her. He could hear her perfectly well without looking at her, but he had learned over time that she appreciated his attention. Now, however, her attention was on the bits of light floating across the computer screen, and she touched another button to make the lights change.

"Darrell Reichart's statement a year ago was that he heard the alarm and that's why he went up to the house. We dismissed it at the time because the evidence didn't support it. The security company's records show that the alarm was triggered at 6:56. I got there at 6:58 and the alarm was still going. The alarm automatically shut off at 7:01, also according to security company records, and I entered the house at about 7:03. Grady and Briggs logged their arrival at 7:02."

Flash listened carefully. It wasn't that he had difficulty following her reasoning; he had an amazing facility with numbers and an instinctive understanding of time, although it had taken him a while to figure out how people quantified it, and why they wanted to. There had never been a problem in logic that he couldn't solve, and he liked to help Aggie figure things out. But this was an easy puzzle and she didn't need his help. He listened to her anyway, because he wanted to know something else.

There were things about people that Flash was not certain he would ever understand. They seemed to have an almost boundless capacity for loving life, like the way Grady loved Aggie and Aggie loved him, and the way they both loved Flash, almost as much as he loved them back. Like the way Grady would build fences on the beach in the spring so the sea turtles would have a safe place to lay their eggs and the way Aggie and Lorraine and all the neighbors up and down the lagoon and even Mo had waded waist deep into the water to try to help a manatee who'd been hit by a boat. Like the people at the dog parade, all dressed up in silly costumes, laughing and talking and marching up and down the beach so that others of his kind would have a safe place to sleep and didn't have to eat out of garbage cans.

And yet, as much as they loved life and each other and all things alive, people were astonishingly careless, almost cavalier, about death. Flash understood death, of course: the dead jellyfish on the beach, the dead fish in the bucket.

The dead squirrel in the yard.

Dead happened, like sunshine happened, like rain and white surf happened. What made little sense to Flash was how people could so easily make dead happen, particularly to those of their own kind. They didn't need to. They just did. A man with a knife on the night of blood and thunder. A man in a car beneath the water. Dead, dead, dead. Dead and gone. Over, full circle.

Except that it wasn't really over, and that was the part that perplexed Flash the most. Aggie and Grady and other people he loved, like Bishop who smelled of fish and dog biscuits, and Lorraine with the sparkly earrings and even Pete—they seemed to like thinking about the dead things, and talking about them, and going over and over them in their minds. They talked about how it had been, and when it had been, and why it had been, and then they watched it on the television and stared at it on their computers and talked about it some more. They couldn't change it by talking; they couldn't change it by thinking. But they did it anyway. They couldn't let it be over.

Flash did not want to think about the knife, or the man in the car. Or the squirrel. But it worried him that until he knew why Aggie did, he would never really understand her. So he listened.

"The thing is," Aggie went on, "Josh also says they heard the alarm from the beach. There is absolutely no record that he and Darrell have spoken since Darrell was taken into custody that night, so they couldn't have collaborated on the story. But if the alarm went off before Darrell went to the house, who triggered it?" She leaned her head back against the painted iron headboard, frowning. "I thought Josh's statement was going to help our case, but it looks like it's only going to cause more problems. Without that knife, we'd be screwed."

She dropped her hand onto Flash's head, stroking it absently. He leaned into the caress, because there was nothing better in the world, not even Pete's hamburgers. She said, still looking puzzled and concerned, "There couldn't have been anybody else in the house. Even if there had been—I'm just saying, even if somebody broke in, triggered the alarm, killed two people with a knife and somehow got out of the house inside of four minutes—Briggs or Grady would've seen him trying to get away." Her frown deepened. "Of course, they didn't see Josh." She stopped petting Flash and rubbed the bridge of her nose, closing her eyes briefly. Then she looked at him. "But there was no one else in the house, was there, Flash?" She smiled a little. "You'd tell me, right?"

In fact, he would have, but he didn't see the point. What was over was over.

Flash's head swiveled as he heard a footstep outside, and a moment later the front door opened. Grady called, "It's me, babe."

Aggie replied, "In here."

Flash heard the refrigerator door open, and then a cabinet.

Aggie said, "Of course, Josh's statement would be a lot more convincing if he hadn't said he heard the gunshot before the knife was thrown out. That right there is going to send his testimony down the tubes, if it comes to that, because we can account for every minute inside that house between the first gunshot and the second, and we know no one threw a knife out the door after we got there." She sighed heavily. "Kids, kids, kids. This is your brain. This is your brain on drugs. Think about that in case you're ever called on to testify for your life in a murder case."

Flash wanted to concentrate on what she was saying, but he couldn't help hearing the beeping buttons of the microwave, and in another moment the whole world was filled with the intoxicating buttery hot smell of popcorn. With an apologetic glance at Aggie, he sprang off the bed and went to join Grady in the kitchen. Aggie turned back to her computer.

A few minutes later Grady entered the room carrying a bowl of popcorn and a bottle of apple juice, Flash at his side. He had stopped next door to shower because the shower in Aggie's house was too small for him—it was almost too small for her—and his hair was still damp. He was wearing gray sweatpants and a faded tee shirt, and he looked exhausted as he sank down onto the bed beside her. "Scooch over."

She put the computer on the nightstand and moved over to make room for him. Flash jumped lightly onto the foot of the bed and waited expectantly. Grady tossed him a kernel of popcorn which he caught expertly midair. Aggie reached into the bowl for a handful. "Did you get any dinner?"

"This is it." He put the apple juice on the little table that was wedged into a corner on his side of the bed, and dropped his cell phone beside it. "How about you?"

"Flash and I stopped by Pete's for burgers." She glanced at him apologetically. "Do you want me to make some eggs?"

"Too tired to eat." He took another handful of popcorn, tossed a kernel to Flash. "You should have seen the moon coming across the bridge. As orange as candy corn. Looks like we've got some weather coming in next week. Monday, Tuesday, at the latest."

She paused with her hand over the bowl, an eyebrow raised in admiration. "How do you know these things?"

"I'm a Grady, baby. I've got the sea in my blood. Also..." He tossed back another half a handful of popcorn. "I watch the Weather Channel. The weekend's going to be nice though. You want to take the boat out?"

Ryan and Pete shared a fifteen-foot cruiser that they kept in the family slip at the marina. Aggie had only known Pete to use the boat twice in the time she and Ryan had been together, and both times had been on family outings with Ryan at the helm. There was only one mariner in the Grady family these days, and it was not Pete.

Aggie munched on a fistful of popcorn. "Umm. Sounds great. We could take a picnic, a bottle of wine..."

"Anchor around Founder's Cove, throw out a couple of lines, hope nothing bites..."

She smiled. "Come in through the bay, watch the sun set..."

"Get home in time to crack open a couple of beers and watch the game."

"The perfect Sunday."

He sighed and reached for another handful of popcorn. "Now, isn't that pathetic? Some guys fantasize about cheerleaders and pom-poms. I fantasize about having a day off on my boat."

Aggie rested her hand comfortably on his thigh. "At least I was with you in the fantasy."

"So was Flash," he pointed out, and Flash thumped his tail obligingly.

"Anyway," Aggie pointed out, "you had a day off last month."

"Yeah. That was the day Briggs called me in to go over Reichart's statement." Grady finished off the popcorn and passed the bowl to Flash, who sniffed around for the last few mostly popped kernels and crunched them up.

Grady uncapped the apple juice and nodded toward Aggie's computer. "The alarm?"

She nodded. "I've been going over Darrell's original statement. The timing just doesn't make sense."

He drank from the bottle. "Yeah. It bothered me too. We always figured Darrell was wrong about hearing the alarm, that he set it off when he came in. Eventually he admitted he wasn't sure about the alarm. "

"But now Josh says the same thing. That they heard the alarm from the beach. I don't see any way they could have collaborated on that."

"Me either."

"So what set off the alarm?"

He shrugged and took another drink. "Could've been anything. It had been going off randomly all week. Could've been Flash barking, like you said."

Flash stopped snuffling around in the popcorn bowl and looked at Grady intently.

"Anyway," he went on, "Richardson says it doesn't matter."

"One druggie corroborating the testimony of another?"

"Right. All we need Josh's testimony for is to substantiate the knife."

Aggie said sadly, "Josh is doing time, isn't he?"

"Oh, hell, yeah."

She sighed and leaned back against the pillows. "You know what I hate about this job? We spend way too much time trying to make our case and way too little time trying to find the truth."

He smothered a yawn. "We know the truth, baby. All the rest of this is just window dressing for the jury."

"I guess." She patted his leg. "You need to get some rest."

He sipped the apple juice thoughtfully. "You know what I was thinking, coming across the bridge tonight?" He glanced at her. "That I don't know how to sleep without you anymore. I can't even remember a time when you weren't here, right beside me. But...you almost weren't. That's what I was thinking about. Not why the alarm went off early or why we didn't see Josh on the beach or whether or not he heard the first gunshot before he saw the knife. Just that."

Aggie shifted close to him, resting her head on his shoulder. "I love you, Ryan Grady."

He kissed her hair. "I love you too, baby." He finished the apple juice and put the empty bottle on the nightstand. "And that's why first thing tomorrow morning I'm going to go back over Josh's statement with him, word by word."

Aggie smiled against his shoulder and slipped her hand beneath his tee shirt, stroking his bare chest. "So," she said, "in this boat fantasy of yours, what was I wearing?"

He started to turn to her, sliding his hand down her shoulder to her hip, and then his phone rang. For a moment neither of them moved. The phone rang again.

Aggie murmured, "You know what else I hate about our jobs?"

"That you can never not answer the phone."

Resigned, she sat up, and he stretched to get his cell phone from the table. His tone was terse. "Grady."

Aggie watched his face change as he listened. He said tightly, "What happened?" Then, sharply, "When?"

Aggie sat up straighter, straining to try to hear the other end of the conversation. She could not, but it didn't matter. She could read in his eyes that whatever it was she did not want to know. He said,

"We'll be right there." And he disconnected the phone.

He looked at her, his expression grim, his eyes dark. "There's been an accident on the bridge," he said. "It's Bishop."

BLOOD AND THUNDER

CHAPTER ELEVEN

The east side of the bridge was blocked off at Island Road by three cruisers, an ambulance, and a rescue truck. Flash bars kaleidoscoped the night and radio static crackled, bouncing off the clear sea air at full volume. Headlights were lined up coming from the mainland, and a half dozen cars waited to go west, but the hour was late enough that there weren't too many cars in either lane. Grady, blasting his siren, swung around a line of rubber-neckers and stopped his cruiser in the middle of the road. Aggie, Flash, and Grady piled out of the car almost before it had stopped moving.

Flash didn't like the swirling red and blue lights; they made his belly feel like he would never want to eat again and tried to make him think of dark, bad times. Aggie didn't like the lights either, and when they were on patrol she hardly ever used them. Flash stayed close to her for that reason, sniffing the air for oranges, even though it meant they had to run toward the lights, not away from them.

"I swear I've never seen driving like that in my life," a man was telling one of the deputies. "After the tire blew, he rode that guardrail for five hundred yards, easy, trying to keep out of oncoming traffic. I thought for sure he was going over. Sparks flying like crazy."

A teenager added excitedly, "Man, you should've seen that tire go. Sounded like a gunshot. Pieces of it everywhere."

Aggie, holding a sweater closed over her night-shirt and the jeans she had hastily pulled on in the car, ran toward the ambulance with Flash at her side. Two EMTs were just lifting a gurney inside. Flash reached it first and jumped up on his back legs to put his paws on the gurney. Aggie was about to call him off when she saw a dark hand reach out from beneath the blanket to pet his head. The knot of terror in her stomach unwound a little.

"Hi, Chief Malone," one of the EMTs greeted her as she reached them. "This your dog?"

"How is he?" Aggie demanded, gasping a little for breath.

"He's fine," Bishop said from stretcher below, and Flash, endorsing that opinion, put all four paws on the ground.

Aggie pushed between the two paramedics and bent over the gurney. He was wearing a neck brace and the bandage on his head had a bright red dot of blood in the center. His skin looked gray in the oscillating light and his lips were tightly compressed against the pain. "Oh yeah, you look fabulous," Aggie said, forcing a smile as she gripped his hand. "You scared us to death. What happened?"

"Front tire blew," he said. "Lost control and hit the utility pole. Airbag banged up my face, nothing serious."

"We're taking him in for X-rays just to be sure," said one of the EMTs.

"Hey, I've had broken ribs before," replied Bishop testily. "There's nothing you can do for them at the hospital I can't do at home. I'm fine."

Flash, having ascertained that Bishop was not injured beyond recovery and that there were no dog biscuits forthcoming, glanced at Aggie anxiously. There was the very faintest trace of oranges in the air, and the lights were pounding at his eyes. Aggie did not seem to notice, though, so when he saw Grady coming to take his place, Flash turned away from the flashing lights and trotted toward the men who were gathered around the twisted remains of the car to see what he could find out.

"Well, you'd better not be fine." Grady came up beside Aggie, looking as relieved as she felt to see their friend alive. "Look at the mess you caused. Traffic backed up on both sides of the bridge, six blocks out of power, and we've got to have the last half mile of the bridge checked out by engineers before we can even open it again." Then he smiled. "Come to think of it, maybe I should be thanking you. If the bridge is closed, I can't get to work in the morning. What the hell were you doing over here this time of night, anyway?"

Bishop grimaced a little with pain. "I was going to meet Briggs for a beer. Halfway across the bridge the front tire blew. Damn thing. I just had a new set put on last month, too. I'll be having a little chat with Henry's Tire and Transmission the first chance I get, you better believe that."

Grady frowned sharply and looked as though he was about to say something, then changed his mind. "Well," he said, "you'd better get on back to town while these guys are still willing to give you a ride. Just leave it to us working stiffs to take care of the mess, like we always do."

Aggie said, "Do you want me to ride in the ambulance with you?"

Bishop was indignant. "I most certainly do not."

"They'll probably admit him overnight, Chief," volunteered the EMT, "given his age and the head injury. You can call the hospital in the morning."

Bishop demanded darkly, "What about my age?"

Aggie smiled and squeezed his hand again. "Try not to give the nurses a hard time. And call if you need anything. I mean it."

The EMTs unlocked the wheels of the gurney and slid it inside the ambulance. Grady touched Aggie's shoulder to turn her away as the ambulance doors closed.

"I didn't want to say anything in front of him," he said, looking worried, "but it wasn't just the front tire that blew. The left front and rear are both out. You couldn't have planned a more dangerous accident. You should see his car. The whole passenger side is torn out. He must have fought like hell to keep control of the car."

"He didn't want to push anyone else over the side," Aggie said quietly. "Meantime…"

"Meantime, it's God's own wonder he didn't go over himself. That was some kind of driving."

Aggie shivered involuntarily, suddenly queasy with the sickeningly sweet smell of the citrusy night air. Flash, who seemed to be busy investigating the battered and worn-down tire rims of the wrecked vehicle, suddenly stopped and looked at her. "Did you call Briggs?"

"He's on his way. The guys said he'd already left the office when the call came in, but they reached him on his cell."

Aggie rubbed her arms against the chill that penetrated the muggy night air and seemed to come from somewhere inside her. "Ryan, you're not going to stay and work the accident, are you?"

"Hell, no. Way below my pay grade." He winked at her. "What's the point of getting a promotion if you can't use it to make your friends do the grunt work?" But his humor faded into resignation as he added, "You want me to go check on him, right?"

She touched his arm lightly. "Just till he gets settled in. I'd feel better."

"You're going to owe me big time."

Aggie replied, "Put it on my tab."

The strobing of the lights was starting to give her a headache and when Flash started to bark the sound was like a needle through her spine. She turned and saw him racing across the road to her, but before he reached her she was flat on her back in a pool of blood, just like that, staring up into the terrified eyes of Darrell Reichart. Wild, harsh breathing pumping his skinny chest in and out, the gun hanging limply between his hands. Something about the gun, something about the way he held it. Then a hoarse whisper, "Lady, are you all right? Lady!" His hair, swinging droplets of sweat and blood as he shook his head, violently, over and over, and the sounds that came from his throat were more moans than words. "No, no, no, no…"

Flash flung his forepaws hard into Aggie's midsection, barking. She gasped and staggered back into the bracing weight of Grady's hand between her shoulder blades. "Baby, you all right?" *Lady, are you all right?* He looked concerned. "You kind of faded on me there for a minute."

Flash barked again. She couldn't answer. But somehow she managed to drop her hand to Flash's collar. She felt the brush of his silky curls against her knuckles, but it took a moment before she could make her fingers obey the command to stroke him. She whispered, "It's okay, Flash."

Flash dropped his paws to the ground, panting, watching her.

"Hey, Cap, you got a minute?"

Grady turned as Brian Holmes, one of the C Shift deputies, came up to him. His face was grim in the strobing lights, and he held an evidence bag in his hand. Grady frowned and reached for the bag. Inside was a small flattened piece of metal. "What's this?"

"Damnedest thing," replied the deputy. "That dog of yours started going all Rambo over the front tire rim, so I got curious about what was setting him off. Looked a little closer and ended up digging this out." Brian jerked his head toward the evidence bag.

"A bullet," he said. "We found it lodged in Bishop's front left wheel. Those tires didn't just blow. They were shot out."

The tension that buzzed through the sheriff's department the next morning was low and angry and urgent, and far too reminiscent of the electric pall that had permeated the office for weeks, no, months, after Aggie was shot. This was completely different, of course. Bishop's injuries were not life-threatening and they had not been sustained in the line of duty; technically he wasn't even part of the department anymore. But someone had targeted one of their own, and in the act of doing so had made them all feel vulnerable, whether they wanted to admit it or not.

Roy Briggs gestured curtly at Grady to close the door of his office when he came in, and went back behind his desk. "Damn it to hell," he said. His voice was tight and angry. "I feel like crap. If he hadn't been on his way to meet me it never would've happened. How is he?"

"Banged up, but okay. Mad as hell. They're cutting him loose after the doctor sees him this afternoon."

Briggs gestured again to the chair in the corner and Grady pulled it up and sat down. Briggs sat in his own chair and folded his hands across his stomach, still scowling. "What've we got?"

Grady had worked until three a.m., slept a few restless hours, and was back at the office by eight, going over the interviews the night shift had collected. His eyes were bloodshot and his face stubbly, but his focus was intense. "Not a hell of a lot. We were treating it as road rage at first, but we can't find a single witness to bear that out. Nobody saw anything to indicate Bishop did anything to piss off another driver, nobody saw any aggressive driving, and Bishop himself didn't see a damn thing." Grady's tone grew angry. "We need two things on that bridge and it's not like I haven't been saying it for the past five years. We need more lights, and we need cameras. If we had—"

Briggs interrupted impatiently, "Talk to the highway department, not me. I'm on your side."

Grady scowled. "It's starting to look like the shooter hit him in one of the dark stretches, probably from the westbound lane. Front tire first, then rear."

Briggs said, "Fancy shooting."

"Maybe. Maybe he just got lucky. Nine-millimeter bullet, anything you hit's going to do some damage." There was a pause as they both considered what damage might have been done had the shooter aimed for the driver, not the tires. Then Grady went on, "Bishop doesn't remember anything that would set any car apart, not that he'd be able to describe it if he did, what with the glare of headlights and all. If we had cameras on the bridge, we'd have license plates, and one of them would belong to the shooter. As it is, we don't even have a complete list of witnesses."

"That time of night on a week day, there can't have been that many people on the bridge."

"The accident was called in at nine forty-five. We stopped traffic on the island side of the bridge at ten o'clock, but the shooter was at home in his jammies by then. So were most of the drivers who might've been behind him and seen something. We did have one witness report a car in the breakdown lane around that time, but nobody else saw it, and by the time the emergency vehicles got there it was gone. If anybody else saw anything, all we can do is hope they come forward."

Briggs said, "Stay on it. If we've got some nut job out there shooting out tires on the bridge, I want him stopped before another night goes by."

"Yes, sir." Grady started to rise, but Briggs stopped him.

"Meantime," Briggs said, "we've got another problem."

Grady sank slowly back into his chair. Briggs's expression was grim. "The Peters kid lied. The knife has been wiped. We've got a DNA match for the murder weapon, but not a single damn fingerprint."

Grady said softly, "Son of a bitch."

"We'll need chain of custody statements from Malone and from you. Did anybody else have access to the evidence before it got here?"

"It was locked in Aggie's desk when I got there," Grady said, "bagged and sealed. You know how she is about documenting things like that. She probably took pictures. After she turned it over to me it never left my sight. "

Briggs nodded. "Routine, but type it up. Nobody wants the evidence thrown out of court because of some foul-up with the paperwork."

Grady sat there, frowning. "No fingerprints? Nada? Not even Josh's?"

"That's what we've got."

"That's crazy."

"It's going to sound even crazier when Richardson puts him on the stand and Josh swears he didn't wipe the knife. Whatever testimony he might offer about what happened that night just lost all credibility."

"Yeah," muttered Grady. "I think I need to talk to that kid."

"I think you need to call his lawyer first."

"Right." Grady rose abruptly.

"Hey, Grady."

He turned.

Briggs said, "Are you going to see him today?"

Grady knew that of course he meant Bishop. "Probably. If the old coot will stay still long enough for me to give him a ride home."

"Tell him…" Briggs hesitated, looking awkward and at a loss for words. Then with a single dismissing twist of his hand he finished, "Never mind, I'll tell him myself."

If he hadn't been so tired, and so distracted, Grady might have smiled. "Probably better."

Briggs frowned, almost in annoyance at himself, and swiveled his chair to the computer screen, clicking the mouse. "Up to the minute updates," he said brusquely. "That includes whatever you get out of the Peters kid."

"You got it."

"And keep the island police in the loop."

"No problem."

That was not a phone call he looked forward to making, because he knew exactly what Aggie would say. And he was right.

"It doesn't make any sense," Aggie muttered to Flash. "The only reason Josh confessed to finding the knife was because he thought his prints were on it. He *told* us his prints were on it, for heaven's sake. You don't lie to incriminate yourself."

Flash gave a soft chuff of agreement, although in truth he wasn't that interested in what Aggie was saying. They were just pulling into the gravel parking lot in front of Pete's Place, and he could smell the hamburger grease from here.

"I sealed the evidence at the scene," she went on, still frowning. "You saw me. It was never out of custody, not for a minute. So the only thing that makes sense is that somebody wiped it down after Josh hid it, and before I found it. Maybe that somebody was Josh. But I don't think so. It just doesn't make sense."

Aggie parked the car and Flash jumped out just as the front door of the bar opened and an entire cloud of good-smelling things wafted out, along with Lorraine Grady.

He waited impatiently while the two women embraced, and was disappointed when, instead of pushing through the door toward the smell of hamburgers, they turned back toward the parking lot. Lorraine held two tall paper cups of coffee with lids on top, and she handed one to Aggie. "Come on, Flash," Aggie said, "we'll eat when we get back."

Lorraine Grady was Aggie's best friend, and Aggie was almost always happy when she was around, which meant that Flash was happy too—except for the funny-smelling e-cigarettes she had recently taken to smoking, which made him want to sneeze. She had short spiky hair that was currently dyed bright pink, and she wore colorful flowy tops and earrings that dangled and jingled when she moved her head, which was a lot. No wonder she made Aggie happy. She made Flash grin when he saw her too.

Lorraine rattled a set of keys. "I'll drive," she said, and Flash fell into step beside the two women. "Mocha latte," she added, nodding her head at the cup in Aggie's hand. "Pete calls it the Surfer Dude, but don't ask me why. I think it's got coffee ice cream in it and he added cinnamon to the whipped cream. I don't care for it myself, what do you think? I was afraid you were going to blow me off again. Jeez, what a week, huh?"

Lorraine tended to talk like that, in multiple sentences without waiting for a reply. Flash liked that; it made it easy to think around her. He thought Aggie liked it, too.

"The least said," Aggie agreed. She peeled off the lid of the coffee and took a cautious sip. "I like it," she said. "Needs more sugar though. And don't think I didn't consider backing out, with everything that's piling up on my desk, not to mention Bishop in the hospital and this new mess with Josh Peters—I *know* you heard about that—but you don't cancel two appointments in a row with Janice Ferguson and live to tell the tale. Not to mention what you'd do if you missed another shoe sale." She grinned and bumped Lorraine's shoulder with her own.

"You got that right, girlfriend. Are we going to run into trouble on the bridge?"

"No, they opened all lanes a little after midnight. No damage at all."

"It's a miracle. How is Sheriff Bishop? We should take him a pie."

Aggie looked surprised. "A pie? What for?"

"Because that's what people do when other people come home from the hospital. They take them pies."

While they chatted, Lorraine pushed the button on her key fob that opened the back door of her vehicle, and Flash trotted ahead. The sooner they got there, after all, the sooner they would get back.

Lorraine lived with Pete Grady, who made the World's Number One Hamburger, in a tall house that overlooked the lagoon. It had a big pine-straw-covered yard with colorful plants and a tribe of chipmunks that Flash liked to track when he visited. There was also a screened pool where she and Aggie would eat salads and cupcakes and laugh a lot, or sometimes have girls' nights out, when they drank wine and talked and got silly. There was always an abundance of talking when the two of them were together, and although Flash didn't always listen to what they said, just the sound of it made him content.

He sprang into the backseat of Lorraine's SUV that smelled like earth mulch and seashells and per-fume and more than a little like the nasty e-cigarettes, and Aggie got into the front. "And can you just *tell* me what's up with that dead body in the lagoon?" Lorraine was saying as she started the engine. "I can't imagine how gruesome. Did you actually have to look at it? No, don't tell me, I don't want to know the details. It was all anybody could talk about all last night at the bar, and reporters everywhere! Seriously, it hasn't been this bad since—well, you know. Jeez, if this keeps up we might qualify to be a real town, not that the Chamber of Commerce will get much mile-age out of a logo that's built around 'major crime scene.' Love that purse. Did you get it at Jo-Jo's?"

By this time Lorraine had swung the car onto Ocean Boulevard, heading toward the bridge, and hadn't paused once to even greet Flash. He reminded her of this fact by balancing on the back-seat and stretching forward to nuzzle her ear. She reached a hand over her shoulder and clucked his chin. "Hello there, gorgeous. Dog biscuits are in the console. Help yourself."

Aggie watched in amusement as Flash nosed open the cover of the console and selected a bacon-flavored dog biscuit, then settled back on the seat to enjoy it. "Online," she said. "I got the purse online. Thanks for driving. You didn't have to, though. I could have gone in with Ryan this morning."

"Like I'd miss the chance to get all the dirt? That's the main advantage of having the chief of police as your best friend, you know."

"Ongoing investigation, no dirt, sorry." She took another sip of the coffee. "I think it's rum ice cream. He should call it Pirate's Bounty."

Lorraine paused at the stop sign, glanced care-lessly in either direction, and made the turn onto the causeway, firing up one of her faux cigarettes as she did. This one emitted a cloud of pink vapor that smelled vaguely, though not entirely, of peppermint. Pete gave her a hard time about the cigarettes, but Lorraine was a twelve-year survivor of uterine cancer, and as far as Aggie was concerned she could smoke anything she wanted—within reason, of course. She suspected Pete secretly felt the same.

"Oh please, ongoing investigation my sweet booty." She waved away a pink cloud. "I probably already know more than you do. Nothing gets past a bartender, my dear. It's not like Mr. Tattoo wasn't the kind of trouble you could see coming twelve miles away, but to get himself killed and locked in the trunk of a car? In *our* lagoon?" She sounded more outraged by this fact than any of the others that had gone before. Like most islanders, she took any invasion by the outside world as a personal affront. "You don't think this is one of those drug cartel things, do you? I mean, could there be more of them? You know, gangs? You're always hearing about that kind of thing on the coast."

She looked genuinely worried, and Aggie assured her, "We don't think the guy was part of a gang." She sipped her coffee. On either side of the car, the sun glinted off the placid waters of the Sound. Easy, so far. "We already have a couple of solid leads. We expect to make an arrest any minute."

Lorraine glanced at her suspiciously. "That's what the news anchor said this morning. Are you quoting yourself?"

Aggie licked a froth of whipped cream from the rim of her cup. "No. I'm quoting Captain Grady."

But tension started to creep into her shoulders as the car approached the grade of the bridge, a long steep climb in which, for approximately twenty seconds at normal speed, you couldn't see anything but sky and water. The optical illusion was that the bridge disappeared at the top and that whoever traversed it would sail into the ocean in fifteen seconds if they didn't stop, stop now and turn around, just put on the brakes and stop.

Aggie could feel her heart start to pound. She sipped the coffee, holding the cup with both hands. Lorraine glanced at her, then went on in her easy magpie way, "You know what I've had an absolute craving for lately? The fried oyster sub at Lola's. I know there's a thousand calories in the dressing alone and let's not even *talk* about the hoagie roll, like I needed another carb in my life right now, but what do you say? Do you think you'll be done by one? Oh, and we can hit the gourmet shop next door afterwards. I love that crab dip mix they sell."

"Sounds great." Aggie took another sip of the coffee but had trouble swallowing. Her nostrils flared with her breath. In and out. In and out. Cold sweat congealed around the corners of her eyes and she could feel her airway narrowing, constricting to a tiny tube through which no oxygen could pass, but it didn't matter because now she was drowning, drowning in her own cold salty sweat, her heart bursting as it tried to squeeze even a few more drops of blood to her desperate, dying brain. Black swirls of nothingness closed in around the edges of her vision. Far, far away, she felt the touch of Flash's nose on her ear, heard his soft query. She couldn't lift her arm to pet him because every ounce of her energy was focused on trying to stop the terror, trying to draw a breath, even one more breath. She couldn't do this. She couldn't. This time she wasn't going to make it.

The first time it had happened was the day she had been officially appointed chief of police, a brilliant November afternoon with sunlight bouncing off the water and bleaching out the concrete of the bridge whiter than white. The radio was on, and Flash, not even a year old then, sat in the passenger seat beside her, drinking in the sea air that flowed through the two-inch opening in the window. She was going back to her little rental house on the mainland to pack up everything she wanted to take with her—which wasn't much—and after that nothing would be the same. This really was the first day of the rest of her life, and she felt good about that.

She must've crossed the bridge a hundred times or more by then. But suddenly that peak came into view, that sharp upward slope into the sky, and she was inexplicably convinced that the bridge would end when she reached the top, leaving nothing but a sheer drop into the water; suddenly her hands were sweaty on the wheel and her heart was pounding so hard that the tires actually wobbled on the pavement when she tried to steer, and she couldn't breathe. Every attempt to expand her lungs was a smothered shriek in and out, in and out, and she was drowning in her own sweat, because she couldn't breathe. She managed to get her car into the emergency lane and to dial Grady's number only because it was a single digit on her cell phone.

They were not lovers yet, but already Aggie had come to understand he was the best friend she would ever have. He had been with her through rehab, through medication reactions, through six weeks of bio feedback and psychotherapy. He slept on her couch for the first two weeks she was home, and she hadn't even had to tell him how much the thought of being alone frightened her when she first got out of the hospital. At first she had been confused by the attention, even mistrusted his motives, but then she had understood, quite simply, that if their positions were reversed she would have done the same. Would have felt the same. They had been through fire together. Their lives would never be entirely separate again. They weren't lovers yet, but they both knew they would be, and that bright November day before the bridge began to slope upward into an endless sky, Aggie was having pleasant thoughts about how it would be when she moved into the little garage house a dozen yards away from Ryan Grady's back door.

When she was in trouble, his was the number she dialed. A single digit.

He arrived with lights and sirens less than four minutes later. It seemed like four hours. But he found her standing stiffly beside the car, her gaze fixed on the glittering water beyond the bridge. Flash poked his head through the open window and her fingers were wound tightly through his collar. She did not look at Grady as he approached.

"I need you to drive me home," she said tightly. "I need you to drive me home and not ask questions."

The breeze coming off the Sound was cool, but he could see the circles of sweat on her shirt, the stains of mascara on her cheeks below the sunglasses. He could hear how hard she was trying to keep her voice steady. The border collie puppy had two paws on the open window frame and was panting anxiously. He inquired calmly, "Is your vehicle operational?"

She nodded her head, once.

"Are you okay? Are you sick?"

"Just take me home, Grady! Just do me this one favor and take me home and don't ask me why! Just get me off this bridge!" She was trembling hard enough now that he could see the quavering in her arm muscles and the jerkiness of her chest as she drew breath. She wouldn't look at him. Or couldn't.

A car whooshed by, slower than normal because of the patrol car lights, but blowing up a gust of wind that tossed around her platinum bangs. The puppy whined. She was holding him too tightly. Grady reached over and gently unwound her fingers from the dog's collar, then reached inside and lifted the little guy out, holding him in his arms as he leaned against the car beside her.

For a moment he said nothing. The water looked like molten silver. The seagulls swooped and dived, and the shrimp boats chugged out to sea with their colorful nets swinging. Another car or two passed them, drivers gawking, but all they saw was an officer assisting a stranded motorist. Aggie stood like a statue beside him, holding herself together with nothing but will and determination. And Grady gave her time.

Eventually he said, "I'll come back with Pete for your car. You need anything from inside?"

She shook her head, hands stiff at her sides.

He said, "But I'm not driving you home."

She whipped her head around to stare at him.

He said, "I'm either going to take you to the ER to get checked out, or I'm going to take you to lunch and we're going to talk this through. I'm either the deputy following procedure, or I'm the guy you tell the truth to. I'm the one you call when things go south. I'm the one you don't keep secrets from."

He reached forward and removed her sunglasses. "What's it going to be?" he said gently.

His gaze was quietly compassionate, but strong. She just stood there, drinking in that gaze, until she felt strong too. Then she said, with an effort, "Do you know a restaurant that allows dogs?"

He smiled and put his arm around her shoulders as he walked her back to his car, Flash still held comfortably in his other arm. "I'm a cop, babe. I have a feeling that's not going to be a problem."

She fell in love with Ryan Grady right there, on the very bridge that she didn't have the courage to cross. She didn't need a therapist of Dr. Ferguson's caliber to help her interpret the symbolism of that.

For almost a year, it had seemed the incident on the bridge was an isolated one. And then, eight weeks ago—which was, not coincidentally, around the time the prosecutor's office had begun prepping testimony for the trial—there had been a recurrence, this time fortunately before Aggie actually got on the bridge. The panic, the cold sweat, the breathlessness, the inability to move. It lasted only a few minutes, and then she was able to turn her car around and drive home. It was then that the fear of unfamiliar doors had begun, and of pools of shadow. But the biggest fear of all was that she wasn't getting better. She was getting worse.

Now they were on the downhill sweep of the bridge, now sky and water and sunshine were back; now, suddenly, Aggie could breathe. The important thing was to pretend it had never happened. Her underclothes were damp with sweat and she had to fight not to shiver in the air-conditioning. The muscles of her chest actually hurt from the struggle for breath. But the important thing was to pretend everything was fine.

If she had been driving, she would have gone over the bridge, she was that close to passing out. She thought about Bishop fighting to keep his car against the guardrail with two blown tires and she had to clench every muscle in her body to keep the shivers from taking over. How many people would she have taken with her if she had lost control of her car? How much longer could she go on like this?

But the important thing was to pretend she was fine.

Flash was panting in her ear, and she reached behind her to stroke his head. He wasn't fooled.

Lorraine glanced at her uneasily. "You okay, sweetie? You want a hit of this?" She held out the cigarette. "I'd offer you something stronger, but with you being a cop and all…"

Aggie managed a smile, or part of one. "Come on, Lorraine, the last time you had anything stronger you were in college."

"A girl can dream, can't she?"

Aggie picked up her coffee cup again and took another cautious sip, still a little shaky. "Next time, tell Pete this would be better with real rum."

Lorraine reached across the seat and gave Aggie's knee a bracing pat. Aggie took a breath, and another, slowly growing steadier. She smiled at her friend, this time more easily. "Listen," she said, "if you're going by Wal-Mart, will you pick me up a bottle of that hot pink nail polish you were wearing the other day? I really liked it."

"Oh, sweetie, pink is not your color. Hot Tamale Red, now *that*'s you. I'll get you some."

Better. She was getting better, bit by bit, every day. She was sure of it.

Almost.

Grady was on the way out the door to the detention center to interview Josh Peters when he was stopped by two of his officers, Axle and King. They were the two who had originally lost the chase with the Charger that had ended up in the lagoon with Lincoln's body in the trunk, so Grady had naturally assigned them to the case, twenty-four seven. He was more than a little pissed off when he did it, so it was perhaps understandable that Axle looked somewhat anxious when he said, "Cap, we got a break in the Lincoln case. You got a minute?"

Grady looked at the door, looked at his watch, then abruptly gestured them back to his office. "What?" he demanded.

King was a fit, determined-looking young black man with two years' military training and six months on the job. Grady was not entirely sure why he should be encouraged by the confidence in the young man's tone as he said, "We've got blood next to a Dumpster in the alley behind Alfonzo's," he said, "and two witnesses who can place Lincoln in the vicinity around two thirty Wednesday morning."

Alfonzo's was a low-rent bar and spaghetti joint on Lawson Street, not far from where Murphy County's finest had lost the Charger in the first place. So far Grady was not overly impressed. "Go on," he said.

Axle stepped forward. "One of the witnesses may have a lead on the suspect."

Now Grady was interested.

"According to our guy," Axle went on, "Lincoln was shooting off his mouth about a sugar daddy, about how he'd already made a bundle for a wet job but that was only the down payment, and he was planning to meet up with his guy that night for the rest."

Grady said, frowning, "Wet job."

"Yeah." King was quick to speak up. "The street buzz is that Lincoln was more than just a penny-ante dealer. He had connections, and wasn't above doing the slash-and-burn work himself when it paid enough. Apparently, somebody was willing to pay enough."

Grady said, "There hasn't been a murder worth mentioning, not an unsolved one anyway, in this county in two years. Where was he supposed to be operating all this time?"

King and Axle exchanged a look. "Sir, from what we've been able to determine," King began.

Axle interrupted, "According to our sources, anyway."

King finished firmly, "Sir, we think the wet work Lincoln may have been talking about was the Reichart murders."

Janice Ferguson was a nationally acclaimed neuro-psychiatrist who specialized in traumatic brain injury. She did not, needless to say, base her practice in Ocean City, Florida. Five days a month, however, she consulted with the Andrew J. Barton Neurology Center, a rehabilitation facility twenty minutes outside the city limits. For this consideration she was granted an office on the ground floor where she occasionally saw private patients. Aggie was one of these.

Aggie did not have very good memories of the Andrew J. Barton Neurology Center, with its glimmering white concrete walkways and sparsely landscaped grounds. The steamy, over-chlorinated therapy pool, the industrial gray linoleum hallways, the frustration-filled PT room where she had slowly, so very slowly, retaught her muscles to respond to the commands of her battered brain. Every time she approached the building there was a part of her that instinctively recoiled. But as frustrating and painful as those early days of rehab had been, she had at least known they would one day end. She could see herself making progress. The same could not be said of the time spent with Dr. Ferguson.

After the usual pleasantries, Aggie dropped into the floral printed wing chair she had come to think of as hers, and took a chew bone out of her purse for Flash. He took the bone over to the sofa, where Janice considerately kept a folded stadium blanket for him, and hopped up on it. When she was being completely honest with herself, Aggie knew that if she had to give up one afternoon a month for psychotherapy—which at this point was both boring and pointless—she could have done far worse than Janice Ferguson.

The doctor took the leather easy chair across from Aggie and took up her electronic tablet from the small table beside it. She had gone to some trouble to make certain that the office, even though it was only a part-time one, had the comfortable feel of a home. The leather chair was upholstered in pale coral, the sofa upon which Flash munched his bone was piled with floral pillows in pastel shades, and a woven rug covered the industrial carpet on the floor. There were plants and lamps, and, except for the desk in the background with its softly glowing computer screen, office phone and fax machine, it might have been a cozy study in any Florida home.

"So," Dr. Ferguson invited, smiling at her, "how are you doing?"

Aggie shrugged. "Great."

"This session is going to run overtime if you can't be more helpful than that. Any headaches? Nausea, dizziness, blurred vision?"

Aggie gave a small laugh. She thought about dropping the cup the other morning, then dismissed it. "Seriously? Every single time?"

"Bear with me. If I don't ask, they cancel my malpractice insurance." And she waited.

"No. None of the above. The average person, meeting me on the street, wouldn't even notice I'm brain damaged."

"So you're great."

Aggie took a breath. "A man was murdered and dumped in the lagoon this week. I arrested a twenty-year-old kid for concealing evidence in a mass murder, and my friend Jerome Bishop was almost killed last night by some idiot who shot out his tires on the bridge. Add to that the fact that I'm scheduled to testify next week against the boy who shot and almost killed me and, yeah, I guess you could say the fact that I'm even sitting here talking to you means I'm doing great."

"That's a lot of stress," observed Janice. "How was the drive over?"

Aggie missed a beat, but just barely. "Lorraine drove," she admitted. "It wasn't too bad. I mean, I got through it. I think I'm getting better."

The doctor slipped on her glasses, nodded, and consulted the notes on her electronic tablet. "That's what you said last time. It must be true, then. So why do you keep coming to see me?"

"Well, there's that whole bullet in my brain thing. Besides, I promised Grady."

"And you always keep your promises."

"I try to."

"How are things with you and Ryan?"

Aggie drew a breath. "He wants to get married."

Now Janice looked up. "And how do you feel about that?"

"Not ready." Another breath. "Scared."

Janice settled back in the chair, crossing her legs. "Why is that?"

Aggie swallowed hard, licked her lips, and glanced at Flash, who paused for a moment in chewing his bone and swiveled his eyes toward her. "I keep thinking," she began. She paused and tried again. "It's just that..." She stopped, closed her fists, then blurted, "Janice, I can't keep on like this. I can't do my job like this. Bishop almost died on that bridge last night, and I'm a cop, for God's sake! If he had needed me, if anyone on that bridge had needed me, I couldn't have helped them, don't you see that? I can't live like this. You've got to fix this!"

Janice replied calmly, "But no one did need you last night, and your friend wasn't killed. So let's deal with what is in front of us, shall we?"

Aggie gave a short, angry shake of her head. "I don't have time! I'm in the middle of a murder investigation. I don't have time to waste talking about Ryan, or my feelings, or anything else I can't do anything about."

"How long have you felt as though time was running out?"

Aggie replied before she could stop herself, "Since I got shot."

Janice looked at her with compassion. "Is that why you're not ready to make a commitment to Ryan? Because you're afraid you won't be able to keep your promise?"

Aggie pressed her lips together, glanced away, and then said, "I have a ninety-eight percent greater chance of having a stroke and dying, or ending up drooling on myself for the next sixty years, than he does."

"Did you look that up?"

In a moment, Aggie nodded.

Janice said, "And Ryan has an eighty percent greater chance of sustaining a debilitating or fatal injury on the job than the average man his age." When Aggie stared at her, she added simply, "You know it's true."

Aggie took a slow breath, and another. Janice waited.

"I need to talk to you about something," Aggie said.

"All right." Janice rested her tablet on the arm of her chair and folded her hands, leaning very slightly into Aggie to indicate her patient had her full attention.

A small frown tightened Aggie's brow. "It's just… these last few days I've been remembering things… about that night, about the shooting, and the hospital."

Janice nodded, encouraging.

Aggie said, "I mean, I remember how you and Dr. Abraham said it was so unusual that I should remember anything at all about that night, but I did, I remembered every detail right up until I got shot. I was able to identify Reichart as the shooter as soon as I could talk. It was crystal clear to me."

"That's one of the reasons your case was so interesting. To sustain a penetrating head wound like that with virtually no cognitive damage isn't unheard of, but it's definitely worth remarking on."

"You're going to testify to that in court, right?"

"I am. Does that concern you?"

"No," she said quickly. "It's not that. It's just that lately, the things I'm remembering about that night…the details are different. It's confusing."

"Do you think you're forgetting things?"

"No," Aggie said, and her tone was a little uncertain as she tried to make sense of it for herself. "It's more like…I'm remembering things. But they're things that didn't happen before. It's like my memories are changing." With every word she spoke she could feel her muscles getting tighter and tighter, and now she looked at the doctor helplessly. "I need to know what's happening with me."

"All right," Janice said, "let's see if we can figure that out." She took up her tablet again. "Would you say these memories started about the same time the panic attacks did?"

"No. After."

Janice said, "Let's talk about the panic attacks for a minute. They only occur with bridges, shadows, and doorways, am I right?"

Aggie nodded.

"Why do you think that is?"

"I don't know." Aggie was distracted by the flashing of the phone on the desk. The phone was not the console kind with blinking buttons, but a low-profile set with a thin white receiver that pulsed with light whenever there was an incoming call. Aggie had noticed it in other sessions, but she had never really appreciated the rhythm of it. Two flashes and a pause. Two flashes and a pause. It was almost hypnotic.

She turned her attention back to the question at hand. Her mouth felt dry. "Janice, I have to testify in a death penalty case in less than a week, and I can't do it like this. I'm not getting better. I'm afraid—I'm afraid I'll never get better. Whatever is broken inside my head, I need you to fix it right now. I can't go on like this."

The doctor made another note, and Aggie said shortly, a little too loudly, "I know that's the second time I said that! I'm repeating it for emphasis, okay?"

Janice smiled gently and held up her tablet for Aggie to see. What she had written was, "Patient feels broken."

Janice said, "I can't fix this, Aggie, you know that. Take a breath. Trust the process. You can get through this. You can fix it."

Aggie drew a breath. And another. She hated this. But she could do it. She had done worse. "It has something to do with change, right?" she said at last. "The bridge, the doors…it's about change."

Janice returned simply, "This is not a test."

"I don't know. Maybe…" Aggie cast around for an answer and Flash stopped chewing his bone and looked up at her, as though trying to coach her. "I think it's that…maybe that I can't see what's on the other side. That's it, isn't it?" Then, "Do you smell oranges?"

Janice said, "No. Do you?"

A slow an uncertain feeling of dread, coupled with a strange disorientation, came over her. She focused on the pulsing light of the telephone to steady herself. She said slowly, "I don't know what's on the other side, and that scares me." It made perfect sense to her now. "I'm afraid of what I don't know."

"Most of us are," the doctor replied kindly. "It's a standard survival mechanism and it doesn't mean anything is broken. Do you think—"

But she didn't finish that sentence, because just then Flash stood up on the sofa and growled. It was such an uncharacteristic sound for him that Aggie almost didn't recognize it. Then he started to bark, and she swiveled her head toward him. "Flash?"

But she did not see Flash, and she wasn't sure the word was actually spoken. What she saw instead was a wild-eyed young man standing over her with a gun. He was wearing red swim trunks and his hair was wet. He said, no, he whispered hoarsely, "Don't do it, lady." As she started to edge away from the puppy crate, her hands held palms out at her shoulders.

"Everything's going to be okay." She started slowly, cautiously, to stand. "Don't be afraid. We're going to take care of this. Okay?"

The knotted muscles in his shoulders seemed to relax a little, and the terror in his eyes was mitigated slightly by desperation, or maybe even regret. "Don't hurt me." His voice was hoarse, rasping. "Don't hurt me, don't hurt me..."

Cautiously, extended a hand toward him. "Give me the gun," she said gently. "Let's not have any accidents. I'm here to help. Let's talk. Everything's going to be okay."

Then Flash barked and she saw out of the corner of her eye that he was standing stiff-legged, barking at the sliding glass door just behind her right shoulder. Instinctively, she swung her gaze toward the door and she saw the reflection of someone standing there, not outside the door but inside the room, just behind the bookcase that blocked her vision.

Tan pants, like Dockers, black boots. And he had a knife in his hand.

He had a bloody knife.

The hand that had been extended to Darrell froze place. She saw the man in the reflection move, turn toward her. A cold and confused horror caught in her throat.

And that was when he shot her in the head.

CHAPTER TWELVE

Grady could tell by the look on his face that Josh had not enjoyed his first night in jail. He and his attorney, a man named Bob Somerset from Tallahassee, were waiting for him at the small conference table in the interview room of the Murphy County Detention Center. Josh was wearing a jail-issue jumpsuit, and he did not look nearly as cocky as he had yesterday.

Somerset spoke before Grady even sat down. "My client has nothing whatsoever to say regarding the statement he made yesterday. We've requested a hearing to have that statement revoked, given that it was made under duress and without the benefit of counsel."

"Yeah, whatever." Grady strode into the room, letting the metal door slam loudly behind him. The chair scraped against the concrete floor as he pulled it out from the table, whipped it around, and straddled it. "I'm here to talk about Lincoln. You know, the dead guy you used to run drugs with?"

Somerset turned to Josh and the two of them whispered together for a while. Then Somerset said to Grady, "My client is not charged with anything associated with that crime."

"That's right, he's not," replied Grady evenly, "which means he's got no reason not to cooperate fully with our investigation."

Somerset leaned into Josh, murmured something else, and then sat back. Grady took that as permission to proceed, so he said, "Did you know Lincoln did time for murder?"

Josh frowned uncomfortably. "Hey, we weren't buds or anything. I barely knew the dude."

"Did he ever say anything to you about getting paid to kill somebody?"

The surprise on Josh's face was genuine. He said, "What?" at the same time Somerset said, "Don't answer that."

Josh ignored his lawyer, probably the smartest thing he'd done in the past twenty-four hours. "Man, that's crazy," he said. "Why would he tell me something like that?"

"So you never heard him mention a sugar daddy? Somebody who was paying him for a big job? Maybe even a job he did a couple of years ago?"

This time Josh hesitated a moment too long.

The lawyer said, "Captain, I think it's clear my client has no information about this matter, nor should he. I see no point in continuing this conversation."

Grady didn't move. He just looked at Josh. "What about you, Josh? Do you see a point?"

Grady could see Josh's Adam's apple bob as he swallowed. He shifted his eyes toward his lawyer and back again. He said, "Okay, look. There's one thing I know. And it's not just me, it's everybody on the street. But I'm the one who's giving it to you, right?" He glanced beseechingly at his lawyer, who seemed too stunned to respond. "I'm the one."

Grady inclined his head, once.

Josh said, "So the word on the street is there's this guy, he can get anything done for you if you're one of his crew. Even, you know, getting rid of somebody. The thing is, you have to be one of his crew. If you are, you pay a percentage. You know, of everything you sell. If you're not, you get busted. Because the thing is, he's a cop."

Grady did not blink. "Name?'

Josh shook his head. "I just know he's pretty high up."

"State? Fed?"

Again, Josh shook his head. "Man, that's not my bailiwick, if you get my drift. I keep my head down and try not to know too much."

"Smart kid," Grady said, and stood. "You'll go far."

He turned the chair around, pushed it back under the table and said, "See you in court, Counselor." And he left the room.

There is nothing sharper than the bark of a border collie, and when Aggie realized that Flash had been barking for some time and that she had not heard him at all, she knew something was wrong. Janice

Ferguson was on her feet but frozen in place, and Flash stood between the doctor and herself, his feet planted and his teeth bared, barking at the other woman in a way that could not be interpreted as anything but threatening.

Aggie gasped, "Flash!" and reached for him. Her movement felt sloppy and uncoordinated, but he stopped barking immediately and whirled around to her. "Flash, come here!"

He lowered his tail to half mast and came to her, looking abashed and concerned, or maybe just guilty. Aggie put a hand on Flash's shoulder, and felt the fine quivering in his muscles. Or maybe that was her. Janice stayed where she was, watching.

Aggie whispered, "Flash, what is it, huh? What's going on?" Then she looked up at the doctor apologetically. "I'm so sorry. He's been acting strange lately. I don't know what's wrong with him."

Janice replied calmly, "That's all right, I think I do. Tell him you're okay, Aggie, and send him back to the sofa."

Aggie looked at her for a moment in confusion, then pressed her face briefly against Flash's neck. "It's okay, Flash. Go sit down."

He hesitated for a moment, looking at her as though to determine the truth of her words. He went back to the sofa and jumped up on his blanket, but he did not take up the chew bone. Instead he watched Aggie, and the doctor, alertly.

Janice crossed the few feet between them without glancing at Flash and took a penlight from her pocket. Aggie tried not to wince as the bright light stabbed first one eye, and then the other, but she couldn't help shrinking back a little. "What are you doing? Why—"

"Raise your right arm for me, straight out."

After a moment, Aggie complied.

"Now your left." Calm, matter of fact voice. "Open your fingers." She rested her hands in Aggie's. "Close them. Squeeze hard."

Aggie recognized the neurological exam, but she could not remember it ever having been performed in the middle of a therapy session before, not even when she was an inpatient. She was confused. "Are we finished? Is our time up?"

"Not quite. Can you tell me what day it is?"

Aggie stared at her. "Seriously?" But there was absolutely no sign of mirth in the other woman's eyes, and so she answered the question. But there was no point in trying to disguise her anxiety so she demanded, "What? Why are you doing this? What does this have to do with Flash? Did something happen while I was..." She broke off in confusion and Dr. Ferguson watched her closely.

She prompted gently, "While you were what, Aggie?"

Aggie gave a brief uncertain shake of her head. "I was thinking...it was another one of those weird memories I told you about. I must have lost track of time."

The doctor nodded and flashed the penlight in her eyes again. "Earlier, you mentioned something about smelling oranges. Has that happened before?"

Aggie tried to smile, but it was a faint attempt. "Well, it's Florida after all." She stopped trying to smile and laced her hands together tightly in her lap to stop the trembling. "Yes. It's happened before."

"How many times?"

"Three, four. I don't know."

Janice crossed the room and sat behind her desk, turning to her computer. That was something she never did in a session. She put on her glasses. She clicked the mouse, scrolled down a few screens, and tapped some keys. After a moment she turned back to Aggie and took off the glasses. "Do you remember what happened just before this episode?"

"It wasn't an episode. It was..." She glanced at Flash. He looked back with his patient, honest gaze. "You got a call. I was looking at the telephone."

The doctor folded her hands atop her desk and leaned forward slightly, her manner compassionate and assured. "I think you're having what we call absence seizures. They're often triggered by flashing lights and can be accompanied by an olfactory aura, like the smell of oranges." She glanced at Flash. "Some dogs seem to be able to sense the aura and predict a seizure, we're not exactly sure how. I think that's exactly what Flash did, and then he was just protecting you until you were able to take care of yourself. "

"That's not it," Aggie said flatly. She pressed her hands more tightly together. "I was just daydreaming. I just...got lost in my thoughts for a minute."

The doctor said, "You were unresponsive for almost five minutes."

Aggie stared at her. "That's not possible." But she hadn't heard Flash barking. She hadn't seen Janice get out of her chair, but she had been standing when Aggie looked at her. "It was only a minute. I was remembering the night of the shooting." Only what she remembered was not the way it had happened. How could she remember something that hadn't happened?

The reflection.

The flash of a patrol car bar; a broken coffee cup. The blinking microwave light. The pulsing telephone. The smell of oranges. Damn it. *Damn it.*

Flash. He had been trying to warn her, every single time.

The reflection in the glass door. He had the knife. *He had the knife.*

Her breath came a little faster. She tried to calm it. Still, her nostrils flared a little with the effort to keep her voice steady as she said, "What does this mean?"

Janice's tone was easy and reassuring. "That's what we're going to find out. I'm sending you upstairs for a CT, and calling in Dr. Abraham for a consult." Dr. Abraham was the neurosurgeon who had first treated her after the shooting. "We may be in luck. He's on duty at the hospital this afternoon, so it's possible he'll be able to meet with you in an hour or so."

"Dr. Abraham?" Aggie's voice was hoarse and her thoughts were swirling, but one thing she was very clear about: it took months to get an appointment with Dr. Abraham. If he was willing to take the time to see her this afternoon, this was serious.

Janice said, "Your friend is waiting outside. Do you want me to talk to her?"

Aggie blinked. "Lorraine is here? She was going to go shopping. We were supposed to meet in the parking lot. Why is she here? Did you call her?"

Janice repeated gently, "Aggie, you've lost time. Our session is over, your friend is worried about you. I'll go with you to explain."

Aggie said abruptly, "I'm going to be sick."

Janice took her arm and guided her quickly to the bathroom, where she dropped to her knees and vomited into the toilet, mostly coffee and bile. Flash sat by the door, making himself very small, and when Janice left Aggie to splash water on her face and wipe her face and use the mouthwash on the vanity, Flash pressed himself close to her leg. It was only his warmth that stopped the shivering enough for Aggie to return to Janice's office.

Lorraine was there, and she turned away from Janice when Aggie and Flash came in. Her eyes were big with alarm, but Aggie spoke quickly, before she did.

"No big deal," she said. "CAT scan, routine, boring as hell. You can go on home. I'll get a ride with Ryan."

Lorraine said easily, "Yeah, okay, no big deal. Room 231, right? Come on, Flash, let's go for an elevator ride." To Janice she said, "I got this."

Aggie protested, "Seriously, Lorraine, everything's fine. You should go home."

She stepped across the room and looped her arm through Aggie's. "Don't lie to me, bitch," she said softly, and pressed her head against Aggie's shoulder in brief affection.

Aggie looked at her, and Lorraine's smile was fierce. "When I was diagnosed," she said, "Pete was in Tampa and my mother was in Pittsburg and my sister was at home with her three kids because we all thought it was routine, you know? But it turned out it wasn't and that was the scariest damn time of my life, so I'm not going home and you're not going through this alone, got that?" She squeezed her arm. "Maybe it's routine. But you're my best friend and I'm here so just shut up and let's get this over with."

Aggie found her throat suddenly too tight, and wet, to speak, so she just nodded. And with Lorraine on one side of her and Flash on the other, she walked to the elevator.

"There's no doubt in my mind that it all leads back to the Reichart case," Grady said. "Two days ago I wouldn't have believed it, but now I don't see a choice. The kid hired it done, and who would he go to but the only connection he had on the seamy side of the beach, his drug dealer? Hell, a guy like

Lincoln could probably be bought for a couple of grand. That's folding money to Darrell Reichart."

"Explains a lot," agreed Briggs thoughtfully. "But something went wrong, which is how the kid ended up covered in his parents' blood facing down the cops."

"You get what you pay for," Grady said dismissively. "So I figure Lincoln came back here for more cash, probably threatening to tell the truth, and got himself killed for it."

"Only one problem with that theory. Reichart's been locked up tight next door for the last twenty-two months."

Grady said evenly, "Not a problem if he had a partner."

"My money's on the Peters kid."

"Yeah, mine too." He frowned. "All that BS about a dirty cop was just to throw us off, waste our time."

Grady's eyes met the sheriff's. They both were thinking the same thing, but it was Briggs who said it. "So why did somebody try to kill Bishop last night?"

It was an amazing thing to see a picture of one's own living brain. Aggie marveled over that while Dr. Abraham talked about quality of life and risk factors and millimeters. Really, millimeters.

In the first seventy-two hours after she was shot, Aggie had undergone multiple surgeries to repair bleeding vessels and relieve swelling, but by the time she was deemed stable enough to allow the surgeons to try to remove the bullet, they had determined the risks far outweighed the benefits. The position of the projectile that had entered her skull was such that it endangered no major functions, but in order to reach it, major sensory nerves and cognitive centers would have to be traversed. The chances of a good outcome were not high. Of course she would be closely monitored and should the position of the bullet shift, options would be revisited.

At age twenty-eight, struggling to hold on to the pieces of her shattered life and desperately grasping at any theory that included the possibility of growing older, holding down a job, falling in love, having babies, walking and talking and doing all the things normal people did, Aggie paid very close attention to the reasons why surgery was not an option. She was far less interested in the part about revisiting those options. But now, it appeared, the time had come to do so.

"We always knew this was a possibility, Aggie," Dr. Abraham said, and she nodded politely and wondered where, in all those sliced-up pictures of her brain, was hidden the memory of Flash chasing a stick into the waves at sunset, or of Grady with his hand on the wheel of his boat and his face turned to the sea. Where was the part of her that could taste fried oysters or laugh at one of Pete's corny jokes? Where was Aggie, in all those slices?

"The good news is that the movement of the bullet has actually made it more accessible." Dr. Abraham pointed with his pencil and Lorraine leaned forward to see, her expression intent. Aggie just nodded.

Maybe, just there, was the part of her that had ranked third at the Academy in marksmanship. Or maybe that was the part of her that could tell the difference between a baby carriage and an armed gunman. Maybe there, just behind the shiny surface of the bullet, was the part of her that swore she'd never forget the taste of her grandmother's apple pie.

Aggie said, "Where's the part that listens to music?"

Dr. Abraham stopped talking and looked at her. He was a small, precise man with sharp features and clear dark eyes, and he did not look at patients; he looked at surgeries. But he looked at her now, and there was even a trace of compassion in his eyes. "Aggie, I know how frightening this must be for you. But from a surgical standpoint this is a much more minimally invasive procedure than it might have been a year ago. I have absolutely no doubt that the bullet can be removed safely with no long-term ill effects, as long as we get to it in a timely manner."

"Today," Lorraine said. Her hands were tightly clasped in her lap, her spine arrow straight. Lorraine, who always took the bull by the horns. Lorraine, who knew what it took to survive. Lorraine, who had no idea what it was like to be terrified of crossing a bridge. "Can you do it today?"

The doctor said, "We'll need to book the OR and assemble a team. But I'd like to get her checked into the hospital this weekend and run some more tests, then schedule surgery early next week."

"Okay," Lorraine said decisively. "Okay, we'll get you checked in and I'll run home and pack a bag for you. Flash can stay with us, of course. I know where all his stuff is. I'll call Ryan and let him know…"

She actually reached for her phone, but Aggie extended a hand to stop her. "No," she said. "Don't call anybody." She stood. "Doctor, thank you. I'll be in touch."

Lorraine just sat there, gaping at her.

Dr. Abraham said, "Don't misunderstand me, Aggie. This is not something you can put off. Even a millimeter one way or another…"

"Yes, I know, severed artery, stroke, vegetable, dead." Aggie's tone was abrupt, and the fingers that were wound around the strap of her purse were white. "I'll call you."

He gave her a card with his cell phone number on it and a prescription for anti-seizure medication, and they left the building.

Flash was waiting for Aggie in the car. Aggie had once explained to him that there were some places in this world that were only for people, which made absolutely no sense to him. But because it seemed to make sense to Aggie he believed it, even though experience had taught him nothing good ever happened when he waited in the car. This time was no exception.

Aggie was quiet when they came out of the big white building, but Flash could smell the tears behind Lorraine's over-sized sunglasses. And there was something about Aggie, dark, sad.

Lorraine beeped the lock on the door with her key fob and Aggie said, "Do me a favor and keep this between us for a while, okay? Ryan has got his hands full right now, and I want to pick my time."

"You don't have—" Lorraine started to say, sounding angry and wet-voiced, and then she cleared her throat. "Okay."

"This is major. I have to get some things taken care of."

"Okay."

Aggie said, sounding stiff and uncomfortable, "I have a living will. It's on file with the hospital. I named Bishop as—you know, the one. You wouldn't pull the plug, and I didn't want Grady to have to do it, so I picked Bishop. I just wanted you to know."

Lorraine pushed up her sunglasses and swiped a hand across her eyes. Aggie went around to the passenger door. Flash put his paws on the back of her seat so that he would be the first thing she saw when she got in. He was, and she absently stroked his chin as she sat down. The darkness did not leave her, and it left a bad taste in his mouth. He sat back and licked his lips.

Lorraine got into the car and rummaged in the console until she found a tissue. She blew her nose.

Aggie said, "I have a little money left over from my grandmother's estate. It goes to Ryan to help him take care of Flash. I downloaded one of those online wills. It's in my desk at the office."

"Shut up," Lorraine said thickly. "I hate you right now."

Aggie smiled, but it was a sad thing that Flash did not understand. He sank down onto the bench seat and tried not to pant. Aggie said, "I love you. Now stop crying and drive."

After a moment, Lorraine started the car and Aggie stretched her hand to the backseat to pet Flash. But her fingers were cold and offered him no comfort, and he was very much afraid that he had failed, today, to take care of her.

Had Aggie had her meeting with Dr. Abraham at the Murphy County Regional Hospital, instead of at the Neurology Center fifteen minutes away, she would have no doubt seen Grady as he pulled up in front of the entrance and got out of the cruiser to greet Bishop. More importantly, he would have seen her. All in all, it was probably best things worked out as they did.

Bishop was waiting in a wheelchair in the lobby, the leather overnight bag Grady had packed for him the night before resting on his knees alongside the fruit basket the department had sent. He looked disgruntled and impatient, but otherwise completely himself, despite the bruised face and the black sling that eased the pressure on his dislocated right shoulder. He started to stand the minute he saw Grady, but a nurse's aide was quick to take the handles of the wheelchair and push him toward the automatic doors. "Hospital rules," Grady heard her say chirpily, and the ferocity of the scowl that Bishop returned made Grady grin.

"I told you I didn't need a ride," Bishop greeted him testily. "I know how to call a cab. And what are you doing using a county vehicle for personal reasons? I'm not riding home in a police cruiser. You want my neighbors to think I spent the night in jail?"

Grady took the bag and the fruit basket and put them in the backseat. "Good to see you're feeling better." He opened the passenger door and Bishop, brushing away the aide's offered assistance, got in. "And this is not personal business. I'm interviewing a witness."

Bishop waited until Grady got in to inquire, "Oh yeah? Who're we interviewing?"

Grady checked his mirrors and put the car in gear. "You."

Bishop stifled a groan as he stretched out his legs. "Well, good luck with that. I must've been over it a hundred times in my head and I swear I can't remember anything I haven't already told you. I hit that dark stretch. There might've been four or five cars in the westbound lane, I can't really say how many were behind me. It wasn't very busy, traffic was well spaced. We were all going five or ten miles over the limit, but who doesn't? Then *bam*. The tire blew. I didn't even know the back tire was out, I was fighting so hard to stay on the bridge. I didn't see a damn thing before that, or after, that could help.

Just traffic. You'd think I was some rookie civilian."
He sounded disgusted with himself.

"Yeah, well, I guess we're all civilians when we're
the one the crime happens to."

Grady went through two intersections without saying anything else, eyes on the road. Bishop
watched him. In time Bishop said, "So what's this
about?"

There was a beat, just a beat, of hesitation, then
Grady said, "We're starting to think outside the road
rage box. Like maybe this wasn't random."

Bishop did not reply for a moment, and when
he did it was with a heavy sigh. "So. You figured that
out, did you?"

Grady shot a quick glance at him, then his eyes
were back on the road. "Yeah."

They said nothing else.

Grady took the turn that led to Bishop's street.
Twisted cypress, sprawling live oaks, two-car garages,
most with boats or boat trailers behind neat enclo-
sures in the side yards. It was a nice neighborhood,
the kind where children grew up happy and well
fed, and when those children came back to visit the
old homestead their parents were still there, put-
tering in the garden, keeping their lawns trimmed,
taking the boat out on weekends. Grady pulled into
Bishop's driveway and got the overnight bag and
fruit basket out of the back while Bishop unlocked
the door.

The curtains were closed, and the interior of
the house was cool and shadowed. Bishop made

his way over to a worn leather recliner and eased himself into it while Grady put the fruit basket on the kitchen table. "You want anything?" he asked, because he knew Aggie would expect him to. "Iced tea or anything?"

"No, I'm good. Help yourself to whatever you can find."

Grady did not. He came back into the living room and thought about opening the curtains, but in the end decided against it. He sat on the edge of the sofa across from Bishop, his hands clasped loosely between his knees, his face somber. He said, "This investigation is taking us places nobody wants to go. But I've got to follow every lead because if I don't, somebody else will."

Bishop just nodded.

Grady said, "Two of his cronies say Lincoln was bragging about a hit he'd done a while back. Said it had paid enough to keep him living large in Mexico for over a year, but now he'd decided to go back to the well. Less than twenty-four hours later he's shot to death in the alley behind Alfonso's and his body dumped in the lagoon."

Bishop was expressionless.

"And that knife Aggie found? The one Josh Peters confessed himself into a corner over and went to jail for? It was the murder weapon all right. Only Josh's fingerprints weren't on it. Neither were Darrell's. Neither were anybody else's. It had been wiped clean. Almost like somebody knew it was about to be found.

"And here's the thing. Word on the street is that back during the Reichart murders somebody was running a protection racket among the dealers, and he was your go-to guy if you wanted somebody out of the way. The way Lincoln was talking right before he was killed, we've got reason to believe he might've worked for this dude, and two separate sources say he was a cop."

Grady watched Bishop's face in the shadows. Nothing.

"Lincoln was murdered the night he was supposed to meet with his payday man," Grady said. "The evidence that could have identified the killer was wiped for fingerprints days before the trial. And now somebody tries to kill the sheriff who was in charge of the Reichart investigation while it was hot." He looked his friend in the eye and said quietly, "Is there something we need to talk about?"

For the longest time Bishop did not reply. And then he said, in a voice that was steady and calm, "You know something? I believe I will have that glass of tea, after all."

Aggie left a plate of pasta warming in the oven for Ryan and a note that said, "At the beach." He ate the parts of the pasta that weren't too crunchy and walked down the street and across to the beach. The night was warm and wild, with crosswinds strong enough to part his hair from side to side and plaster his tee shirt to his body. The surf thundered and slapped against the shore, sending spittles of foam into the air that were visible half a block away. It had been dark for two hours, but the night was brilliantly clear, the moon almost full. He could taste the salt in the air and the electricity on the horizon.

Grady found Aggie near the crossover, tossing a soggy tennis ball for Flash in the moonlight. He came up behind her, wrapped his arms around her waist, and kissed her neck. He said, "Thanks for dinner."

Flash raced up and dropped the tennis ball at his feet. He picked it up and tossed it hard. Flash was after it like a streak. Aggie said, "How does he do that? I can't even see twenty feet ahead."

They had to raise their voices to be heard over the wind and the sea, but it gave a peculiar kind of intimacy to their conversation, leaning close, talking loudly. He said, "Did you get my messages?"

"Most of them. Sounds like you had a busy day."

"Not a good kind of busy. I don't like going to bed with more questions than I woke up with."

"Murder for hire. That's one thing we never considered."

"It doesn't change anything. The kid was still the doer, had to be. He's the only one with a motive."

"It's a death penalty case, Ryan." There was the mildest reprimand in her voice. "It changes something."

Flash returned and Grady pried the tennis ball from his jaws, tossed it again. "I know, babe," he said wearily. "I'm just a worn-out cop trying to do his job."

"I guess Richardson is having kittens over this whole thing."

"He asked for a postponement, but the defense wouldn't have it. The judge agreed. So it's up to us fine folks in blue—or khaki as the case may be—to find out what really happened before the trial is over."

"No pressure there."

This time Flash dropped the ball at Aggie's feet. She picked it up, paused to rub his ears, and then tossed it. Spinning and fighting the wind, it went half as far as Ryan's had. She said, "I talked to Bishop before I came down to the beach. He said you got him settled in at home, and he's getting around fine. He's pissed because the insurance company can't deliver his rental car before the weekend, although where he thinks he needs to drive I couldn't say."

Grady didn't answer. When Flash returned with the ball, he stepped forward to retrieve it, and tossed it again.

Aggie said, "You don't still think this was a random shooting, do you?"

He replied simply, "No."

She slipped her arm around his waist, and rubbed his back briefly. They watched together as Flash raced back down the beach toward them. Silver sand, foaming surf, indigo night. Ryan said, "That storm's moving faster than they thought. NOAA will probably issue an alert tomorrow sometime."

"Weather Channel?"

"Seaman's instinct."

"Good thing we didn't plan on taking the boat out this weekend, then."

"I guess."

Flash dodged an incoming wave with the perfect timing of a choreographed dance, never breaking stride as he ran back to them, the tennis ball in his teeth. Aggie said, "Ryan, if anything happened to me, you'd take care of Flash, right? And I don't mean just feed him and throw the ball for him, but, you know, talk to him. Give him a job. Love him. Right?"

He groaned softly. "You know I hate it when you talk like that."

"Come on, it's a fact of life. It's our jobs. I just need to know."

"I will. You know I will." He reached down, took the ball, and threw it again, far, far, down the beach.

"And you won't go all Grady over the whole thing."

"What the hell does that mean?"

"You know. You have this tendency to get a little dramatic when things happen."

"I do not." He sounded testy.

"I think it's sweet. One of the first things I loved about you."

"Well," he admitted, "maybe I do. A little."

"So hold it together, man up, and do the right thing. Because if you don't I'll haunt your ass."

"Yeah, well, right back at you." He drew her to him and kissed her hair. "Baby, I'm beat. I'm going in. Where're we sleeping tonight?"

She smiled quietly in the dark. "Go on, sleep in your own bed. I'll be up in a while, after I read about a hundred more e-mails from the sheriff's department."

He turned back toward the street, muttering, "I hate this."

"What was that?"

"I said 'I love you,'" he returned. He had gone a couple of dozen yards up the beach before he turned and called to her, "Hey, I almost forgot. How'd it go with Doc today?"

Aggie dropped to her knees and opened her arms to Flash, who ran into them, squishing the wet tennis ball between his teeth. She buried her face for a moment in his damp, briny fur, and then stood, smiling at Grady across the night beach. "Great," she called back. "Everything was great."

CHAPTER THIRTEEN

Aggie did not spend the next hours reading e-mails. Instead she used Ryan's password to access the sheriff department's files on the Reichart case: ballistics reports, CSI photos, autopsies; her statement, Grady's statement, Briggs's, Darrell's statement. Some of these she had looked at before; most she had not. It was never good police procedure for a victim to become involved in investigating her own crime, and she'd known Bishop had it under control. Besides, it had always been an open and shut case. The perpetrator was in jail. What was there to investigate?

Until now.

She went to bed at three a.m., only because her eyes were too tired to focus on the screen any longer. She let Ryan think she was asleep when he kissed her cheek at six thirty and whispered, "Gotta go, baby. Don't get up. I made the coffee."

She murmured, "Thanks. You be careful out there."

"You, too."

"Ryan." She turned over, shielding her tired eyes with her forearm. "If you're around the jail today, you might see me."

He looked back at her curiously. "Are you going to talk to Josh?"

"Maybe. I don't know."

"Need a ride? Want me to wait?"

"No, go to work. I might not even have time to go today. I'm just thinking about it."

"Well, give me a call if you decide. Maybe I'll take you to lunch."

"Oh, boy." She turned over and plumped the pillow beneath her cheek. "I've had a craving for vending machine food lately."

He paused on his way out to scratch Flash's ears. "Take care of my girl, buddy." And to Aggie he said, "Have a good day."

She smiled sleepily. "You too."

But her smile faded as soon as he was out the door. She propped a pillow behind her head and stared at the place he had been. Flash jumped up lightly and lay down beside her. She dropped her hand to his neck, twirling her fingers lightly in his fur.

"Flash," she said softly, "we might have made a terrible mistake."

His attention quickened. He had made mistakes, just a few, and he didn't like them one bit. The skunk in the park, that had been a mistake. The chow mix with the sneaky look in his eye that Flash hadn't seen until too late was another one. He had never known Aggie to make a mistake, and wasn't entirely sure she was capable of it.

"The ballistics report says the bullet was fired from ten feet away, at a sixty-degree angle. But it wasn't. Darrell Reichart was standing right in front of me. Four feet away at most. You remember that, don't you, Flash? I was kneeling beside your cage, and when I looked up Darrell was standing over me with a gun. He was right there."

Flash watched her and listened.

"Nobody ever thought to ask me," Aggie murmured, stroking his fur. "They asked me what I saw, but they didn't ask me where he was when I saw him. They thought they already knew. They had the evidence. The problem with that, of course, is that even if they had asked me, would I have remembered? Do I remember now? Or is this all just a figment of a little piece of metal in my brain?"

Flash watched her alertly, tracking her questions, trying to figure out why they were so important to her. For some reason that made her smile, and she scratched the base of his ear right where he liked it. That made *him* smile. She said, "And that's not even the real question, is it? The real question is did Darrell Reichart kill his parents? And if he didn't, who did?"

She blew out a big breath and sat up, ruffling his fur as she did. "The problem is, it's starting to look like we might not ever know the answers to either of those questions. And if we did, it wouldn't matter."

A quiet sense of relief swept through Flash as he realized Aggie had finally come to think about the whole thing the same way he did. He knew exactly who killed the two people from his puppyhood, and he had always known it didn't matter. He was glad this meant they didn't have to think about it anymore.

What he didn't understand was why this seemed to make Aggie so sad.

Aggie left Mo in charge of the office and assigned Sally Ann to be her driver for the day—a situation that did not sit well with either of her two employees. Mo felt that as long as there was some lunatic shooting out tires on the bridge there was only one person qualified to drive the chief of the police around and that was herself. Sally Ann felt, probably with some justification, that if she left her well-organized office in the hands of an amateur all day there wouldn't be anything left of it when she returned. Aggie mollified them both by pointing out that since Mo was the only one authorized to enforce law and order on the island, she had to stay, and that Sally Ann could use the time to update the island's emergency plan at the courthouse, which was always a priority at the beginning of hurricane season.

Another trip across the bridge. Another endless ellipsis of heart stopping terror, of not knowing how she would humiliate herself, of bursting lungs, shaking limbs, terror; just terror. She put on her headphones and pretended to watch a video she'd downloaded on her iPad about civic volunteer organizations. Sometimes that helped. This time it only made her nauseous and shaky and, by the time they crested the bridge on the down slope to Ocean City, wondering how many more times her heart could be expected to pound out blood at five times its normal rhythm before it simply collapsed. And wondering if it even mattered.

Sally Ann, of course, noticed nothing. That was her job.

Aggie left Sally Ann in the office of the Planning and Safety Director, pulling ledgers from the shelves and busily making copies, and she and Flash walked down the street to the sheriff's office. The morning was hot and lead-colored, smelling of diesel fuel and fish and heavy with the weight of the coming storm. She'd opted for civvies for the trip across the bridge, which was only proper protocol, but before she'd walked the two blocks to their destination, her crisp white blouse was damp with sweat and her feet squished inside her faux-alligator pumps. Flash, on the other hand, was grinning with the excitement of the city and the smell of the storm. He loved going new places and smelling new things, and Aggie had said they were going to Grady's work.

Grady wasn't there. Flash could tell that the minute they walked through the glass door with its shiny linoleum floor and the bright overhead lights. There was a hint of his presence, a confluence of familiar smells that reminded him of Grady, and that made him feel better about being here with Aggie. But there were other things in the air, too, things he didn't much like at all, and those made him very uneasy.

There was a counter with a window on one side of the wall, and a woman came to it when she saw Aggie, greeting her happily. She said something nice about Flash and he glanced up at her politely, but mostly his nose was to the floor, trying to make sense of all the conflicting information left behind by the footprints there.

Dogs receive hundreds of thousands of scent input signals every second, much like a human in a stadium might hear hundreds of thousands of voices all at once. Focusing on, analyzing, and understanding the meaning behind every single one of those signals would overwhelm even the most astute canine—or human—brain. But occasionally there will be a hint of something interesting, familiar, important. Something that stirred a memory or resonated with an emotion. So Flash ignored the smell of shoe rubber and coffee and dust and oil and soap and paper and computers and leather belts and floor polish, all of which were familiar and unimportant. He focused on the smells of people, each with its own distinct signature beneath the perfumes and shampoos and laundry soaps they used to disguise it. Dozens of them, hundreds. Some sad and sour, angry and afraid; some confident, tired, bored, easy, excited, such a great churning swirl of scents, all of them coming together to form a picture that made absolutely no sense to him.

He wondered why Aggie would want to come to a place that smelled so much like blood and thunder. He wondered why Grady would want to work here.

A couple of men in uniform came through the double doors at the end of the hall and took turns hugging Aggie, then knelt on the floor to pet Flash. One of them said, "So this is the famous Flash. We've seen a few pictures of you, dude."

And another one said, "I remember Grady brought him by when he was still little enough to fit in one hand. He grew up to be a looker, didn't he?"

Aggie smiled at him in a proud way, so he sat up taller and kept his best manners. Aggie said, "Flash, these are two of Murphy County's finest. They're the ones who keep the bad guys off the streets."

That interested Flash, even though he wasn't quite sure what it meant. He'd never met a bad guy, not that he knew about anyway. He'd met some sad ones, some mad ones, some confused and really messed-up ones. But he didn't think any bad guys lived on Dogleg Island.

One of the deputies got to his feet, grinning. "You got that right. Because if we don't get them, they're sure to get you."

Flash wondered if a bad guy was anything like that chow mix with the sneaky look. Things were starting to make a little more sense to him.

Aggie wrinkled her nose. "That's a terrible slogan. I sure hope you're not in charge of public relations."

More people came through the double doors, wanting to hug Aggie and talk to her and pet Flash. One of them had a package of cheese crackers that he wanted to share, and Flash didn't object to that at all. Another one brought him half a donut, which was the kind of treat he rarely got at home. In the middle of all this Aggie said, "Well, I don't know who's out keeping the streets safe if everybody's in here catching up on old times, but the sheriff is expecting me." She opened the double doors that led to a big room filled with desks and computers and other people in uniform. "Flash?"

Flash looked regretfully at the donut he had barely tasted and followed Aggie down the hall. It still made no sense to him why she wanted to be here, but if Aggie thought it was okay, his place was by her side.

Roy Briggs stood up behind his desk when she came in, opened his arms wide in welcome, and then came around and enveloped her in a big teddy-bear hug. "You look great, Chief," he said, stepping back. And then, looking at her more closely, added, "Are you?"

Aggie tried for one more smile. "Yeah. I think so. More or less."

Flash sat still as a statue and ever alert, right at the threshold of the office. Roy nodded in his direction. "Boy, he sure grew up, didn't he? Think he remembers me?"

"Flash remembers everything," Aggie said, and smiled in his direction. Flash just sat there, doing his job.

"Well, he looks like a hell of a guard dog. Must be a lot of company for you."

Aggie agreed that he was and then, small talk over, she sank into the guest chair before his desk, clasping her hands together in her lap. "Roy," she said, "I don't want to waste your time. I know you're in the middle of a couple of major investigations. I'm here because I'm about to step on one of them."

He sat on the corner of his desk, his expression intent and interested. He nodded at her to continue.

Aggie tightened her fingers in her lap. "I've asked to see Darrell Reichart. There are some things I need to ask him about his statement, things that don't make sense in light of…well, in light of some of the things I've started to remember. I know this is your case. But it's personal to me. I just wanted you to know why I'm butting in."

He gave a dismissive flick of his wrist, frowning. "Aggie, you know we don't stand on protocol around here. Whatever you need. But what is this? What do you mean you've started to remember things? What kind of things?"

She found herself floundering, picking her way around the edges of the truth. "I don't know. I'm not sure. I just…" She looked at him helplessly. "The thing is, Roy, if I have any doubt about how accurate my memories are, I can't let Richardson put me on the stand. I can't perjure myself. And if I tell the truth about what I remember…I'll blow our case."

Roy leaned forward, his expression intent. "My God, Aggie," he said softly. "What do you remember?"

She took a breath, released it slowly, and gave a short shake of her head. "Not yet, okay? Right now I just need to look into Darrell's eyes while he tells me what happened that night. I know he's not going to take the stand, so I won't hear it in court. But I need to hear it. "

Roy nodded, trying to look as though he understood, but looking mostly concerned. "Grady's out chasing down a lead in the Lincoln case," he said, "but I can call him back in. Or I'll go over with you, if you want. I'm not crazy about the idea of you talking to that whack-job by yourself."

Aggie smiled wearily and tilted her head to him. "In the first place, I won't be by myself, I'll be in a roomful of lawyers and guards. And in the second place, this is why I couldn't work here anymore, remember? I'm a big girl and I can take care of myself. But thank you for worrying."

Briggs thumbed his nose, looking briefly embarrassed. "Habit, I guess. Sorry."

She stood up, pressing her palms down the seams of her slacks in a quick, nervous gesture. "Thanks, Roy. Don't call Grady."

He gave a single nod of reluctant consent. "Keep me informed."

She tightened her smile and nodded in return, and she and Flash left the office.

They walked three more blocks and paused outside a big gray building that, even before they entered, already smelled like the saddest place Flash had ever been. Aggie took a nervous breath. "Well, this is it, Flash," she said, and dropped her hand to his head. "This is where they keep the bad guys so that the rest of us are safe. No place for you and me, I guess."

Nonetheless, she opened the door and the two of them walked inside.

Aggie signed in, presented her ID, deposited her cell phone and her keys in a small plastic box— everything else she had left with Sally Ann—and signed a receipt for them. There was some discussion about Flash, but it didn't last long. Aggie won just about all of those kinds of discussions.

The deputy who came to escort them back to the interview room liked dogs, and talked about a woman with a therapy dog who sometimes came on Sunday afternoons, and how it really lifted the inmates' spirits. He thought they should do more of that, maybe even get one of those cell dog programs started like you saw on TV. Aggie smiled and agreed with him, even though it was easy to tell she was not in the least bit interested in the conversation. The deputy took them down a concrete and metal hallway that smelled like antiseptic and sweat, fear and despair, and a hundred other things it was best for a dog not to think about, then opened the metal door to the small conference room. Four people already sat at a table and another deputy stood off to the side. He said, "Just push the buzzer when you're finished." The door closed with a heavy click.

Aggie and Flash crossed the room, Flash hanging back a few steps, being cautious, taking things in. Aggie knew Allen Edwards from the prosecutor's office, and recognized two of the members of the defense team, who quickly rose to introduce themselves. Between them sat Darrell Reichart.

He had spent six weeks recovering from abdominal surgery which included the loss of his spleen, fourteen inches of intestine, and part of his liver, and a certain gauntness still lingered in his face. But his hair was freshly barbered for his upcoming appearance before the twelve men and women who would decide his fate, his eyes were clear, and his shoulders were straight. Without the gray county jail jumpsuit he wore, he might have been mistaken for any MBA student on any college campus in the country. Aggie waited for a reaction to set in: dread, anger, fear, hatred. She remembered lying on the ground, choking on her own saliva. She remembered lying in a hospital bed, counting the dots in the acoustical tiles over and over again, hundreds of thousands of times. She remembered pushing herself along, inch by inch, on a walker with muscles that were so weak she couldn't even get to the toilet by herself. She remembered the first time she looked in a mirror and some bald cone-head space alien had looked back. She thought about the bullet in her brain that even now could take her away from Grady and Flash, that could mean she'd never see another sunset over the Gulf or throw another tennis ball or hear Grady say "scooch over" or speak another intelligible word, ever, and she waited to feel something for the person who was responsible for it all. But she felt nothing.

She looked down at Flash, wondering how he felt. Wondering what he really remembered.

Flash looked back up at her, wishing he could tell her.

The development of a young dog is both efficient and practical. He begins to learn as soon as he is born, and to remember shortly after that. The first four weeks of a puppy's life are centered around survival. By eight weeks the boundaries of his world begin to expand exponentially and his brain experiences the most rapid growth it will ever undergo. Everything that he encounters during this time becomes a lesson, and the lessons are never forgotten.

The woman with the kind face and the sing-song voice who brought Flash food and took him for walks in the sand had only been in his life for a week before the blood and thunder came, but he remembered her fondly. The man who lived with them sometimes he remembered less well, and the boy who smelled like chemicals and unhappiness was most confusing of all. But when Aggie said the name Darrell Reichart, he knew exactly who she was talking about, and when he looked at the young man sitting at the table now he knew precisely who he was. He looked different. He smelled different. But he was the same.

What Flash didn't understand was why he was in this place, where the bad guys were kept.

"Chief Malone, this is really quite irregular," said the lawyer called Martinez, who seemed to be the senior man present on Darrell's behalf. "You're not even authorized to investigate this case."

"I'm here with the full permission of the Murphy County Sheriff's Department."

"Discovery has already been filed," he went on huffily. "We start testimony next week. My client is not required to answer any more questions related to this case and, to be perfectly frank, will not be allowed to do so. So I honestly don't see the point of this meeting."

Flash looked at Darrell. Darrell looked back. He almost seemed to smile a little. "Nice dog," he said. "My mom had a puppy that looked a little like that." And his smile faded into something sad and quiet again.

Flash felt bad for him, and started to walk over to him. Darrell lowered his hand as though to reach for Flash, or to pet him, but the guard stepped forward quickly and snapped, "Hands on the table. Ma'am, control your dog."

Darrell put his hand back on the table, and Flash returned to Aggie. Aggie stroked Flash's neck in gentle reassurance, but her eyes were on Darrell.

Allen Edwards cleared his throat. "Shall we get started?"

She sat down in the wooden chair across from Darrell. Close enough to touch the hands that were resting on the table in front of him. She looked at Darrell. He looked back.

She said, "Do you remember me?"

He didn't even glance at his lawyers. "I know who you are."

She said, "You told the police that you came up the steps from the beach through the east-facing sliding glass door and that the burglar alarm was already sounding before you entered the house. Your friend Josh corroborates that."

Allen looked startled and leaned toward her as though to stop her, but she ignored him. Darrell said nothing.

She went on, "The house was dark but the sun was coming up. You found your parents' bodies lying across your path, between the door and the sofa. You knelt down to examine the bodies, which was how you got their blood on you."

Nothing. He didn't even flinch.

"The alarm stopped automatically. We know that because the last set of fingerprints on the keypad was your mother's. No one turned it off. I knocked on the front door and announced myself approximately thirty seconds later. You claim you didn't hear that. I entered the house and turned on the lights, and that's when you picked up the gun that was lying next to your father's body. Do you remember any of this?"

He glanced at the lawyer on his right, who nodded slightly. It was all in the record. "I remember."

"Then what did you do?" Aggie asked.

"What do you mean?"

Martinez said with an air of pained forbearance, "We've been through this multiple times. We're all busy people here, so unless you have something new to add…"

Aggie insisted, "Did you stand there over your parents' bodies with the gun in your hand, waiting for what you thought was the killer to appear, or did you move forward when you heard me coming through the house?"

Martinez said, "Don't answer that."

Aggie surmised that question had already been shown to be a dangerous one for the defense, probably because Darrell had no clear memory of what he had done or where he had moved during that time. Any attempt he made to answer it would not cast him in a favorable light. So Aggie just nodded.

She said, "You saw me, but in your impaired state you didn't recognize me as a police officer, again according to your statement. I asked you to hand over your weapon. You said…" She took a folded piece of paper from the pocket of her slacks and read, "You said, 'don't do it, lady.' Then you began to plead with me not to hurt you."

After a moment, and another glance at his lawyer, Darrell nodded cautiously. "I remember that."

"Of course you do. You've probably read your statement, or heard it read to you, a hundred times by now, like everyone else involved in this case." She kept her eyes on him. "Did you say anything else? Anything that wasn't in your statement?"

He just looked at her.

Martinez sounded bored. "Darrell, I would advise you to—"

Aggie spoke over him. "Maybe you said something to me after it happened. After I'd been shot. When I was lying on the floor."

Darrell's eyes held hers. Martinez said, "Chief Malone, I hardly see…"

Darrell said, "I asked if you were all right. I didn't know what had happened, so I remember saying, 'Lady, are you all right?' Is that what you mean?"

Aggie sat back in her chair. Allen Edwards, next to her, turned a page in his file folder, and then glanced across the table at the defense attorneys. "That wasn't in the original statement."

"No," Aggie said softly, looking at Darrell. "It probably didn't seem important at the time. But it's something you're not likely to make up. And two people can't mis-remember the same thing."

"I'm not sure I understand the relevance," Martinez said. "This can't possibly have any bearing on my client's guilt or innocence. If anything, it demonstrates his compassion for the victim."

Aggie said quietly to Darrell, "You didn't pull the trigger, did you? You didn't shoot me."

And before either of his lawyers could speak, Darrell answered levelly, "No ma'am."

She said, "Do you know who did?"

"There was somebody else in the house. Like I said, the sound of the gunshot came from behind me. I never saw who it was. But somebody was there."

Aggie held his gaze for another moment, then nodded.

Allen Edwards said, "Aggie, this is nothing new. This is the same thing he's always claimed. And as the defense well knows..." He passed a stern look to the men across the table. "There is absolutely no evidence to indicate anyone was in the house that night aside from the victims, the accused, and the first responders."

Aggie said, "Yes. I know." She stood up. "Thank you for your time, gentlemen."

The defense lawyers, trying not to look as puzzled as they no doubt were, began to gather up their folders and confer in low voices with each other. Aggie turned to Allen. It actually hurt her throat to say the words. "You and I," she told him, "need to have a talk with Mr. Richardson."

Flash knew his place was with Aggie, but he couldn't help looking back once more over his shoulder at Darrell Reichart before they left the room. The conversation had cleared up a lot of things for him, and made some things even foggier. He thought he was starting to understand about bad guys now. The ones who made people dead, or tried to. And they had to be locked away so they wouldn't do it again. So that he and Aggie could be safe.

The footprints in the sand. The man in the lagoon. The man with the knife. The thunder in the night.

(The squirrel in the yard.)

Dead.

What he didn't understand was why Darrell Reichart was locked up in that dark place of hopelessness and fear, while the bad guys were laughing down the street, in the place where Grady worked.

A fine flurry of beach rain had begun by the time Aggie got back to the island. The rain and gusting winds continued the rest of the day, bringing with them the early gloom of a false sunset. The Weather Service issued an advisory in advance of the tropical storm that was gathering in the Gulf and was expected to make landfall within twenty-four hours. Aggie and Sally Ann started working the phones, notifying businesses to stand by for possible emergency measures, while Mo, who had been cooped up in the office all day, made her rounds on foot.

Most of the islanders had weathered too many storms to be much alarmed by a routine alert, but the Wedding Chapel was the exception. While it was certainly possible to move seventy-five chairs, a few hundred yards of bunting, and twenty floral arrangements to their indoor backup facility, the fifty-plus pounds of shrimp and lobster could not—simply could *not*—be expected to survive without refrigeration, so exactly what did the island emergency plan have to say about that? Not to mention the guests themselves, most of whom were staying in the Beachcomber Inn on the other side of the bridge and might be stuck there if the island was cut off, as it had been for three weeks after Hurricane

Rita. Aggie assured the frantic owners that nothing even approaching the magnitude of Rita was heading their way, but suggested they buy ice and keep the weather radio on just in case. She intended to do the same.

"This is what I like about our job, Flash," she murmured as the two of them made their way home to the rhythmic swish of the windshield wipers a little after six. "You go looking for a cat, and you end up finding a murder weapon. You give a deposition that could free a mass murderer in the morning, and save the wedding shrimp in the afternoon. Never a dull moment."

She meant it to sound funny, but Flash could tell she didn't feel funny at all. She felt tired, and sad, and a little sick. He rested his head on her knee for the rest of the drive home.

Grady's house was dark and his parking space empty when she arrived, so Aggie went to her own cottage and made scrambled eggs for Flash and herself—mostly for Flash. She heard Grady's car pull up about an hour later, and saw the sweep of his headlights on her window. She waited for him to come in, but he didn't, so she put on her raincoat and walked with Flash across the drive.

She could hear the sound of the television, turned low, in the living room and made her way through the darkened house toward it. Grady was sitting in the big chair in front of the fireplace drinking beer from a can while the blue and white lights of the television flickered across his face and the weather reporters excitedly chatted about the gathering force of Tropical Storm Andy.

"Too bad," she observed. "I only missed it by a few letters. I always wanted a hurricane named after me."

He said, without looking at her, "They retire the names of the storms that do the most damage."

Grady lifted the can to his lips and took a long drink. He said, without much expression at all, "When were you going to tell me?"

To Flash, the tension in the room felt like lightning bolts waiting to happen. He eased up to Grady, sat uneasily, then pressed himself against Aggie's calf as she came around the big chair to the sofa and sat down, linking her hands between her knees. She said in an odd, constrained voice, "I tried to call you a couple of times. I wanted to explain."

He kept his eyes focused on the television, and took another drink.

She said, "The last couple of weeks I've been getting these memories, flashbacks really, about that night, the night of the shooting. I thought I remembered everything when I gave you and Bishop my statement that day, you know, before I went into surgery, but now I'm not so sure. Ryan, I think there may have been somebody else in the house that night. Darrell might be telling the truth. I don't know if he killed his parents or not. But I remember seeing somebody reflected in the glass of the sliding door, and he had the knife. I didn't see his face. But he was standing in exactly the position the prosecution is claiming Darrell was standing when he shot me. Only he didn't. He couldn't have. Darrell was standing right in front of me, and if he had shot me from that distance, he would have blown my skull apart. That's the truth. That's what I remember. And I had to tell Richardson. I had to tell him because if he put me on the stand and asked me to swear to the truth of my original statement I couldn't lie. And because the defense would have destroyed my testimony on cross and they should have. I was the strongest witness in the prosecution case, and now we have no case. I'm sorry."

Grady lifted the can again and took a long drink, emptying it. He said in a curiously flat tone, "Do you think I give a shit about Darrell Reichart? Do you really think that's what this is about?"

Flash shivered.

Abruptly, Grady crushed the empty can in his fist and hurled it toward the fireplace. Every muscle in Aggie's body stiffened. For the longest time there was nothing in the room but the sound of breathing and the murmur of television voices. Then Aggie said in a voice that was very tight and very subdued, "Who ratted me out? Lorraine or Richardson?"

For a moment Grady didn't reply. Then he said stiffly, without looking at her, "It was Briggs. He'd just come from a meeting with Richardson and I had to hear from my boss that my—that you were facing life-threatening brain surgery and you hadn't bothered to mention it to me."

Aggie lowered her head. Flash pressed close to her. She said in a small tight voice, "I had to tell Richardson about the seizures, about the diagnosis. Otherwise he wouldn't have known how important it was not to put me on the stand."

"You walked out on the neurosurgeon. You refused to schedule."

"Ryan, I—"

"So that's it? You just die? I don't get a say?"

Her eyes went hot and wet. "Ryan, don't."

He surged from his chair, his jaw tight, his eyes furious. "I'm your first phone call, goddamnit! I'm the guy you don't keep secrets from! I'm the one you call when things go south! You don't get to do this, do you understand me? You just don't!"

Aggie stood up. Her eyes were flooding, and every breath she'd ever wanted to take was compressed in her chest. She tried to reach for him, but she couldn't make herself do it, so she just stood there helplessly while everything they'd ever built together slowly shattered into sharp, irreparable shards.

At length Grady swung away, picked up his jacket from the chair where he'd tossed it. His voice was harsh. "I've got to get back. They need help securing the marina before the storm."

Aggie wanted to cry *Don't leave me, don't do this, don't make me face this alone.* But what she said was, "You've been drinking. Be careful crossing the bridge."

He left her without looking back.

A little after midnight, Flash heard Grady's step in the hallway and sprang off of Aggie's bed, the one with the lace pillows that smelled like flowers and, tonight, like tears. He wasn't sure why she was sad, but it didn't matter. His job was to stay close and take care of her until Grady returned. So he did.

Grady took off his utility belt and put his gun and cell phone in the drawer next to the bed. He sat on the edge of the bed to remove his shoes, but then didn't. He just sat there. "I don't know how to sleep without you," he said into the dark.

Rain spattered on the tin roof with a brief gust of wind, and then was quiet. He touched her shoulder, but she did not turn over. He leaned close, brushing away a strand of hair that was caught in the dampness near her temple, and released a slow, unsteady breath. He squeezed his eyes tightly closed, as though holding back pain. Then he said huskily, "Aggie, I need you to promise me something."

For a moment she didn't reply. Then she whispered, "I can't. I can't make any promises now." Her voice sounded wet and choked.

"This one you can."

He leaned over her, turned her toward him gently, and put a hand on either side of her damp, hot face, fingers curled lightly against her skull. The refracted light of low-hanging clouds filled the room with a silvery gray illumination, and Aggie could see sparks of raindrops in his hair and on his face. His eyes were dark. "Promise me," he said, low and tight, "you won't ever let me make you cry again.

Kick my ass. Slash my tires. Sink my boat in the harbor." Slowly he lowered his forehead to hers until his breath flooded her face, his heartbeat smothered hers. "Just don't do this," he whispered. "Just don't cry. Don't let it be my fault."

Aggie wrapped her arms around him and pressed her head against his shoulder and squeezed her eyes tightly shut against the last of the tears. She whispered, "I was just so scared. I'm sorry, I was just so scared."

And he whispered back, breathing hard, "I was too, baby. I was too."

They held each other, breathing. She said at last, thickly, "Okay. I promise. I'll slash your tires. But I won't sink your boat. Flash likes your boat. So do I."

He kissed her face and then lay down beside her fully clothed and drew her into his arms. They stayed like that for a long time, holding each other, saying nothing. Flash jumped back up on the bed and nestled near their feet.

After a time Grady said quietly, "When are we going to do this? The surgery."

She entwined her fingers through his. "When I decide."

Another long silence. At last he said, "Okay."

Grady tilted his head back against the pillow, gazing into the dark. He said, after a moment, "There's something I need to tell you. When I heard you'd changed your testimony, that you were supporting Darrell's claim about a second gunman...all I could think was, *I shot that kid.* If you're right, then he was innocent and I shot him. I shot to kill."

Aggie lifted herself onto one elbow to look at him. "Grady, you shot an armed gunman who was high on crack and refused to halt or drop his weapon. Just because he didn't shoot me doesn't mean he was innocent. We won't know that until a jury decides."

He took a slow breath, in and out. He turned his head to look at her. "Then we'll never know," he said. "There's not going to be a jury. There's not going to be a trial. It's over. Darrell Reichart hanged himself in his cell three hours ago."

CHAPTER FOURTEEN

People liked to say that everything happened at once. In Flash's experience, things happened more or less in the order they were meant to. Clouds gathered, rain fell. The telephone rang, trouble came. They got in the car, adventure began. It was all pretty predictable, from his point of view.

In the minutes before the weather alarm sounded, Grady was making scrambled eggs and bacon, and Aggie was buttering toast. Her voice was a little shaky as she said, "Darrell had no reason to kill himself. His charges had just been reduced from three to two. He had a good chance of getting off." She took a loud breath, blew it out. The hand that held the butter knife stopped. "I was the last person to see him alive. It was me."

Grady turned bacon in the pan. "You weren't. The jailor brought him supper. Darrell saw his attorneys. Richardson and Briggs saw him after that. You weren't the last one. It wasn't you."

Aggie pushed a hand through her rumpled hair. It was dark outside and rain still splashed intermittently against the windows, but inside Aggie's cozy kitchen it smelled of bacon and butter and good solid mornings. Aggie, unfortunately, could not see that.

She said quietly, "He wasn't like I expected. He was—I don't know, he seemed like a regular kid. All this time I'd made him into a monster and he was just this quiet, skinny kid. Polite. He called me ma'am. Flash even liked him. He tried to pet Flash, but the guard wouldn't let him. He was just—not what I expected."

"Flash likes everybody," Grady replied patiently. "It doesn't mean anything. And of course he was polite. He had a jury to impress."

"It's just that—after all this time, now he's dead. It doesn't make sense. Grady, I swear when I saw him he was as calm as—"

That was when the weather radio claxon started to blare, followed almost immediately by the buzzing of both Aggie's and Grady's telephones. Grady turned off the burner with one hand and checked his phone with the other. Aggie turned off the radio alarm and started scrolling through her messages.

"Well, that's it then," Grady muttered. "An official Category One hurricane, scheduled to make landfall by four p.m. Damn, that's high tide."

For the next few minutes they did nothing but work on their phones. Grady scooped some eggs and bacon into Flash's dish and waited for it to cool. Aggie added toast. Flash watched the dish fixedly until Grady set it on the floor in front of him. At that point he didn't stand on ceremony, but helped himself.

Grady disconnected his phone and glanced at Aggie. "Briggs wants us to report in for assignments by seven. I'll probably be assigned right back here, but I'd better help Pete board up the bar before I go in, just in case I get stuck over there."

As it happened, Pete's Place was located on the highest elevation on the island, which wasn't saying much, and was far enough toward the center of the land mass to be safe from most storm surge. It had therefore been designated the only emergency shelter on the island, and was always secured first—which was both good and bad for business.

Aggie said, "I'll check in with him later, but tell him to e-mail me before nine if he's running low on emergency supplies. And don't forget the storm shutters on your place."

"Damn, those things are a pain in the ass. What're you going to do about evacuating the island?"

"Voluntary until noon, then I'll see how it looks. I just texted Briggs and the radio station."

"How much help do you think you'll need from the department?"

Aggie worked the keys on her phone. "I'm calling in the volunteer fire and rescue squad to close off the beach and low-lying streets. I think I'll be okay, but if you guys need something to do we can always use more men on sandbag duty."

"I'll put the word out."

Aggie continued to scroll down her messages until she found the text she was looking for, then emitted a small exclamation of triumph. She held up a finger to Grady as he started to speak, and pushed another button. "Hey, Mo," she said in a moment, "sorry to wake you. Storm's coming. I'm declaring a state of emergency in about an hour, but before I do, would you stop by Mike's Motors and pick up a generator he's holding for us? You're driving the pickup, right? Yeah, okay. Deliver it to the Wedding Chapel on First Street. I know, I'll make sure they're waiting for it. Thanks, you're the best."

Grady turned a portion of eggs and bacon on to a piece of toast, topped them with a second piece of toast, cut the sandwich in half and slid the dish in front of Aggie. "Eat that," he said.

"Okay, thanks, I will." She punched more buttons on her phone.

He made a similar sandwich for himself. "I mean it. You're not leaving here until you do."

Aggie said, "Hey, Sally Ann, sorry to call so early but…you are? You did? Okay, thanks. See you at the office."

Grady said, "Just in case we end up closing the bridge, the emergency plan is to stay with Lucy, okay?"

Aggie wrinkled her nose. Lucy was Grady's sister, mother of the twins from hell, and the most unlikeable person Aggie had ever known. "I'm chief of police," she said. "I don't leave the island."

"We'll get a couple of deputies over here to take over security. It'll be fine."

"I'm not moving in with Lucy. Not for a day, not for a night, not for an hour. I'll meet you at Pete's."

"Bishop's then. He's far enough inland."

She looked up from her phone, straight at him. "We won't close the bridge unless it reaches Category Two. If that happens, our plan is to shelter in place. That's always been our plan."

Grady said, "Not anymore. Not this time."

"That's crazy. You don't just change the plan. Anyway, it doesn't matter, we're not closing the bridge, and the whole thing will probably be back down to a tropical storm before it even gets here. So it's a moot point. But don't forget to lower the shutters on your place."

Grady placed his hands palms down on the counter. He said, very quietly, "A hurricane is going to hit this island at four o'clock this afternoon. I want you on the other side of the bridge by two. I can't argue about this. Two o'clock. Okay?"

Aggie looked at him for a moment without speaking. Then she said, trying hard to keep her expression neutral, "Because the hospital is on the other side of the bridge."

She saw the muscles of his jaw tighten. She said wearily, "Damn you, Grady."

Flash looked up from licking his dish.

Aggie started to turn away, but Grady caught her wrist, lightly. She looked back. He said, "Listen. I don't think you get it. You're the strongest, bravest, smartest woman I've ever known, but I don't think you get it. If I lose you, if this thing in your brain explodes and I lose you because you were on the wrong side of the bridge or because I wasn't there or for whatever reason—it's over for me. Everything changes. Whatever life I might have had, whatever kind of man I might have been, I can never be that again, because losing you will change everything. You don't get it. You're not just living for you anymore. Can you understand that?"

Aggie looked at him, helpless and confused. She didn't know what to say. She didn't know what he wanted of her. So she just told the truth. "I'm chief of police. These are my people. I can't leave."

His lips compressed, and his hand fell away from hers. His phone buzzed and he glanced down to check the message, but not before she saw the bleak shadow of pain in his eyes that she never, ever wanted to see in the eyes of anyone she loved.

"Okay," he said, and when he looked back at her his expression, like his tone, was carefully flat. "I'm heading to Pete's, then across the bridge. I'll be back as soon as I can." He picked up his egg sandwich and turned for the door. "Flash, make sure she eats."

The door opened and closed on a surge of warm wind and the sound of pounding surf, and Flash jumped up on the bar stool, staring at Aggie. He continued to stare at her until she picked up her sandwich and ate it.

Well, most of it anyway.

Some habits were hard to break, and Jerome Bishop still got up at five o'clock every morning, even though he hadn't had to be at work at six in over a year, even though he knew there would be no fishing today, and wouldn't have been even if a storm hadn't been headed this way. It was pitch dark outside the windows and rain pattered on the roof in fits and starts. A good day to stay in bed.

He was stiff and sore and walking like an old man, and with one arm in a sling it took longer than it should have to make coffee and butter toast. Eventually, though, he hobbled back to the living room with a saucer of whole wheat toast balanced on top of a mug of coffee. He put the dishes on a lamp table, eased himself into his recliner, and reached for the remote control. The face of the early-morning female news anchor filled the screen.

"...confirms today that Darrell Reichart was found dead in his jail cell yesterday evening of an apparent suicide. Reichart was being held in the Murphy County Detention Facility charged with murder in the deaths of his parents Leah and Walter Reichart. Testimony in that case was scheduled to begin next week. Ellen Freemont is standing by at the Murphy County Courthouse. Ellen, what can you tell us?"

Bishop leaned forward and pushed the button on the volume control repeatedly as the scene switched to a windblown-looking blonde in a windbreaker standing before the backlit courthouse; dark skies overhead, silver streaks of rain illuminated by erratic flashes of lightning. She looked sober and intent as she spoke into the camera, despite the gusts of wind that tossed her expensively styled hair from side to side and tugged at her jacket. She said, "Thank you, Erin. At this hour, we can report that Darrell Reichart, who was accused of brutally killing his parents at the family beach house almost two years ago, was found hanging from a crossbar in his cell last night in the Murphy County jail as jailors made a routine final check. The victim apparently used his own clothing to fashion a noose and stepped off his bunk to hang himself. The Murphy County Sheriff's Department has issued a statement saying that the victim was not under a suicide watch, and that they will be conducting a full investigation into this matter. Erin, as you know, Leah and Walter Reichart were discovered stabbed to death at their beach home on Dogleg Island and their son Darrell, reported to be under the influence of methamphetamines and crack cocaine at the time, was discovered at the scene with a weapon and was wounded when he tried to flee. Murphy County Deputy Agatha Malone was also seriously wounded in the confrontation and, interestingly enough, Erin, we have learned that Officer Malone paid Darrell Reichart a visit yesterday afternoon in the jail before his death. We have no information as yet about what was discussed at that meeting, but a brief statement from Reichart's attorney says that as of five o'clock yesterday afternoon Darrell was in good spirits with a strong hope of proving his innocence of all charges in court. We'll continue to bring you developments as we have them but, as you can see, Erin, with the approaching storm it promises to be a busy day at the Murphy County Sheriff's Department and new information is likely to be slow in incoming."

The camera switched back to the somber-faced anchor at the studio. "Thank you, Ellen Freemont, for that up-to-the minute report on this developing story." The camera shot widened as she turned to her colleague at the desk, a good-looking auburn-haired young man with second-string-anchor-hopeful written all over him. "Speaking of weather, Stuart, it is wild out there today! What's the latest on this storm?"

"Well, Erin, we do have some things to talk about. Tropical Storm Andy has been upgraded to a Category One hurricane as it makes its way to the Gulf Coast, and is expected to make landfall by four o'clock this afternoon…"

Bishop pushed the mute button and sat back, staring but not really seeing as the enthusiastic young weather person made his way across the set to the weather map. He knew the Murphy County jail like he knew his own kitchen; he knew the pro-cedures and the safeguards. Nothing like this had ever happened on his watch. There was no reason it should have happened now. With all the public-ity this case had gotten, Darrell Reichart would have been under round-the-clock surveillance had there been even the slightest risk of suicide. What had gone wrong?

He picked up the phone, looked at the time, and considered the calls he could make. He considered the one call he didn't want to make. He considered sitting back, drinking his coffee, and watching the story unfold on the news like the ordinary citizen he was. He was retired, for God's sake. This was none of his business.

But before the energetic young weatherman had even finished going through the graphics on storm surge, wind speeds, and rate of movement, Bishop was dialing a number.

Aggie was surprised to see so many cars parked in front of her office before six a.m., and even when she saw the knot of people huddled under umbrellas around the door to the police station it took her a minute to figure out why. When she got out of the car and a television camera light almost blinded her, though, she understood.

"Chief Malone! What is your reaction to Darrell Reichart's suicide?'

"Chief Malone, is it true you were the last person to see him alive?"

"What did you say to him?"

"Chief, is it true you were the one to bring new evidence against him just this week? Do you think that's why he did it?"

Aggie flipped up the hood of her rain jacket and started toward the reporters, Flash by her side. "You all are up early," she said by way of greeting, then flinched and put up a hand to protect her face from the microphone someone thrust toward it. Flash stopped and gave the impudent reporter a hard blue-eyed stare.

"Chief, we need something for the eight o'clock news break. Just a quick statement for the folks having breakfast at home."

The blinds to the office were closed but light peeped through the edges, so Aggie surmised that either Sally Ann or Mo was inside, possibly both. When she reached the front door, she heard the dead bolt click open and knew it was Mo, who had no patience for or sympathy with the "bunch of deadbeat fools," as she called reporters. Aggie turned before going inside and raised her voice slightly to be heard. "If you have any questions about the Reichart case, you should take them to the Murphy County Sheriff's Department. If you want a statement for the eight o'clock news, here it is: Dogleg Island is under a hurricane warning as we anticipate Hurricane Andy to make landfall along our coastline this afternoon. As of now, we are calling for a voluntary evacuation of all low-lying areas, which includes virtually all of the island. We will be taking emergency measures throughout the morning. For a full list of those measures, including cancellations and school closings, go to our website at www-dot-doglegisland-dot-gov. I'll issue an update with more details at nine o'clock."

"Chief Malone, is it true you found the murder weapon in the Reichart case? Do you think that's why Darrell killed himself?"

"Were you shocked that he wasn't under a suicide watch?"

Aggie held up her hand and called out, "We're not going to serve coffee, ladies and gentlemen, so if that's what you're waiting for, you all better finish up your business and get out of the storm. Evacuation means go home."

She turned to open the door and someone called out, "How did you feel when you heard the man who tried to kill you was dead?"

She froze with her hand on the door handle for just a second, and then pushed inside. How did she feel? *How did she feel?*

"Good for nothing deadbeat fools," Mo said loudly, glaring at the door as Aggie closed it behind her. "You want me to get my gun?"

"No thanks, Mo, I don't think that will be necessary." Flash shook out his coat and Aggie unzipped her jacket, wiping raindrops from her face with the back of her hand. "Did you get the generator delivered?"

"Would I be here if I didn't?"

"Right."

"Hi, Chief!" Sally Ann greeted her happily. "What are the chances, huh? We just got our emergency plan updated and we have a real emergency to use it on!"

"Well," Aggie reminded her, "we did know the storm was coming." *How did she feel?* Seriously?

"The point is, I've got all the flyers printed out and the public information announcements ready. I just need you to fill in the details."

"Good job, Sally Ann." She poured coffee into an oversized mug with a picture of a border collie on it and took it to her desk, flipping through the papers there. How did she feel? The problem was, she didn't know. And maybe it was a good thing that she didn't have time to find out. "Okay, Mo, let's start getting these flyers out. You take Main through Marine, I'll take Ocean. Some of the businesses won't even bother to open today, so make sure you tape one on every door and window." She rummaged in her drawer for tape. "Find out who's going to need help boarding up and keep a list so I can notify the volunteers. If anybody asks about evacuation, tell them the west-bound lanes across the bridge will be open until noon."

She found the tape and gave it to Mo, who replied with a surprised, "Ya'll closing the bridge?"

"No, but it doesn't hurt to put a little scare into folks who think they can wait until the last minute to make up their minds. The last thing we want is a traffic jam on the bridge, in case something does happen."

"Yes sir, Chief, on it." She opened the door and paused to call back, loudly enough to be heard by the reporters still milling about, "You sure you don't want me to shoot some of these worthless fools hanging around on our doorstep?"

"No thanks, Mo," she called back. "But check back with me in an hour, in case they're still here."

Mo gave a satisfied nod and closed the door behind her.

How did she feel? How the hell did they imagine she felt?

Aggie turned to Sally Ann. "Okay, Flash and I are going to hit the streets. You're in charge of Command Central, okay?" Sally Ann's eyes grew so enormous with self-importance behind the thick-framed glasses that Aggie had to smile. "Just hold down the fort till I get back. Here's the info for the website. Be sure to double-check the emergency numbers before you post them. And here's what I want you to record for the automatic phone system but *don't* start dialing yet. I want to wait for the latest from the weather service after sunup. Check with the Utilities Commission to see how many generators they can have standing by and—oh, never mind, I'd better talk to them myself. Just call me on my cell if you need me."

Sally Ann was scribbling furiously on her notepad, but as Aggie stopped by the door to put her jacket back on, Sally Ann looked up. "Chief," she said, "I guess you're relieved, huh? About the trial, I mean."

Aggie stared at Sally Ann. Relieved. Was that what she felt? Relieved?

She said abruptly, "Call me if you need me." And she and Flash went out into the storm.

CHAPTER FIFTEEN

Flash loved storms. Once he and Aggie and Grady had been on the boat in the middle of the ocean when the sky got dark and the wind and rain blew and he could tell even Grady was worried, just a little, but the way Aggie laughed into the sky with her face all wet with rain, and the way Flash's fur bristled whenever the lightning flashed, and the way the sea tossed them high and then low...well, there was just no way to explain it. But he loved storms.

So it was hard not to feel good when he and Aggie went out into the rain, even though he knew Aggie herself wasn't all that happy about it. Not like she'd been on the boat, holding onto Grady and laughing into the thundering sky. It occurred to Flash that maybe the reason Aggie wasn't laughing now was because she wasn't holding onto Grady.

They cruised through the wet shiny streets of Dogleg Island all morning to the intermittent rhythm of the rubber wipers scraping the fine blowing rain from the windshield. Occasionally a big gust of wind would make the patrol car shake sideways, and every now and then Aggie would get out with a handful of papers that showed a map of the evacuation route and some emergency numbers and warned people to boil their water for two days after the storm passed, and she would hand those papers out to people on the street or tack them up on closed doors or put them in mailboxes. They knocked on a lot of doors, and Aggie said things like, "Yes ma'am, the evacuation is voluntary, but you don't want to be crossing that bridge with sustained winds of fifty miles an hour…" and "Yes sir, I know that, but you can't judge the amount of risk a storm might do by its category. We're probably going to lose power, and if the streets flood, we won't be able to get supplies in…" And, "No ma'am, you're wrong. There is a one hundred percent chance that the storm will make landfall somewhere within a hundred miles of Murphy County, and when that happens we will definitely be affected. The best thing for you to do is pack enough for three or four days…"

Aggie kept her phone on speaker, and voices were bouncing back and forth all over the place. Sally Ann, Mo, Zeke from the volunteer fire department, someone called Kelly from the Red Cross. And Grady, sounding terse and busy: "Malone, we need your status ASAP re: requisite personnel for the coming emergency." And then Grady, sounding not so terse but just as busy, "Four car pile-up on Highway Forty-Four. Clearing the evacuation route will take approximately two hours, forty minutes." There was a pause then, "Call me."

Joe the shrimp man wasn't in his usual place, which was probably just as well. They had doors to knock on and people to talk to and important things to do. That did not mean, however, that there wasn't time to stop by Pete's Place for an early lunch. There were big sheets of plywood over all the windows, but Pete had spray-painted in orange across the front of one of them, "Open for Business Til Storm Hits. Drinks Half Price After That." Flash could smell the hamburgers before Aggie even opened the car door. There was nothing, absolutely nothing, better than the scent of hamburgers on electric storm-tossed air.

The wind parted Flash's fur and slicked his ears back as he and Aggie ran toward the door, but it didn't do anything to slow his pace. Aggie, though, with her head ducked against the wind and her jacket puffed out with it, had to grab at the handrail on the porch and used both hands to pull the door closed after they entered.

The bar didn't officially open for another hour, but there were four or five people inside already, most of them with "RESCUE" stenciled on their jackets, some of them filling coolers with wrapped sandwiches and bottled water. They greeted her with, "Hey, Chief" and "How're the roads?"

Aggie replied, "Mo called in some flooding beachfront, so we're going to start closing roads as soon as we check all the houses. Two, three hours at most."

Pete poked his head out of the swinging door to the kitchen. The whole room was awash in delectable aromas. "Hey there, Ags, Flash." He called back over his shoulder, "Honey, Aggie's here." He came out of the kitchen in his slightly stained cook's whites, wiping his hands on a towel. "Trying to get an inventory stacked up," he said, "for when we lose power. How's it looking out there?"

Aggie said in her firm police-chief voice, "This is a designated emergency shelter. No hurricane parties. No half-priced drinks."

Pete grinned and bent to scratch Flash's head. "Yes ma'am." The way he said it let everyone know he'd do exactly what he wanted to, the way he usually did. "How're you doing, Flash? Bet you could use a hamburger long about now, huh?"

Flash barked an enthusiastic affirmative and Pete straightened up, still grinning. "Smartest dog I ever met."

Aggie took out her notebook. "How are you fixed for supplies? Do you need anything?"

"We're running low on vodka."

She gave him a stern look. "How's your water tank? Have you got propane for the generator?"

"Sweetheart, we are the best-prepared small business on the Gulf Coast, thanks to you and your emergency plan. How about some lunch? We're not going to be able to run the freezer on the generator, so we're cooking up everything now. I sure hope folks are hungry."

One of the rescue workers picked up the cooler full of sandwiches and called, "Thanks, Pete!" as he headed for the door.

Pete waved him on and replied, "There's plenty more where that came from."

Aggie smiled at him. He was always the first to donate food, water, and hot coffee when there was a crisis, and he never had to be asked. "Thanks, Pete," she repeated.

He shrugged. "Like I said, we're emptying out the freezer. Besides, it's good PR." He winked at her. "Who do you think they're gonna call when it's time to throw that big anniversary party or cater that wedding, huh?"

Aggie laughed a little, and looked back at her notebook. "Okay, the Red Cross said they could deliver a dozen stacking cots, along with blankets and pillows, by noon. How's your first aid kit? Can you think of anything else?"

The kitchen door opened again and Lorraine came out, pulling off her white apron, tossing it on the bar, walking straight to Aggie without a word and grabbing her close in a fierce-armed hug. Aggie hugged her back.

Lorraine stepped away and said to Pete, "Get out of here. Girl talk."

Pete glanced at Flash. "Come on, man, let's see about that burger."

That sounded fine to Flash and he started to follow Pete out of the room when Aggie said, "No dogs in the kitchen."

Pete looked at him regretfully. "Sorry, Flash, I'm afraid she's right about that one." He pointed to a sign over the swinging door that Flash couldn't read. "Employees only. I'll bring it out to you."

Both Lorraine and Aggie smiled as Pete went through the swinging door and Flash jumped up onto a barstool to wait. But Lorraine's smile faded as she looked back at Aggie. "Are you mad at me?" Before Aggie could answer, she went on, "Sweetie, I swear I wouldn't have said a word to Ryan if he hadn't already known. But when he asked me flat-out what the doctor said, I couldn't lie. Don't hate me, but I couldn't lie."

Even if she hadn't looked so miserable, even if her eyes hadn't been so filled with pleading, Aggie would have forgiven her. She hugged her friend again and said, "I'm not mad. I don't hate you."

"I tried to call you…"

"I know. Yesterday was crazy, and then the storm…"

"I know."

They stepped apart and just stood there for a moment, their smiles filled with weariness and relief.

Lorraine said, "Ryan was pretty upset when he was over here this morning."

"I know. He wants us to see the storm out at Lucy's, of all places."

Lorraine winced. "Well, I can see how that would be out of the question. But…"

"But it's close to the hospital and he's afraid that if the island is cut off by the storm and something happens…"

"He's just trying to take care of you."

Aggie shook her head, hard. "I'm chief of police. I don't bail while the island is in a state of emergency. He knows that. Besides, you can't live your life being afraid of things that might happen but probably never will."

It was only half a second later that Aggie heard her own words, and was embarrassed by them. But Lorraine's smile was gentle and understanding as she reached into the pocket of her jeans and brought out a small bottle of pills. "You forgot your prescription," she said.

Aggie couldn't quite meet her eyes as she took the bottle from her. "Thanks," she said. "I mean, for not sending them home with Ryan."

Lorraine replied, "That I *knew* you wouldn't forgive me for."

Aggie looked at her. "I'm going to take care of this. I am. But…" she struggled for the words. "This last year or so…I never thought my life could ever be this good. I don't know if it ever will again. Maybe…I don't know, maybe you only get one second chance, and this was mine. I just want to hold on to it a little longer, you know?"

The kitchen door swung open and Pete served Flash's hamburger at the bar. Lorraine swiveled her head toward them and Aggie could see her press her lips together, but when she looked back at Aggie her smile was in place. "Sometimes," she told her firmly, "when life is that good, that much better than you ever thought it could be or that you ever deserved— then that's exactly how hard you have to fight to keep it. Got it?"

Aggie tried to smile, but couldn't quite manage it. So she just nodded.

Lorraine slipped her arm through Aggie's and gave it a squeeze. "Come on. Sit down and have something to eat. I made you a grilled cheese, and who knows when you'll get another chance?"

"Thanks," Aggie said, but just then her phone rang. She answered it, and Flash, watching her face change, ate faster. She said, "Okay" and "Right" a couple of times, then hung up the phone. By that time, Lorraine was already back from the kitchen with a grilled cheese sandwich wrapped to go. Aggie smiled gratefully as she took it. "Thanks. The traffic light on Ocean just blew down. Mo says she's got people working to get it out of the street, but I'd better get over there. Flash, let's—"

But Flash was already by her side, licking his lips and ready to go. This was an emergency, after all, and they were on the job.

Bishop spent most of the morning trying to talk himself out of the picture that was starting to come together in his head. He was just an old man housebound on a rainy day with nothing to do. He was missing the action. He was just trying to make himself feel relevant again. The kids he once had commanded were out there in the thick of the storm— metaphorically and literally—and he was feeling left out. Watching too much television. Reading too many thrillers. This was Murphy County, Florida, for God's sake, the place that time forgot. Things like this didn't happen here.

Except that they had. Except that somebody had hired a hit man to kill a dentist and his rich wife. Then, a week before the trial, that hit man ended up stuffed in the trunk of a car that was pushed into the lagoon. Then Bishop started poking his nose in where it didn't belong, putting pieces together, and he almost ended up in the Sound. Now the only suspect they'd ever had in the case, the one who had been safely locked up in county jail for almost two years, was dead.

It was over. There would be no trial. They'd never know the truth.

According to the excited newscasters who couldn't put enough weather maps on the screen or show enough stock video of palm trees bent to the ground and cars floating on flooded streets, a hurricane was coming this way. But as far as Bishop was concerned, it had already hit.

You weren't sheriff of a small county like Murphy for over twenty years without making a few friends. One of them was the jailor at the Murphy County Detention Center, now on administrative leave pending a full investigation into the death of Darrell Reichart. From him, Bishop learned about the last minute order to move the prisoners upstairs last night due to the possibility of flooding, and how, during the chaos and disruption of the routine, it was entirely possible that someone might have gotten in to see Reichart without a pass. Another one was now the clerk at the county prosecutor's office who had transcribed Aggie Malone's revised deposition, and she wasn't above a little gossip while stuck at home waiting for the hurricane. From her, Bishop learned that Aggie had practically handed Darrell Reichart's attorneys their case on a platter wrapped up in a silver bow. The prosecution had lost their star witness. Yesterday afternoon the chances of Darrell Reichart walking away from two counts of homicide had just gone up one hundred percent.

And then he had killed himself.

Briggs had left the door open to the office the day that Bishop came to see him. Deputies, clerks, civilians were in and out, passing by, sitting at desks within easy earshot, so many Bishop couldn't even begin to picture their faces. Anyone could have overheard. And who was standing nearby when Briggs and he made their plans to meet for a drink? Who would have known what time he would be on the bridge?

They'd all assumed the shots had been fired from a passing car, difficult to do under the best of circumstances. What if the shots had been fired from a stationary position, in an abandoned vehicle in the breakdown lane or by someone on foot? On that dark stretch of bridge either one would be easy to miss. What if someone knew what time he would be driving by and waited for him?

And what if that person had done it because Bishop was getting close to taking the investigation in a direction they didn't want it to go?

Those were only some of the questions that kept knocking at his brain like insistent visitors wanting to be let in. Too many questions, and most of them, now, would never be answered.

The investigation into the Reichart murders had ended with the arrest of Darrell Reichart. Now that there was no trial, no suspect, no case to be proven, the questions would never be asked. The investigation was over. The case was closed.

Because Darrell Reichart was dead, there would be no more questions.

He had two more calls left to make. He didn't want to make either one of them. Because once he did, there would be no turning back. Two pictures stared up at him from his phone, each of them a single push of a button away. The problem was, he didn't know which button to push.

Over the next three hours, Hurricane Andy gained intensity as it bore down on the Gulf Coast, spawning tornados, water spouts, and severe lightning. A utility pole went down on Second Street, leaving ten blocks of the island without cable television or landline telephone. An uprooted palm tree sailed through the window of an unoccupied home on Turpin Road, and a woman and her two miniature poodles had to be rescued from her car on flooded Sea Turtle Lane. The lagoon began to seep into people's backyards, lapping at their patios and barbecue grills. The ocean churned over the seawall. And the storm had not even made landfall yet.

The sheriff's department sent four men to help with traffic control and emergency relief. Grady was not among them.

At noon, Aggie ordered a mandatory evacuation of all beachfront residents from Gulf Boulevard to Ocean, and from Harbor Road on the north to Beachside Park on the south, an area of about three square miles. The good news was that it was still too early in the year for most of the beachfront houses to be occupied, and aside from one exceptionally stupid group of college students who Mo had to threaten to evacuate at gunpoint, most of them had had the good sense to leave the beach that morning. Nonetheless, every one of the houses would have to be checked before the storm arrived, which was still on schedule for high tide. Aggie divided the grid into three sections: Mo took beachfront, Aggie took the section from Egret to Ocean, and one of the deputies took the park to Island Road.

The lights were on at 1312 Egret. Flash swallowed back the sound he wanted to make in the back of his throat as they pulled up in front of the house. He recognized the cat.

Aggie said, "Flash, I'll just be a minute. No need—"

But he bounded out after her into the rain. No way was he missing this.

The door opened just as Aggie lifted her fist to pound on it. She found herself face to face with

Bernice Peters, who looked at least ten years older than when Aggie had last seen her. Partial shelter was offered by the upper deck, but rain still streamed around her and popped on the hood of Aggie's raincoat. The ocean was like the sound of constant thunder, and she had to raise her voice to be heard. "Mrs. Peters," she said, "I'm sorry, but you're going to have to leave. This area isn't safe."

The older woman just looked at her, weary and sallow faced. She said, "Josh bonded out of jail yesterday."

Aggie squinted a little against the rain that dripped into her lashes. "I want you to know how sorry I am about everything that happened with Josh. I know how it must have upset you."

She said, "His parents wanted me to put up my house to make bond for him." She sniffed. "I told them to put up their own house. I'm ashamed I ever knew that boy. He was dealing drugs out of my house. He was using my car tag to run contraband across the bridge. And now you think I should go wait out the storm with them in that fancy condo they rented on the other side of the bridge? I'm just fine where I am, thank you very much." The brief defiance that had lit her eyes faded then, and left her looking tired and sad. "You try to do the right thing. You try to live a good life. But in the end, it all comes down to who you trust. You remember that, and maybe when you're my age you won't be standing here all alone in a storm wondering where you went wrong."

Aggie said, "Mrs. Peters…"

She peered at Aggie sharply through the curtain of rain. "Is it true what I heard on the TV, about that boy Darrell killing himself in jail?"

Aggie said, "Yes ma'am, I'm afraid it is."

Bernice Peters gave a single nod. "Well, evil be to him who evil does. And yes, I know I butchered that quote."

Flash slipped past Aggie a few inches into the doorway, sniffing for the cat. He found it peering from behind the sofa, fur bristled. He backed off.

Aggie said, "Mrs. Peters, I understand if you don't want to leave the island. But if you stay here other people will have to put their own lives in danger trying to keep you safe. We've set up a temporary shelter at Pete's Place Bar and Grill. They'll have water and electricity for the duration. Please let me take you there."

She nodded slowly. "I want you to know I don't blame you for any of this. I think you're a good girl just trying to do her job. And that's why you should know that poor boy didn't hang himself in jail."

Aggie stared at her. "What? What are you talking about?"

Bernice Peters looked at her with eyes that were tired and patient, standing firm while the wind parted her hair this way and that and raindrops slashed at her slippered feet. "I know most people think my grandson walked all over me, that I was too old to watch out for him the way I should when he was here…given the way things turned

out, maybe they're right. But I always kept an eye
on his friends. Most of them coming back, summer
after summer, like the Reichart boy, who'd been
hanging out with Josh since he was fourteen. They
used to go canoeing and fishing in the lagoon, and
the other boys used to joke about never letting
Darrell tie off the boat because he couldn't tie a
knot. I noticed he wore Velcro tabs on his sneakers because he couldn't tie his laces. Josh said it
was some kind of disorder, like dyslexia, but I don't
know. I think a lot of times doctors just make up
names for what they don't understand. I do know
that in all the time I knew him he never once wore
shoes with laces. And you can't make a noose without tying a knot."

Aggie just stared at her in the rain.

The cat crept forward from behind the couch,
making its way toward the door. Flash took a step
back and sat down, watching it. Bernice Peters bent
down and scooped up her cat. "I'm not leaving without Oscar."

Aggie said, "Umm, yes ma'am, I understand.
If you'll get him packed up, I'm sure we can make
arrangements. Do you want me to take you to the
shelter?"

Bernice made an impatient gesture with her
head. "Go on, you've got better things to do. I know
my way."

Aggie's phone rang. She looked distractedly
from the phone to the woman at the door. "Please,
Mrs. Peters, the tide is rising and..."

"Child, do you think I'm an idiot? My suitcase is already in the car. Go on. You've got other people to pester besides me. Do your job."

Aggie cast her a grateful look as she started down the stairs. "Flash, let's go."

Flash, confident the cat was safe, trotted after her back into the rain as Aggie pushed the button on her phone and said, "Malone."

The answer sounded as though it was coming through a tunnel, which in fact it was. "This is Captain Grady of the Murphy County Sheriff's Department with a private message for Chief Malone."

Aggie's heartbeat speeded, and she was sure the exhalation of her breath included with it the release of the entire morning's tension. Grady. It was Grady. "Go ahead."

"The evacuation route is clear. I will be relieving B-Shift Deputy Wallace on emergency island assignment in approximately forty-five minutes. Do you need anything from the mainland? Candles, wine, chocolate-covered cherries?"

Aggie caught the rail midway down the steps and closed her eyes in brief, intense gratitude. A gust of wind almost knocked her backwards and Flash pressed against her leg, steadying her. Static crackled on the phone. "Just you," she said. And, because she was afraid he might not have heard she repeated, louder, "Just you."

In the background, Aggie could hear a steady loud drumming, and she realized it was the sound of rain on the roof of Grady's car. He spoke loudly to be heard above it. "The accident screwed up the assignments. But the plan is on schedule. We shelter in place. And our place is together."

Aggie stood still in the wind and the rain and she smiled like a schoolgirl into the phone. "I love you, Ryan Grady."

"What?"

Holding the hood of her jacket tightly closed over the phone against her ear, Aggie started toward the car. "Grady, listen, I'm here with Bernice Peters and she just told me something about Darrell Reichart…" Static crackled.

"What? Baby, you're fading. What did you say?"

Aggie raised her voice. "He couldn't tie a knot! That's what she said. You need to check into it—medical records, school records—" More static.

"—Only caught about half of that. Say again."

A gust of wind yanked the hood off of Aggie's head and rain soaked her hair. "I'll tell you when I see you!" she shouted back. "Hurry home!"

"What?"

"I said hurry—"

But the line was dead, and he was gone.

Bishop spent three hours changing the channels, watching the lights flicker, listening to the wind roar, limping around the house, debating himself. *Old man. Trying to be relevant. None of your business. Out of touch.*

And trying to push out of his head the scene he'd never forget, the EMTs forcing an airway down Aggie's throat when he arrived, her body convulsing, the blood pooling on the floor. The girl, the *child,* who'd almost lost her life on his watch. He had sent her into harm's way. Was he supposed to just to ignore that?

In a twenty-year career, a man made a lot of decisions. Some good, some bad, some on the cusp. Some he would regret. Some he'd thank God for. But maybe the thing about getting old was that you got to look back, to see the big picture, to choose which decisions you'd make differently. And maybe to know that if you'd chosen differently, a twenty-eight-year old girl wouldn't be lying on the floor in a pool of blood with a tube being shoved down her throat.

A big limb from one of the live oaks crashed across his driveway with a crack and a thud. He supposed it was a blessing his car was already sitting in the junkyard. He checked the backup generator and his refrigerator. Milk, cereal, some steaks in the freezer. Bottled water in the pantry. It wasn't as though this was his first hurricane.

He dug out the cardboard box again and sat at the dining table where he could still see the television, spreading out his notes on the case. The transcript of the radio chatter from that night. Aggie and Grady flirting with each other, Bishop letting them; it hadn't shown the department in a particularly good light when it all went into the record, but this was a small county on the far end of civilization where protocol often played second fiddle to people. That was just the way it was. Aggie going in, describing the situation. Chatter about the puppy in a cage. Grady talking about carpets and expensive sofas. Aggie replying that the television was still there, that Roy could stop looking for it. Grady saying he was coming around. Then nothing. Bishop calling for Aggie to report. Nothing. Then from Grady, *Shots fired.*

Frowning, he went back over the transcript again. What was it about it that was bothering him? What was it that was off? He remembered every minute of that night. He had been over it, Grady had been over it, Briggs and Richardson and everyone in the prosecutor's office had been over it again and again. It was impossible that they had missed anything.

And yet, he was almost certain they had.

At one thirty he saw a news scroll inch across the bottom of the muted television set: *Emergency Alert… Emergency Alert…From the Murphy County Sheriff's Department…The east-bound lane of the Cedric B. Grady Memorial Bridge will be closed at 2:00 p.m.…Mandatory Evacuation of low lying areas of Dogleg Island is in place… Emergency Alert…Emergency Alert…*

Bishop stared at the screen. He stared down at the papers in front of him. And he picked up his phone.

Aggie was responding to a report of a live wire down on Lighthouse Lane when Bishop called. By regulation, all electrical wires were buried on the island, but special permits were granted for above-ground electrical during the construction phase. The fire department was on its way but had encountered debris in the road on Island Road, delaying their progress, and then they got another call on the lagoon side. Aggie told the fire chief she would check out the Lighthouse Lane situation and report back, then she put Bishop's call on speaker.

"Bishop, are you okay?"

"Aggie, is Grady with you?"

Flash swiveled his ears toward the speaker when he heard Bishop's voice, and Aggie leaned forward over the steering wheel, as though doing so would make the voice clearer. The phone crackled and whined with static.

"No," she said, raising her voice to be heard across the uncertain connection. "He's on his way. What's wrong? Kind of in the middle of something over here."

With the typical unpredictability of a storm such as this, the rain had lightened to little more than gusting sea spray, and Aggie kept her windshield wipers on low as she carefully navigated the flooded streets. But the sky was greenish purple, and the wind was a steady, screeching roar outside her window. She gripped the steering wheel and strained to hear what Bishop was saying.

"Aggie, listen to me. The morning you were shot, you said you saw someone else in the house. Someone reflected in the window."

"What?" She said that not because she couldn't hear him, but because she couldn't believe what she was hearing. "How do you know that? Why—"

"This is important. You saw someone. Do you remember anything else? Maybe an odor, a smell like lemons or oranges?"

She stared at the radio speaker for just a moment too long. A gust of wind slammed the car sideways and she fought the wheel to keep it under control. Flash struggled for balance on the passenger seat. "Oranges," she repeated, a little breathlessly. And more loudly, "Did you say oranges?"

Static hummed and whistled. "Aggie, you're breaking up…try to call you back."

Aggie practically shouted, "Bishop, what are you talking about? Why—"

"It's in the transcript. Where was he?"

"Bishop, I can't hear you! What—"

"—only four people in the house that night! The transcript—two—the radio! If Reichart wasn't the shooter, then—"

Aggie waited, hands gripping the steering wheel, windshield wipers squeaking, wind roaring. There was nothing. The line was dead.

She pushed the call-back button repeatedly and got nothing. She tried to dial the office. Again, nothing. "Damn," she muttered.

Aggie radioed the office and learned that cell service was out all over the island, as was electricity. Sally Ann had two county deputies and Mo helping her prepare to move police headquarters—including important documents and electronics that had not already been removed—to higher ground. By this time Aggie had already reached the scene of the downed electrical wire, which clearly was no longer a problem now that the island had lost electrical power. She told Sally Ann she was on her way back in and signed off.

That was when she turned the corner and realized where she was. She couldn't prevent a chill that ran up her arms and her legs and actually caused her hands to shake on the wheel of the car. 210 Harbor Lane. The home of Walter, Leah, and Darrell Reichart.

Harbor Lane was starting to look like more of a fast-running stream than a street as currents of water whooshed past her wheels. It wouldn't be safe to stay here much longer. The smart thing to do would be to make a quick left onto Pine, to head back inland, and that was what Aggie intended to do, except that just then her headlights flashed through the murkiness and picked up a county patrol car parked in front of 210 Harbor Lane.

She slowed her own car to a stop and just sat there, staring at it.

It was spooky, almost like déjà vu. The dark skies cast a predawn gloom over the scene, and the swirling rain and mist simulated fog. Aggie had to blink to assure herself she was not hallucinating. It was almost as though she had traveled back in time, come around the corner, and discovered her own patrol car parked in front of the house at 210

Harbor Lane. As though she were a silent witness to the woman she once had been, the woman who was about to get out of that car and walk up to the door, the woman who had no idea that once she did her life would never be the same.

Aggie pulled into the drive behind the patrol car and just sat there, hands on the wheel, watching the car almost as if she expected her younger self to get out, to slam the door, to walk to the garage and shine her light inside. The girl with a firm, athletic figure and raven black hair. The girl who thought she could conquer anything but refused to admit a secret crush on a certain deputy. The girl with so much spunk and sass and hope and courage who was about to get out of that car and walk inside that house and take a bullet in the head.

Would Aggie have stopped her if she could?

Flash shifted in his seat and made a low sound in his throat, as though reminding Aggie that they were still on duty. Aggie drew in a sharp breath and pressed her palms against her eyes, which she was surprised to find were wet with tears. "Right," she said. "Let's check this out."

She got out of the car and started up the walk toward the house. But this time she wasn't alone. This time Flash walked beside her.

The wind made an almost musical howling sound around the house, but the buffer of the structure between herself and the beach seemed to wrap them in a vacuum, protected from wind and rain and the thunder of the ocean, enveloping them in damp mist and the echo of their own footsteps. Flash trotted close beside her, his coat shiny and wet but his ears alert. She saw what she thought was the flash of a flashlight beam inside the house, but it might have simply been lightning. She cupped her hands and called, "Hello! Hello, inside!"

She didn't expect an answer, and she didn't get one. She went onto the porch and put her hand on the doorknob. It was open.

That boy didn't hang himself in jail.

Aggie pushed opened the door. In the greenish purple light, the shadow of the enormous chandelier lay like the broken bones of a skeleton on the floor. A flash of lightning brought the parrot painting briefly to life with raptor beaks and pterodactyl wings. Flash pressed close to her leg.

Did you smell oranges?

Aggie could feel her heart beating. Her rain jacket clung to her limbs like a clammy veil. She swallowed hard. She called out, "Hello! Chief Malone of the Island Police!"

The house smelled old and musty and cold. It did not smell like oranges. It smelled like blood.

She called again. "Hello! Who's here?"

Maybe it was Grady. It had to be. Two deputies were helping at the office, the other two were assigned to the bridge. Who else would be here?

She moved out of the foyer and into the main room. *Don't go there, don't go there.* Don't stand on the floor where your own blood still stains the tile, don't look at the carpet with its chalk marks and dark, dark smudges. Don't look at the reflection in the window.

A gust of wind rattled the windows. Lightning flashed again briefly and brilliantly, and in that flash she thought she saw something…She was sure she did.

Did you smell oranges?

The puppy in the crate, barking. Turning her head toward the window. The reflection in the glass. Black boots. Khaki pants. A knife in one hand. A gun, slowly turning to point at her, in the other. And as she raised her eyes, all too slowly, as he turned to look at her, even more slowly, she almost could see his face. And wasn't that what she had been trying to forget all this time? The memory of his face?

There were no oranges now. The puppy had grown to be a full dog, and he pressed his hot wet body against her knee. But clearly reflected in the window glass against the background of an exploding, crashing sea, she could see black boots, khaki pants. And a gun.

Aggie, there were only four people in that house…

He turned, started to round the corner.

She whispered, "Grady?"

CHAPTER SIXTEEN

Sometimes understanding comes slowly, in small bits of truth and torn scraps of information whose jagged edges seem to bear no relationship to one another. Sometimes the mind, working so hard to unravel the problem, to put those jagged pieces together into some kind of coherent whole, obscures the very picture it wants so badly to see. And other times, often when it's least expected, the picture comes together in a single flash of insight, a sudden understanding, a moment of truth that changes everything.

That was the way it was for Flash as they stood there in the living room of the house where once blood had splattered and thunder had roared, where he had tried to chew through the bars of a cage to escape the smell of death and violence. As the man who had shot Aggie came around the corner of the room with another gun in his hand, everything that had puzzled Flash, everything he had been worrying over and trying to figure out, suddenly made simple, brilliant sense.

Just because it was done did not mean it was over. Dead was not the end as long as the truth was still missing. This was why Aggie and Grady and Bishop talked about it so much. This was why they could not let what had happened in the past be buried in the past, even though they sometimes tried to pretend it was.

The squirrel in the yard.

The man in the lagoon.

Sometimes you had to go to the dark place and face the thing that terrified you the most for the sake of someone you loved. It was all becoming clear to Flash now.

Because a bad guy was a bad guy whether he sat behind a desk and made jovial conversation, or whether he walked around a corner holding a gun. Because someone had to keep the bad guys off the streets, so that he and Aggie could be safe.

Because if they didn't, it could happen again.

Grady stopped his car in front of the barrier that blocked the emergency lane and got out, ducking his head against the rain that pounded on the plastic cover of his hat as he splashed across the road to the first of the three cruisers that blocked all lanes of the Cecile B. Grady Memorial Bridge. The officer inside the car got out when he saw Grady coming, and Grady shouted to him, "I need to get across! Help me move the barrier."

"You can't!" the officer shouted back. "We've got water over the causeway a mile in!"

Rain pounded, whipped and slashed sideways. Grady held onto his hat with both hands to keep it from blowing off. "How much?" he called loudly, even though the deputy and he were now almost face to face.

"Impassable in that vehicle! Truck, maybe, but we're not authorized to let anything other than fire and ambulance across."

Grady's lips tightened in raw frustration as he looked from his car, useless now, to the dark, white-cap-whipped Sound beyond the bridge. At its peak, the bridge was thirty feet above the water, but at its lowest span was barely six. If the Causeway was going to flood, it would be at that five-hundred-foot-long low point at the base of the peak a mile from the mainland, and any vehicle with a low clearance would be swamped within minutes. "Damn it," he said. Then, raising his voice to be heard, "What's the situation on the island?"

"They just radioed the cell tower is down and so is the power. All communications are on the emergency band. Sheriff Briggs is over there now."

"What?" He thought he hadn't heard correctly. While Bishop had been the kind of sheriff who'd liked getting into the thick of things now and then, Briggs was definitely more of the administrative type. It would take more than an ordinary hurricane to make Briggs leave his post. "Why? Did they call for assistance?" They had already sent support personnel to the island, and Briggs knew that Grady was on his way. What could have gone wrong?

"Sir, I only know what I've been told. The sheriff called in half an hour ago and said he was rendering assistance on the island and put Simmons in temporary command on this side."

Grady drew breath for more questions, then changed his mind and waved the officer back to his car. Grady turned and ran, head down against the wind, to his own vehicle. He switched his car radio to the emergency band and picked up the mike. "This is Captain Grady calling Island Police. Come in, please."

He got nothing but static.

"Grady's not coming," Briggs said, stepping around the corner and in front of Aggie. He spoke in a disconcertingly conversational tone that was hard to reconcile with the pistol he held pointed at her. "Sorry about that. I'm sorry about everything, really, and I hope you know I mean that. I never meant for it to go down this way, but it is what it is. And at least none of us have to sit through a long trial."

Roy Briggs, overweight, balding, bad knee. A big harmless teddy bear of a man, but a lot smarter than most people gave him credit for. At least that was what Grady always said. He wore leather duty chukkas to support his bad ankle, and back in the day when he rode patrol he'd sometimes have to wrap his knee in a liniment ointment that smelled so strongly of citrus that you could tell where he'd been five minutes after he'd left. He always made her think of orange candy. She'd forgotten that. She'd forgotten a lot of things.

Aggie just looked at him, feeling sad and still and tired. And, oddly, unsurprised. "Oh, Roy," she said.

He said, "You don't carry a gun anymore, do you, Aggie? Police chief of a little place like this, there's really no need. But unzip your jacket so I can make sure."

She unzipped her jacket and pulled it back to show him her waist and shoulders. He nodded and she pulled it back on. He gave a small smile of approval. "I didn't think so. You never were much of one for deadly force, were you? The guys used to tease you about that at the firing range. You'd never take the kill shot. Always aimed for the shoulder or the leg, just like they taught you at the academy." His tone grew regretful. "I miss those days sometimes, I really do."

She said, "What are you doing here? Did you leave something behind the last time?"

"The only thing I left behind Josh Peters found on the beach. But you already know about that. It was just luck, really. I heard you give your position on the radio and knew you wouldn't be able to drive by the house if you saw my car here. You'd have to check it out. And here you are."

She said quietly, "I wouldn't have guessed you. I never would have thought it was you."

His expression, in the greenish gloom, was deeply regretful. "I wish that were true. For a while I thought it might be. I mean, you remembered everything else except me. I thought I might even have been wrong, and you hadn't seen me after all. Then I thought maybe we'd get lucky, and maybe you'd never remember."

"Is that why you pushed me to take this job? Because you were afraid if I saw you every day, I'd start to remember?"

"Partly," he admitted. "But mostly because it made me so sad to see you. I hated what happened, I really did. And I hate what I have to do now."

Grady tried another frequency, and another. Beads of sweat mingled with the rainwater on his face and the windows of his car started to steam up. The rain roared on his roof and then went silent. In a way the silences were worse than the thunder of rain. He switched back to the emergency band. "This is Captain Grady of the Murphy County Sheriff's Department calling the Island Police. Come in."

This time he got Mo, and he let his muscles sag in relief. "Mo, what's the situation over there?"

Her voice came back through the crackle of static. "We just got headquarters set up in the emergency shelter. Supplies are holding out. Near as we can tell, about half the residents evacuated before noon. We're getting ready to close the bridge at Island Road. All we can do now is wait it out. What's your position?"

"On the other side of the bridge." Grady wiped his face with his sleeve, which only made it wetter.

"The causeway's flooded at the low point. Can you put the chief on?"

There was a pause and he thought he'd lost her. "She should be on her way in. Do you want me to try to raise her?"

"No, I'll do it." He started to sign off and then said, "What about Sheriff Briggs? Is he with you?"

This time the pause was even longer. "Is he supposed to be?"

"Didn't he check in with you?"

"No, sir, Captain. Far as I knew he was on the other side of the bridge."

Grady hesitated, frowning. "Thanks, Mo. Let me know if either one of them call in. Grady out."

He tried Aggie on her car radio. Nothing. His muscles started to tighten again. On impulse, he tried Briggs. Still nothing. Odd, but there was a storm. Anything could happen. In growing frustration, he peered through his wet windshield at the sheriff's department vehicles blocking the bridge. Two cruisers and a large-wheeled SUV, the kind they used in backcountry emergencies and for beach rescue. He wondered if...

That was when his phone rang.

He checked the caller ID and answered, "Bishop, what's wrong?"

"Are you alone?"

Grady frowned. "I'm in my car. What—"

"Listen to me." Bishop sounded tense and upset. "I think Aggie might be in danger. That thing we were talking about the other day...there's something I didn't tell you."

Briggs said, "I've been over and over that night in my mind. What if I'd done it differently? What if I'd shot Darrell and claimed a justifiable homicide? I would have been a hero, saving a fellow officer's life. But there was the knife. How would I explain picking up the knife? You'd already seen me with it. There was no point in wiping it down, too late to try to throw it out. They were never going to find Reichart's fingerprints on it. He never touched it. A long inquiry, a lot of questions…maybe they never would have been able to connect me with the murders, but a thing like that could ruin a man's career. And I couldn't afford to have my career ruined. You didn't know it, but I could see you from where I stood. I saw you turn your head, I saw your face change when you recognized me. I had to make a split second decision, and I did the only thing I could think to do."

Three police officers had answered the call. But after they approached the house, only two of them were in radio contact. That was what Bishop had meant about the radio.

Where was he?

"Of course," she said, understanding. Out of the corner of her eye, she saw a glimmer of movement reflected in the window, but she kept her gaze focused on Briggs. "You were in the house all the time, not checking the beach. That's why you didn't answer any of our radio transmissions."

"I had to check the scene," he said, "and a good thing I did. The fool had to get out so fast he left the knife behind. I found it and was about to take it down and throw it in the ocean when that kid Darrell came in. And then you."

"Something went wrong with the timing," Aggie said, thinking it through slowly. "I wasn't supposed to take the call."

"Nobody was supposed to take the call," Briggs elucidated patiently. "It was change of shift, by the time we got there it should have been all over. But that crazy-ass Grady, he was a bull after a heifer in heat and nobody could tell him anything. He used to arrange all our shifts so that he could see you, even if it was just for a few minutes. Hell, I didn't mind, all about young love and all that, but that night...well, it got complicated."

Aggie stared at the gun in his hand. "You switched the guns. Darrell had a thirty-eight. That's what I was trying to remember."

He nodded. "While Grady was blubbering over you, I came in to check on the suspect. I switched Darrell's gun for mine. Not my service pistol, but a backup like this one."

Aggie said, "So it was a murder for hire, after all. You hired Lincoln to kill the Reicharts, and when he got greedy, you killed him. But why? What did they do to you that you wanted them dead?"

He gave a dismissive shake of his head. "You don't get it. Not everything is black and white. This was business, that's all. It was Walter Reichart who came to me, wanting his wife dead. His business was in trouble and he stood to inherit millions. It wasn't a big deal; I had a few operatives on the string and knew how to make it happen, anonymously, of course. We always met at night, maybe he could've given a general description of me if he'd had to—but why would he?—but I wasn't worried about it. And then he recognized me a few days later in uniform when I came to investigate the false alarm. He wasn't even supposed to be in town, and I thought it would be a good excuse to have a look around, get the lay of the land for myself. That's when it all started to unravel. He thought it was a setup, tried to cancel the whole job, then when he left that message for Bishop at the office, I knew he was getting ready to bolt. He'd already paid me fifty thousand cash, and I'm sorry to say that was more than his life was worth. So the plan had to be accelerated, and both of them had to die. It was a close call, but I might have held it together if it hadn't been for the kid Darrell. And you."

He said, his face filled with sorrow, "Oh, Aggie, you should have died. It all would have been so much easier if you had just died."

Bishop said, "That investigation we had into the corrupt cop, back in the nineties. I told you we never turned up anything, and we didn't. But I never told you who I suspected."

Grady watched a piece of sailcloth fly by overhead, twisting in the wind. In the background his radio crackled on low, terse voices back and forth handling the multiple details of a county in crisis as best they could. Grady listened for the only voice he wanted to hear, but it didn't come. "Bishop, listen, this is not—"

"Briggs," Bishop said.

Grady stopped talking.

Bishop went on, "Not long after the investigation closed, I discovered Briggs carrying a backup weapon. Maybe you can get away with that in New Orleans or Atlanta, but a small county like this—something was off. It didn't make sense. I should have fired him, but I didn't. He'd been with me longer than anybody on the force, and otherwise he'd been a solid deputy...so I gave him a warning, kept it out of his record. Let it slide."

Grady said, "I don't understand what—"

"His backup was a nine-millimeter Luger," Bishop said tightly. "The same kind they found on Darrell Reichart the night Aggie was shot. The bullet they took out of Arthur Lincoln was a nine. So were the bullets they dug out of my tire rims. You know that once a man develops a preference for a weapon, especially an emergency one, he almost always sticks with it. Replaces it with the same kind if he loses it. "

Grady's hand tightened on the phone and he pressed it so hard to his ear that his head hurt. "There's no way to determine whether those bullets—any of them—came from the same gun. The nine is a popular cartridge, maybe the most popular on the market."

Bishop said, "Do you remember when Aggie gave us her original statement? She was so clear about every detail. She said Darrell had a thirty-eight special in his hand. I have it in my notes right here. And then you said something like, 'Are you sure it wasn't a Luger?' And she said she really didn't know, and from then on she just referred to it as a pistol. But she was staring at that gun for fifteen, twenty seconds. She got every other detail right."

Something about the gun...

Grady could hear the hiss of his own hard slow breath. "What are you saying?"

"The radio," Bishop said. His voice was tight with impatience. "That night after you three split up, you and Aggie never lost radio contact with me, but Briggs was off the radio until after the shooting. He said he was out of range on the beach, but what if he never went to the beach at all, but straight to the house through the east set of steps? He would have had to turn off his radio."

"Bishop, this is crazy." But Grady listened. He listened.

"When I started digging into the Lincoln case," Bishop went on rapidly, "I told him I suspected a link with the Reicharts. That very night somebody took a shot at me on the bridge—while I was on my way to meet him. Maybe I was getting too close. That knife Aggie found, the murder weapon. It went from her hands to yours, right? Did you turn it over to the technician yourself?"

Grady stared at the sheet of rain glistening off his window. Now he could feel his heartbeat, shaking his chest. "You were there. You saw me sign it over to Briggs."

"But before it made it downstairs, it had been wiped."

"We don't know that. It could have happened before Aggie ever took custody."

"You know it didn't. If the killer was going to wipe the knife at the time of the murder, he would have wiped off the blood too. If Josh had done it, he would have no reason to confess he'd ever been at the scene."

Grady watched his breath condense on the windshield, forming rivulets that dripped like raindrops mirrored on the inside.

"Then Aggie goes to see Darrell in jail, confirms his testimony, and six hours later the boy is found hanging in his cell. Guess who found him?"

Grady was silent.

"Right," Bishop said, "it was Briggs."

Lightning flashed across the big wall of windows. Surf exploded in white foam tornadoes above their heads. Aggie said, "You were a good cop, Roy. You're a good sheriff. I don't understand."

The smile the other man returned was tight and bitter. "Damn right I was good. A good cop making less than thirty thousand a year busting kids half my age who were earning that in a night. Watching them get back out on the streets in two years and start it all over again. But it wasn't about the money. It was about being smarter than them. Better than them. Beating them at their own game. I know everybody else looked at me and just saw a fat cop with bad knees past his prime. But out on the street they called me Boss. That's why I hate what happened. I never wanted to get you involved, or Grady. I liked you both. And as long as the evidence was stacked against the kid Darrell, as long as the prosecution was asking all the wrong questions, we still might've gotten away with it. But once you started remembering, once you gave them the testimony they needed for reasonable doubt…well, we couldn't have a trial, that's for sure. And I couldn't take a chance on just how much longer it would take you to remember everything."

Another thunder of surf crashed against the shore. The windows rattled.

Aggie said, "We can't stay here. The storm surge will swallow this house before the hour is over."

He nodded thoughtfully. "That would solve a lot of problems, wouldn't it? But I'm not the kind of man who goes down with his ship. I'm the kind of man who lives to fight another day. So this is what is going to happen. You and I are going to start across the bridge. Everyone knows your situation, you needed emergency medical assistance. It was lucky I was here. But midway across, you have one of your famed panic attacks. You fight me, escape the car. I tried my best to stop you, but you flung yourself over the bridge and were lost. There will be a full-honors funeral. Grady will be devastated, but he'll survive.

I think we all knew that eventually it would end this way. After the shooting, you were broken. There was no coming back from that. But life will go on for everyone else. It always does."

Aggie breathed in, she breathed out. For some reason the words echoed in her head: *You don't get it, do you? You're not just living for yourself anymore.* Her hand slipped into the pocket of her jacket.

He said abruptly, "Where's that dog of yours?"

Aggie didn't blink. "In the car."

Briggs lifted the gun sharply, steadying it on her chest. "No, he's not. I saw him come in with you."

Out of the corner of her eye, she could see Flash reflected in the window, head low in the classic border collie crouch, coming behind Briggs. She said, "If you shoot me, there'll be an autopsy."

He said, "True. The last thing I want to do, believe me, is to shoot you. But I didn't want to shoot you the first time. I'll do what I have to."

Flash knew what he had to do. Because somebody had to keep the bad guys off the street. He saw his moment. He crouched low, tightening his muscles, and sprang at Briggs with all his might, teeth bared.

And that was when Briggs swung around and shot him in the head.

CHAPTER SEVENTEEN

Sometimes everything really does happen at once. Flash crashed into Briggs and his teeth sank into flesh just as something screeched past his ear and he fell to the floor, shaking his head with blood spraying everywhere, which was just as Aggie tore her gun from her jacket pocket, took her firing stance, and pulled the trigger all without taking a breath. Briggs stumbled backwards with a bright red stain growing on his shirt, looking stunned and disbelieving, and Flash started to lunge at him again, but all he could do was stagger around in circles, shaking his head. Briggs fell into a lamp and it made a splintering sound as it crashed on the floor, Briggs collapsing in a heap atop it. The ocean thundered and lightning flashed, and Flash did not see anything else.

Aggie stumbled across the room to Flash, slipping on blood spatter, dropping to the floor beside him. He was on his side, his chest pumping shallowly, his head dark with sticky wetness, his eyes open, barely slits. "It's okay." She stripped off her jacket and tucked it around him. She couldn't even hear the sound of the storm for the roar of her own breathing. "We're going to get you help. Hold on, Flash, stay with me. Stay with me…"

He was limp and heavy in her arms as she struggled to her feet and, shielding him with her body as best she could, she ran out into the storm. She never once looked back at Briggs.

Flash heard the car door slam and they were out of the rain, but the storm still sang wildly in his head and blue and red lightning swirled before his eyes. He was on the floor of the car, wrapped in Aggie's jacket, which was not where he belonged, not at all. He tried to push himself to his feet and was surprised when his knees went out from under him. He tried again.

He heard Aggie, gasping for breath with little sounds that resembled sobs, start the engine and shout into the radio, "This is Chief Malone of the Island Police requesting emergency assistance at—"

A torrent of rain and wind broke through the car as the door flew open and the microphone was snatched, wires and all, from the dashboard. Aggie roared out a furious scream and twisted to fight the intruder while rain and wind slashed through the car. Flash saw Briggs's face, shiny and white and torn with fury and pain, and the pinkish water that dripped from his fingers as he grabbed for Aggie's throat, and he ground out through hard, closed teeth, "You should have taken the kill shot, Aggie."

Flash surged to his feet with a roar of his own, digging into the car seat with his front claws, jaws open and teeth bared. The quick flash of terror on Briggs's eyes was all it took for Aggie to twist away, to slam the car into gear and turn the wheel hard. Briggs yelled at her, "You'll never make it, Aggie! You'll never make it across the bridge!"

Aggie gunned the accelerator and the swinging car door struck Briggs across the torso before slamming shut. The tires caught traction and she swung the car onto the gleaming asphalt. Flash sank down onto the passenger seat, panting, resting his head between his paws with lights and sound and electric thunder whirring all around, beside Aggie, where he belonged.

Grady said dully, "On the phone this afternoon, Aggie said Bernice Peters told her Darrel had some kind of disability. Couldn't tie a knot. That's what she meant. You can't hang yourself if you can't tie a knot."

"In the past week, we've lost the murder weapon and two key suspects—Lincoln and Reichart. Josh Peters has lost all credibility. The only person left is the eyewitness. And she just changed her testimony. She was safe as long as she couldn't remember. But now…"

Grady's voice was hoarse. "He's on the island with her. And the bridge is closed."

"What's that? Say again."

And that was when Grady heard on the radio the voice he had been listening for. He turned up the volume. "—Island Police requesting emergency assistance at—" And then nothing.

Except it wasn't entirely nothing. What followed next sounded like a scream.

Five minutes from Harbor Lane to the bridge. She'd driven it a thousand times. Ten thousand. All those nights of beach patrol with Ray Charles on the CD, hamburgers at midnight, watching the deep blue surf curl and crash on the shore at Beachside Park. Cruising the silent streets, lights going out, peace coming in as sure and powerful as the tide. Chatting with the dispatcher on the radio as the stars blinked on, hundreds upon thousands of them in dazzling three-dimension. Watching the dawn creep slowly in and fill her with a secret happy anticipation because it meant Grady would be there soon with his stupid flirtations and silly passes. Turning the cruiser toward Island Road and the bridge home. Five minutes.

Five minutes with dry roads and clear visibility. Five minutes with lights and sirens. With rain and wind lashing at the windshield and water over the tires and someone you loved bleeding on the seat beside you, it took a lifetime. Flash's lifetime.

Aggie's lifetime.

A lifetime of dog parades and beach volleyball and watching Flash chase sticks into the surf; of fireworks on the Fourth of July and sunsets on the beach and salt spray on her face. Waving at neighbors from her patrol car while Flash sat proudly in the seat beside her, watching the tourists trek down to the beach with their lawn chairs and lobster-colored shoulders, waking up to the smell of coffee and the sounds of Grady in the kitchen. *Her lifetime.* Hers and Flash's and Grady's. And someone had tried to take it from her.

Her tires lost traction and the car skidded and swayed as she made the turn onto Island Road. Wind pelted the windshield with a blinding curtain of rain, and then stopped. Her wipers scraped dry glass. Up ahead she could see the two sheriff's department's cars that had been assigned to guard the bridge, their blue lights pulsing. One of the deputies, in a bright yellow rain poncho, got out and stepped forward, waving his arms at her.

You'll never make it across the bridge.

She stretched her hand across the seat and rested it on Flash's wet fur. He was panting fast and hard and occasionally fine shivers trembled through his muscles, but when she touched him he turned to look at her, his eyes filled with expectation and faith. She tightened her fingers in his fur.

"Yes, I will," she whispered.

She flipped on her lights and siren and gripped the steering wheel with both hands. "*Yes I will!*"

She pressed down on the accelerator and the deputy stepped quickly out of the way as she swung her car between the two cruisers and onto the bridge.

Grady wrenched open the door of the SUV that was parked across the bridge and demanded of the startled deputy inside, "Get out!"

When the young man hesitated a second too long, Grady grabbed his arm and yanked him out of the vehicle and onto the pavement. "Sir, you can't—"

Grady shouted against the wind, "Watch me!"

Grady slammed the vehicle in gear and swung around the barrier, taking up the radio mike at the same time. "Island Police, this is Captain Grady of the Murphy County Sheriff's Department. Come in, please, Island Police—

A crackle of static, then, breaking through on the emergency channel, a whoosh of breath. "You can't save her this time, Grady. She shot a police officer and she's going down. This is Sheriff Briggs requiring emergency medical assistance at 210 Harbor Lane, Dogleg Island." Another whoosh of breath. "I've been shot. The assailant has fled the scene in an island police cruiser, identified as Chief Agatha Malone...all available units respond..."

Grady looked at his cell phone, useless in his hand, and slammed it against the wheel as he accelerated across the bridge. He saw blue lights in his rearview mirror. He thought about what Aggie would do, the smartest woman he had ever known. He thought about Bishop. He picked up the microphone.

"All units, this is Captain Ryan Grady, assuming command as per regulation six-twenty-three-point-one-eight." He hoped he got the numbers right. Aggie would know. "The sheriff is down. Repeat, this is Captain Grady assuming temporary command. All units, acknowledge."

There was a flurry of activity on the radio. "Unit nine, acknowledging." "Yes sir, Captain. Unit Four out." "Unit twelve, acknowledging. Awaiting orders." Then, "Unit six reporting an Island Police cruiser just traversed the barricade at a high rate of speed westbound on the Cedric B. Grady Memorial Bridge..."

Grady said, "All units, this is Captain Grady. The east-bound lanes of the causeway are underwater. Do not attempt to cross. Repeat, do not attempt to cross. Island-side units, respond to 210 Harbor Lane with emergency medical assistance." The blue lights in his rearview mirror fell back.

Grady pressed the microphone button again. "Chief Malone, respond. Aggie, are you there?"

A whoosh of breath over the staticy airwaves. "She's crazy. Everybody knows it." Whoosh. "She'll never make it...nobody will believe her...I've got her now." *Whoosh. Whoosh.* "This is Sheriff Briggs requesting..." And then silence.

A gust of air rocked the big vehicle back and forth. The windshield wipers slashed and whitecaps surged on either side of the causeway, splashing over in places and forming little rivulets of themselves that the tires of his SUV plowed through at its own risk. Grady said into the microphone, "Island units, 210 Harbor Lane is a crime scene. Approach with caution. First responders, search the premises for a nine-millimeter Luger and bag as evidence. Do you copy?"

A hesitation, then, "Unit twelve, approaching the scene. Copy that."

Grady pressed the button on the microphone again. He said, "Aggie, if you can hear me, everything is going to be okay. I'm on my way…"

The peak of the bridge loomed ahead like a giant ski slope. Once the apex was reached, the skier would sail off into the void, into the vast empty vortex of churning seas and flashing skies. Aggie's hands seized on the wheel and her foot pressed on the accelerator. She could hear her own breath, and she could hear Flash's breath, rapid, uneven. And on the radio, she could hear the whoosh, whoosh, of another breath.

It's about change, isn't it? Her own voice now. *It's because I can't see what's on the other side.* But on the other side, the great green-black sea roared and swirled and flung its furious foam onto the concrete. On the other side, eddies swelled and ebbed. On the other side she heard Grady's voice, "Everything is going to be okay. I'm on my way…"

She crested the apex. She reached out to grip Flash's fur. "It's okay, Flash. We're going to be okay."

And the thing was, he believed her.

She braked on the down slope just as a wave of water rose to meet her, slamming into the windshield, spinning the car around. She felt the jolt and heard the scrape of metal as the cruiser slammed into the bridge barrier and she saw a sheet of water crash over the windows. She thought she was going over. She turned the wheel, shoved the gear into Park, and unfastened her seatbelt. She turned to reach for Flash and what she thought was, *It was worth it. Every minute was worth fighting for...*

The driver's side door of her car sprang open suddenly and Grady was there, rain streaming from his face. He caught her shoulders and dragged her from the car. She stumbled and lost her footing in the water. Blue lights flashed through the storm and shimmered on the water. She caught herself against the car door and cried, "Flash!"

But Flash was there, cradled in Grady's arms as he emerged again from the interior of the car. The wind screamed and tore the hat from Grady's head; rain pelted them like bullets. "It was Briggs," she said. "He tried to kill me. He tried to kill me...and Flash..."

Aggie flung herself against Grady and wrapped her arms around the both of them and held on tight and the last thing she heard Grady say was, "It's over, baby, everything's okay, it's over now..."

She remembered thinking, before the night started to pulse and whirl about her, how very much she wanted to believe it was.

CHAPTER EIGHTEEN

The first words Aggie spoke after surgery were hoarse and groggy. "Where's Flash?"

Grady was on one side of the bed, holding her hand. Lorraine was on the other, holding her other hand. Aggie saw the almost identical looks of joy and relief that lit up their faces, and the way Grady surreptitiously swiped at his eyes with the back of his hand before pretending to glance casually at his watch.

"Well," he said, "it's a little after one. I'd say he's holding down his usual stool at the bar, waiting for his lunch." Aggie smiled weakly and Grady added, "He sent you this." He leaned in and kissed her cheek.

Lorraine said anxiously, "Aggie, do you remember what happened? You scared us half to death."

"You had a seizure," Grady said, his voice husky. "After the bridge, after we got you out of the car…"

"Emergency neurosurgery—"

"In a hurricane—"

"You're fine, baby, it went great. They got the bullet—"

"The doctor has been here every time you woke up…"

"They just moved you down from ICU today. You're going to be back on your feet in no time."

She closed her eyes, listening to the sound of their voices, feeling their hands, strong and tight on hers. She murmured, "But Flash? He's okay?"

Grady lifted her fingers to his lips and kissed them. "He didn't even need stitches. The bullet grazed his skull and cut a notch in his ear, but I think he's kind of proud of it. He can't wait to see you."

Aggie smiled a little drunkenly. "Yeah. Me too."

With a great effort, she pulled her fingers free and fumbled with the bulky bandage around her head. "Oh, God," she groaned softly. "My hair."

Lorraine beamed and squeezed her hand. "Sweetie," she said, "do I have a wig for you."

Aggie drifted back to sleep, still smiling.

Dr. Abraham came in to perform the familiar battery of tests, and pronounced the surgery a resounding success—thanks to his brilliance, it was clear, and no thanks at all to her careless disregard for his orders, her reckless behavior, and her foolish refusal to take the anti-seizure medication he had provided. He expected her recovery to be rapid and complete, and she should be home resuming normal activities within ten days.

Aggie slept and ate Jell-O and toddled to the chair by the window with Ryan and an orderly holding her up. Every day she grew a little stronger. Ryan showed her pictures and videos of Flash on his phone. Lorraine brought her lipstick and painted her nails bright red, and when the doctor removed the bulky bandage, she brought a collection of pretty scarves that she fashioned into turbans. She brought more videos of Flash that made Aggie laugh.

Dr. Abraham told her that the bullet he'd removed from her head had been turned over to the police as evidence. Ryan told her that ballistics had matched the bullet taken from Lincoln's head to the nine-millimeter Luger pistol that Briggs had on him when he was transported to the hospital. That had been more than enough to secure a search warrant for his home, where they found a thirty-eight special registered to Walter Reichart wrapped in butcher paper in the back of his freezer. The gun showed no evidence of having ever been fired. A further forensics investigation of Briggs's finances showed several hundred thousand dollars in unexplained cash deposits had gone through his bank accounts over the past twenty years. Roy Briggs was arrested before he left the Emergency Room, and within seventy-two hours had given a full confession.

Dr. Janice came by and they talked for a long time. Afterwards she smiled and put away her tablet and said, "Well, it looks as though I've lost a patient. That's a good thing in my line of work."

Aggie said, "Don't take this the wrong way, but I'm not going to miss you. And thanks."

To which Janice replied, "Well, I will miss you and Flash." But she was smiling. "And you're welcome."

Hurricane Andy left its mark on Murphy County and the surrounding coastal areas, but it was nothing they hadn't seen before. The bridge was opened within twenty-four hours, and electrical service to Dogleg Island was restored within the week. The damaged cell tower was already being rebuilt; cleanup of the streets and residences was almost complete. Several of the beachfront homes had sustained considerable damage, and a few were determined to be beyond repair. 210 Harbor Lane was one of those. Speculation was that the house would be torn down and the lot cleared. Aggie would not be sorry to see it go.

Ryan slept in the fold-out chair beside her bed, holding her hand, leaving her only to shower and change and check on Flash. He followed the investigation via telephone. He conducted meetings with prosecutors and investigators in the corridor outside her room. He did his paperwork on his laptop while she was sleeping.

He brought her chocolate-covered cherries.

Bishop came to see her, bearing a big bouquet of flowers, and Aggie hugged him until she lost her strength and had to sink back onto the pillows, smiling at him, until she regained her breath. Grady got up to offer his chair, while Lorraine fussed around looking for a vase for the flowers. Bishop said, "Good work, Chief."

Aggie replied, "Yeah, well, we couldn't have done it without you."

He shook his head, sobering. "I let him slip through my fingers, Aggie. Something told me all those years ago that he was off, but I let it go. Didn't want to see it. Didn't want to believe it. That's what I came to tell you. I'm sorry, honey."

Grady said quietly, "Yeah, well, I wasn't much better. When you told me about the bad cop I should have pushed harder, should have gone further." He glanced at Aggie. "That was the only part of our investigation I didn't share with you. I didn't want to believe it, either. Didn't even want to think about it."

Aggie moved her head slowly back and forth against the pillows. "It's easy to look back and see what we should have done, or could have done. Most of the time, though, we're wrong. You couldn't have stopped him, any more than you could have stopped me from going in the house that night." She frowned a little, thoughtfully. "You know, it's funny. I was thinking about it the night of the storm, about how if I had it all to do over again whether I would still have walked into the house, and you know what?" She looked at Ryan, and he smiled and twined his fingers around hers. "I would have. I wouldn't change a thing."

Bishop nodded, understanding, and they were quiet for a moment. Then he looked at Grady. "I hear he confessed to the Lincoln murder, and Darrell Reichart's too."

Grady nodded, his expression grim. "He didn't have a choice. We had the ballistics match on Lincoln, and we found the piece of telephone cord he used to strangle Reichart in his car. My guys are collecting testimony that goes back ten, fifteen years about the protection racket he was running, and we've got leads on at least two other killings, both out of county, one of them out of state."

Aggie said, "What I don't understand is why he would keep Walter Reichart's gun. That was the only material evidence that could tie him to the shooting."

Bishop said, "My guess is that he kept it as insurance. If everything else failed, he could always plant the gun on someone else. Josh Peters, maybe." He glanced apologetically at Grady. "Or you."

There was a solemn moment while they all considered this. Then Aggie said, "What's going to happen to the department now? With Briggs in jail and his second-in-command under an official reprimand for invoking a regulation that doesn't actually exist..." She glanced at Grady disapprovingly. "Well...who's running things?"

"Oh, the regulation exists, all right," corrected Bishop with a mild twinkle in his eyes. "It goes into effect automatically every single time the president of the United States declares this nation to be under siege."

Grady helped himself to a chocolate-covered cherry from the box on the bedside table. "As far as I'm concerned, the only downside to that reprimand is that it didn't come with time off. And it's anybody's guess who's running the place. It's a mess. State police and investigators everywhere, maybe even a few Feds, I don't know. You can't go for coffee without tripping over somebody in a suit. Who knows how long it'll be before things start to look anything like normal again, if they ever do. As for who's going to be tapped to run the place now that the sheriff's in jail, the only thing I know is that it's not going to be me. I've heard a few rumors, but I couldn't say for sure." He looked at Bishop.

Bishop agreed somberly, "It's a mess all right. Not just the scandal in administration, but the whole department is bound to fall under scrutiny. It's a PR nightmare. The longer the investigation goes on, the more rocks that are turned over, the worse morale is going to get. A man would have to be a fool to walk into something like that." He tried to hide a rueful grin. "Of course, I guess I've been called worse than a fool. And I've been thinking lately that maybe retirement is overrated."

Aggie's face broke into a grin. "Oh, Bishop, that's good news! If anybody can get the department through this it's you."

"Nothing's certain yet," he warned her, and just then Lorraine pushed through the door with the big vase of flowers in her hand.

"The nurse just gave us the five-minute warning," she said, holding the door open with her hip. "But until then, sweetie, are you up for one more visitor? Or maybe two?"

Aggie gave a small cry of delight as Flash came through the door, followed by Pete on the other end of his leash. Flash was wearing a navy blue vest stenciled in white letters that read: Dogleg Island Police Department. The minute Pete unsnapped his leash he trotted over to the bed and sprang up onto it beside Aggie. She wrapped her arm around him, laughing, hugging him, while Pete and Ryan grinned at each other across the room.

"Flash," she whispered, over and over again into his fur, "oh, Flash, I'm so glad you're here. I missed you so much."

Aggie checked the scar on his head, which was still red and angry but soon would be covered by hair, and his torn ear. Flash checked out the small bandage on her head beneath the scarf, and the tube in her opposite arm, and finding her to be relatively undamaged, he grinned his relief. She grinned back.

"Pete, thank you!" Aggie twined her fingers through Flash's fur, and she couldn't stop beaming. "How did you get him in here?"

"Hey, he's a full-fledged member of the police department now. The Council voted on it yesterday." He nodded toward the vest. "It's Kevlar, by the way. We don't want another incident like the last one."

Aggie laughed and hugged Flash again, hard. Then she looked up at Pete uncertainly. "Does that mean I still have a job? I mean, I was involved in a shooting, and I'm taking all this medical leave, and my name is going to keep coming up in association with Briggs...there's bound to be trouble."

"Honey," Pete told her firmly, "the only trouble we'd have on the island is if we tried to remove you from office. The way you handled the storm, facing down an armed gunman and bringing a corrupt sheriff to justice...You're a genuine homegrown hero over there. But you always were."

Aggie hid her pleasure by burying her face once again in Flash's fur. Hero? She still wasn't sure. But homegrown...she could live with that.

Bishop congratulated Flash on his promotion and kissed Aggie's cheek before saying good-bye. "We're wearing you out, honey. Get some rest and get home. I'll see you soon."

"Wednesday night supper," she said.

He chuckled. "Maybe not this Wednesday. But you bet."

Lorraine said, "He's right, sweetie, we should all get out of here. This is all a bit much for someone just getting over brain surgery."

Aggie protested, but the fatigue was creeping up on her, and she wasn't sure how much longer she could stay awake. She hugged Pete and Lorraine, but held on to Flash when Pete picked up his leash. Pete smiled at her, shrugged, and draped the leash over the IV pole. "Get back to work," he said. "Both of you."

When they were gone, Grady kissed her fingers and said, "Lorraine's right, this is a lot of excitement for one day." He hesitated, looking uncertain. "Honey, tell me if this is too much shop talk, but there's something I've been wondering. Bishop reminded me of it just now." He paused, but she looked at him curiously so he went on, "I understand about the flashbacks, and why you had to go to Richardson if you thought your statement was wrong. But when you went to see Darrell, you said it was because you remember him saying something *after* you were shot, right?"

"That's right. It wasn't in his statement, and I hadn't told anybody about it, so I knew if what he remembered saying to me after I was shot was the same thing I remembered, it had to be true. He asked me if I was all right. I remember him standing over me looking scared out of his wits with the gun at his side and asking if I was all right. It was such a weird thing to say." Her brows quirked together in a half frown, trying to dismiss the unpleasant memory. "That's what first made me start to think something might be wrong. That we'd made a mistake."

Grady said carefully, "You remember that. You remember seeing him."

She nodded, stroking Flash's fur, threading her fingers through his soft curls. "And the next thing I know you're there, holding my face in your hands, yelling at Bishop on the radio, so scared, crying..." She smiled at him gently. "I felt so bad that I made you cry. I wanted to tell you everything was going to be okay, but then Roy came in..." Her smile faded.

Grady studied her with an odd look on his face. "You remember all this?"

Now it was her turn to look puzzled. "Why?"

He took a breath as though to speak, hesitated, and released it. He said, "Baby, when I got there you were unconscious. Your eyes were closed, you were unresponsive. I don't see how you could remember any of that. Not me, not Roy, not Darrell...not any of it."

She stared at him. "But I do. I remember every detail."

For a moment they just looked at each other, puzzling over it, finding no answers. Then Aggie said, forcing a tired smile, "Well, you know what Dr. Janice always used to say. The landscape of the mind is alien terrain. Or something like that."

He smiled back at her, and leaned in to kiss her nose. "You're fading, babe. I'd better get going too and let you get some rest."

Aggie said, "Yeah, okay." She stroked his cheek, which was covered in a fine stubble of blond beard. "Go home, shave, get something to eat. And come back."

He smiled and kissed her lips lightly, tenderly. "Don't you worry about that." He got to his feet. "Come on, Flash, let's go."

Flash regarded him with steady patience, but did not move.

Aggie said, "Let him stay."

"You know they won't allow that."

"Just until the nurse comes in. Pete can take him then."

Grady gave a wry shake of his head. "You always get your way, don't you?" He reached across the bed and ruffled Flash's fur. "Take care of Aggie for me, dude. I'll be back in a couple of hours."

He glanced back as he reached the door. "Do you need me to bring you anything?"

The day had taken its toll, and Aggie could feel her strength draining. She hated that and fought it. She wasn't finished yet. "Actually," she said, with an effort, "I do." She met the question in his eyes steadily and said, "A preacher."

He looked surprised, and then a little concerned as he turned back to her. "Sure, sweetie. I never thought to ask…"

She added, "And make sure he has a license."

His expression grew cautious. "What kind of license?"

Aggie smiled. "A marriage license, you dope."

It has been said that, next to human beings, dogs are the most adaptable species on the planet. This may be due in part to their ability to retain lessons from the past and apply them to new situations, while at the same time living most of their lives almost entirely in the present. Flash would never forget the lessons he had learned on the night of blood and thunder. He understood things now that he hadn't before. He knew what was important. And in these past days without Aggie, he had learned at lot, paramount among which was the fact that he never, ever wanted this to happen again.

Now, as Flash watched Grady's eyes start to smile and heard Aggie's breath stop, just a little, when Grady walked toward her, he knew that everything was, in fact, okay. He wasn't thinking about bullets or bad guys or keeping the streets safe. He was thinking about how good it made him feel inside, how easy and right, to see the way Aggie's face went all soft and happy as Grady said, "Scooch over," and stretched out on the bed beside her.

Aggie rested her head on Grady's shoulder and curled her fingers around his. "I can't believe it's over," she whispered. "But it is. It really is."

Grady kissed her fingers gently. "And just in time for the good part. Are you really going to marry me, Malone?"

She murmured, "You bet I am, Ryan Grady." And closed her eyes.

Flash got up and walked to the foot of the bed, settling himself between their feet, where he belonged. Maybe life on Dogleg Island would never be quite as simple as it once had been, but everything was going to be okay. He understood what a bad guy was now, and why it was important to keep them off the streets. He knew what his job was, his and Aggie's.

The only thing he didn't entirely understand was why Grady and Aggie still seemed confused about how Aggie knew what had happened that dark, bad night in the long-ago time. Aggie's eyes might have been closed, but Flash's eyes had been wide open, and he remembered every detail. So of course she would too. It was all perfectly clear to him. He knew what Aggie was thinking, and Aggie knew what he was thinking. They took care of each other that way, he and Aggie.

But Grady sure was right about one thing. Right now, here in this moment, back with the two people he loved most in the world: This was definitely the good part.

About the Author

Donna Ball is the author of over a hundred novels under several different pseudonyms in a variety of genres that include romance, mystery, suspense, paranormal, western adventure, historical and women's fiction. Recent popular series include the Ladybug Farm series and the Raine Stockton Dog Mystery series. Donna is an avid dog lover and her dogs have won numerous titles for agility, obedience and canine musical freestyle. She divides her time between the Blue Ridge mountains and the east coast of Florida, where she lives with a variety of four-footed companions. You can contact her at www.donnaball.net.

MM

Buo
Jan 116
Liv app 9/17

MB
SEP - - 2022

CPSIA information can be obtained at www.ICGtesting.com
Printed in the USA
LVOW07s0851120915

453937LV00001B/32/P